Siddharth Maheshwari is an  avid reader, he harbours a great science, geography and art. H him to places all over the glol cultures of the world. He enjoys theatre and Sufi music and loves spending time with his family.

His first book, *Lynchpin: The Best Laid Schemes of Mice and Men*, published by Leadstart Publishing, was a political thriller and was well-received by audiences across Amazon and social media.

Siddharth Vishwanath is an entrepreneur by profession. An avid reader, he is deeply interested in history, philosophy, science, geography and art. His love for travelling has led him to places all over the globe, appreciating and imbibing cultures, while striving to enjoy a hearty time with nature and fellow adventurers and while on flight.

His next book, 'Encounters the Ancient Mysteries of the Aztec, Inca, Babylonian, Egyptian, Sumerian, Tibetan', and a collection of diverse short stories based on humanity, life, love, sacrifice and relationships.

VEIL OF SHADOWS

SIDDHARTH MAHESHWARI

Om Books International

First published in 2023 by

Om Books International

Corporate & Editorial Office
A-12, Sector 64, Noida 201 301
Uttar Pradesh, India
Phone: +91 120 477 4100
Email: editorial@ombooks.com
Website: www.ombooksinternational.com

Sales Office
107, Ansari Road, Darya Ganj,
New Delhi 110 002, India
Phone: +91 11 4000 9000
Email: sales@ombooks.com
Website: www.ombooks.com

Text copyright © Siddharth Maheshwari 2023

ALL RIGHTS RESERVED. This is a work of fiction. All characters and events in this book are fictional and are a result of the authors' imagination. Any resemblance to any individual or event is purely coincidental. No part of this book may be reproduced or transmitted in any form by any means, electronic or mechanical, including photocopying and recording, or by any information storage and retrieval system, except as may be expressly permitted in writing by the publisher.

ISBN: 978-93-5376-885-0

Printed in India

10 9 8 7 6 5 4 3 2 1

To my father, Shri Anand Kumar Maheshwari,
and the journey of life we have shared so far.

Contents

Prologue		ix
1.	I Came, I Saw, I Left	1
2.	The Gambler	4
3.	Hunted for Sport	10
4.	Broken Wings	15
5.	Daytime Nightmares	22
6.	A Crack in the Glass	25
7.	Good Morning! You Are Going to Die	31
8.	The Gathering of the Clouds	39
9.	A Thief in the Night	44
10.	The Not So Grand Entrance	49
11.	Let's Disappoint Each Other	53
12.	In the Dark	56
13.	Who Cares if They Die?	61
14.	Riddles in the Dark	68
15.	A Walk in the Woods	74
16.	The Pit of Despair	80
17.	Delusions of Happiness	90
18.	The Whispering Room	95
19.	The Plot Thickens	102
20.	I Spy from the Corner of My Eye	108

21. Killing Time	113
22. T Is for Trauma	117
23. Dead Ends	127
24. The Cloudburst	130
25. Be Still, Be Quiet	140
26. Things to Come	143
27. Into the Tunnel	148
28. Outfoxed	150
29. Race You	157
30. On the Doorstep	160
31. Never Trust the Silent Ones	162
32. A Time to Kill	166
33. Deathly Silence	169
34. Dead Men Tell Tales	171
35. In It Together	176
36. Time Zero	180
37. Midnight Coffee Race	184
38. Tread Lightly	190
39. Big Little Lies	196
40. Bitter and Sweet	201
41. Dying to Meet You	206
42. The Scars Remaining	211
43. Queer Lodgings	215
44. Hello Again	218
45. An Unexpected Party	224
46. Three Blind Mice	226
47. Sea of Greed	229
48. Red Herrings	234
49. Well, That Didn't Work	239
50. Walk through Fire	247
Epilogue	252
Acknowledgements	260

Prologue

On a sunny winter afternoon in January, as the sun's warm rays bathed a corner office in the National Investigation Agency's headquarters, its chief, Director General of Police Vishal Chauhan, was going through the latest list of the most wanted criminals in India. Heaps of files and papers were scattered around his room and on his desk. A yellow coffee mug stood on one side of the table, with steam still rising out of it, and the intense aroma of the brew filled the room. Ignoring the clutter as he sipped his hot coffee, the DGP scoured the list that the intelligence unit regularly released and updated.

The NIA had domestic jurisdiction and consequently had to regularly share data and intelligence about terrorists that were operating overseas, especially in neighbouring countries, with the nation's foreign intelligence agency, the Research and Analysis Wing (R&AW).

As DGP Vishal Chauhan flipped through the pages of the newly published report, thinking about the life most of these young, impressionable men had wasted by choosing to go down this heinous path of hate and crime, his mobile phone rang. He glanced at it and saw the call was from a "Private Number". After the phone rang desperately and vibrated for almost thirty seconds, making it impossible for the DGP to ignore it, he answered the call.

'Send your team to Vrindavan tonight,' a disguised and hushed voice spoke. 'House number seventy, behind the Banke Bihari temple. You will find Mirza Ghulam Khan.'

'Who are you and who is this Ghulam Khan?' enquired the DGP while straining his ears, as he realized that his informer was most likely using a handkerchief to distort his voice.

'He is the financier of multiple terror networks. He is number five on your recently updated most wanted list of terrorists, Mr Chauhan. You don't have time to play games,' the voice on the other end replied quickly.

'How do I know this is not a trap?' asked the DGP.

The voice just drew a heavy breath and cut the call.

That night a team of five NIA agents drove to Vrindavan, the pious city of five thousand temples, also known as the city of widows. The city was hauntingly quiet at night, there were no tourists, hawkers, priests or the endless lines of devotees who regularly arrived at God's doorstep to barter with him. Even the cows and monkeys that roamed the streets with almost equal rights as humans were nowhere to be seen. As the clouds covered the moon, the five agents, who had parked their SUV near the Banke Bihari temple complex, stepped out of their vehicle and stealthily moved towards the designated house.

In the pitch dark of the silent night, where neither the footsteps of the commandos nor the rustling of the wind was heard, a molly black cat with haunting green eyes sat observing the men move with agility as they appeared and disappeared into the darkness. The cat was used to people who came to pray and the priests who extravagantly explained the pious rituals. They would either shoo her away, run away from her or occasionally throw stones at her. But never had the old cat, often considered an omen of bad luck, seen five humans move as fluidly as the wind. Her animal instincts kicked in, and she correctly identified them as a pack of hunters out to kill.

The numbers were written with chalk on the gates of most of the houses and shops in the lane. As the agents neared house number sixty, one of them, with the help of his buddy, climbed up onto the low roof of the single-storey brick house. These houses were easy to scale, and the team needed one man at a vantage point. As the rest of the team ventured ahead, the agent who was on the roof was now in the direct line of sight of the old cat. It had decided to silently observe without interrupting the hunt.

A few moments later, the agent who was moving across roofs parallel to the team below tapped his earpiece twice to indicate that he had a message to share. One officer looked up and saw him raise his index finger. This indicated that there was one man standing outside house number seventy. The team maintained radio silence. The officer then tapped his teammate, who was in front of him, on his right shoulder and held up his index finger, to communicate the message. Without breaking a sweat, almost as if this was a simple household chore, the team advanced, and at the turn of the corner came upon the man standing guard. The lone man was wearing a Pathani suit and was smoking a cigarette. He had a handgun, which although he had concealed under his kurta, was discernible by the distinctive shape it created around his waist. From the corner of his eye, the guard made out the commandos who had seamlessly blended with the darkness around them. But he had observed them a tad late. Before he could raise the alarm or even reach for his gun, the leader of the commando team whipped out his knife, placed a hand over the guard's mouth to muffle his screams and carved his guts out. The karambit, a special knife used by the armed forces, easily ripped through the guard's stomach and intestines, as if going through a pound of butter. In under thirty seconds the blood loss and the wound triggered internal haemorrhaging, ensuring the guard's swift departure to hell.

The agent who was on the roof stayed there to ensure no one could escape from the roof while the team operated below.

One of the commandos silently picked the lock on the front door. But the door had also been secured with a tower bolt. The leader realized that they would have to lose their element of surprise and barge in. A small charge was placed on the door, such that the blast would blow a hole inwards, with the shrapnel flying inside the house. The fuse was lit, and a meek blast was heard. Enough to wake up the occupants inside but not loud enough to wake the nosy neighbours from their deep sleep.

The small house had just one bedroom, a small pantry and an even smaller bathroom. The bedroom and bathroom were across each other while the pantry was down a dimly lit corridor. With the commotion of the break-in, the three guards inside jolted off their mattresses. One was sleeping in the pantry, another in the corridor and one inside the bedroom on the right side of the bed. But before any of them could reach for their weapons, the commandos deftly moved in and fired their silenced guns, quickly identifying the bodyguards by their similar uniforms and response reactions. Muffled thuds were heard as the team methodically put two rounds in each of the guard's chests. The shots were precise and aimed at the heart. The effect was an instant and not terribly painful death.

Two of the four commandos who had entered the small bedroom and shot the guard within now encircled Mirza

Ghulam Khan, who stood as tall and unwavering as a redwood tree. He was an old dog and accepted the consequences of his way of life. He did not shudder while death stared him in the face. He had the guts to look at his killers with equal ferocity. Although he was surrounded, Ghulam was not going to give up easily. He deftly took out a knife and charged at the officer in front of him. A terrible fight ensued with two officers trying to grab and subdue Ghulam. Their instructions were to capture and interrogate, before terminating him.

After several minutes of fighting, the tall, burly man was brutally hurt and bleeding from being stabbed by his own knife by one of the officers, but Ghulam was nowhere close to giving up. Not wanting to cause any more commotion, the team leader shot Ghulam in the leg. He was careful to miss the main arteries. Ghulam squealed as the bullet penetrated his leg, just above the knee, but did not bend. He did not want to give his killers the satisfaction of subduing him. There was rage in his eyes, and he glared at the team leader for cheating in the fight. The other officers, taking a cue, punched him in the stomach with the butt of their rifles and then heaved him up onto a chair. Without wasting time, the commandos began Mirza Ghulam Khan's interrogation. According to the intelligence received by the NIA chief, time was of the essence and so was the need to maintain absolute secrecy. Therefore, the commandos were not to extract the prisoner and move to a secure site. They also made no attempt to patch up his wounds or stop his bleeding.

The notorious financier realized that his end was near. He looked up at the team leader with bloodshot eyes and in a hoarse voice said, 'Will you please stop the bleeding?'

The leader shook his head and replied, almost like a doctor to his patient before operating on him, 'No. We will kill you.

If you cooperate, I will make it quick and painless, otherwise I will ensure that you bleed slowly and have the most painful death possible.'

The leader's cold and calm reply made Ghulam shudder. Without further ado the leader resumed the interrogation and Ghulam began answering his questions.

Following a short, five-minute conversation, the terrorist financier, who as per the NIA list was dubbed the 'Jack of Clubs', was shot cleanly in the head and executed.

After the commandos left, the cat slowly made her way into the small house and saw the gory massacre that the hunters had left behind. Although not really used to warm human blood, she still licked at it and relished its taste.

Later that night, acting upon the recently gathered intelligence, DGP Vishal Chauhan formulated a plan and called up an old friend of his. The phone ring reverberated around the quiet house in the hills.

1

I Came, I Saw, I Left

The warmth of the late afternoon spring sun had made the fat rat drowsy, but the whiff of buttered bread and juicy chicken legs woke the rodent from his slumber. Salivating, he ascended to the street from the sewers below. Sniffing the air, he quickly dashed down the pavement towards the shisha bar located on Shalimar Road in the Gulberg district of Peshawar, Pakistan. He came to a halt at the entrance of the shisha bar and saw a giant sitting on the pavement. He felt threatened by the presence of the giant who was occupying space in his territory. He was unsure if the giant was going to lay claim to the fallen breadcrumbs and the juicy chicken bones with tiny slivers of meat still dangling from them that had been tossed out by the two large, unruly men who were sitting at the table right next to the pavement.

It was the sole occupied table in the shisha bar. The two men were wearing Pathani suits and each was smoking his own shisha. They were eating chicken legs with buttered bread, while sipping on mint tea.

The giant had a long beard, was wearing rags and probably smelt worse than the rat. As the rat scurried towards the scraps of food and started gnawing at them, a plump lady in a black burqa, her body rhythmically moving with each push of the rickshaw's pedal by its malnourished driver, passed by the shisha bar. Looking down upon the giant she opened her purse and threw a few coins at the old fellow. The man quickly collected the metal pieces and raised his clenched fist to his temple to thank the generous woman. The woman rapidly blinked her kohl-rimmed eyes, visible through the slits in her niqab, as she swayed by on the rickshaw. The rat wondered why men ignored food and chased pieces of metal, which they could not eat.

Between the bubbling of the water in the shisha pot, the chewing of the food and the sipping of the hot mint tea, the giant could hear what the two men were talking about in hushed voices. He picked up the name 'Hamid Ansari' from their conversation and was sure that the two had used the Pashtun word for 'transfer' while discussing their plans. The said transfer was to take place in the next nine hours on the outskirts of Darjeeling, India. The giant further picked up that the leaner of the two was arranging for the transfer, while the heavier one was going to be personally present in Darjeeling to receive the package. The two men then got up and hugged each other thrice and called upon their God to bless their path ahead. The leaner one left first in a white SUV which had an emblem depicting a markhor eating a snake against a background of the half moon and star of the Pakistani flag painted on its doors, indicating that the individual was from Pakistan's elite Inter-Services Intelligence agency. The heavier one then left, without paying the bill—the café was not going to present a bill to a top ISI officer and a notorious arms dealer. He drove off in a white pick-up parked outside the shisha bar. He now had to prepare for his flight to India.

After they left, the beggar-cum-giant too decided to get up and leave, to the rat's relief. The beggar walked down the road slowly with the help of his walking stick. Once he was out of sight of the café, Vikram discarded his stick, false beard and the rags he was wearing. Wearing only the loose, filthy pyjamas that hung from his waist, R&AW's undercover agent Vikram Aditya Singh picked up his pace and dashed towards the car that he had parked in a lane behind the pharmacy situated up on the road.

Vikram got in and after quickly changing into a Pathani suit, drove north towards the Continental hotel on Khyber Road.

2

The Gambler

For the past four days, Ranbir Roy and Vikram had been in Peshawar, tailing the arms dealer Jahangir Niazi. A year ago, the secretary of R&AW, Wasim Khan, had successfully recruited the duo into the spy agency.

One week before, R&AW had picked up a local arms pimp, Keshav Thakur, in Nepal. He had been supplying weapons to the local gangs of Uttar Pradesh and Bihar. The interrogators did not even have to make the effort of intimidating him; Keshav had instantly spilled the beans on the entire nexus. Keshav had even informed R&AW that he had met Jahangir Niazi a while ago in Nepal. Niazi had told him that he would be in Peshawar as he was planning something big along with the ISI and had given Keshav the opportunity to be involved in their plan. Providing illegal weapons to local goons was one thing, but aligning with his country's adversary was not something Keshav was comfortable with. Therefore, and to

Jahangir's dislike, he had passed up the opportunity. Since he had not shown an interest, Jahangir had not revealed any of his plans.

R&AW promised Keshav that if his information proved fruitful, they would let him walk free, with the condition that if they ever found him involved in pimping arms again, they would execute him.

When R&AW's local assets had spotted Jahangir in Peshawar, Keshav had walked free.

That morning, Vikram and Ranbir had landed in Peshawar to tail the target and to see whom he was meeting.

Jahangir Niazi was a notorious arms dealer. He was an exceptionally resourceful person with contacts in all the right places in the bureaucracy of Pakistan. His contacts made sure he never got caught, helping him remain a step ahead of his adversaries. He had grown up on the streets and his rough upbringing had helped him develop tradecraft abilities that made him elusive and shrewd. Jahangir had been on R&AW's radar for quite some time, but this was the first time the spy agency had received any credible intel on his location, and his nefarious intentions towards India had allowed the hunt to be sanctioned.

At 4.30 p.m., Pakistan local time, Vikram entered the hotel room where Ranbir and he had been staying. He first drank two glasses of cold water then looked at Ranbir, who had been watching a news anchor report in grotesque detail and with cold fervour on a coup that had taken place in Myanmar, leading to the country's democratic leaders being put under house arrest.

Ignoring the news, Vikram said, 'I saw Jahangir Niazi meeting a senior ISI agent.'

'How do you know he was from the ISI?' enquired Ranbir.

'I saw the famous markhor insignia on the car in which he drove off,' replied Vikram. 'Anyway, I heard them talk about a "Hamid Ansari" and they definitely used the word "transfer". It seems this said transfer is being facilitated by the ISI and is to take place in about eight hours from now in Darjeeling. Also, Jahangir confirmed that he would be flying to India and would be present to take delivery of the package.'

Ranbir pondered the information. A few minutes later he called up Secretary Wasim Khan and the Joint Secretary for the Pakistan desk Arvind Ghosh to update them on these developments.

Fifteen minutes later, Ranbir received a call from Arvind Ghosh with Wasim Khan also on the line. Ranbir put the call on speaker.

Grimly, Arvind said, 'Professor Hamid Ansari is our top nuclear scientist, and he is presently in Darjeeling working on a highly classified nuclear fusion programme.'

Vikram, the ever inquisitive, enquired, 'What is so secretive about nuclear fusion? The world knows about it, and scientists around the world have been trying to harness the energy from fusion reactions for years.'

Taking a deep breath Arvind responded, 'It is arduous to achieve power through nuclear fusion; and harnessing that power has been mostly theoretical. It takes immense temperatures and pressures to cause positively charged atoms of lighter elements like hydrogen to fuse, thereby generating fusion energy. And unlike nuclear fission, fusion has no radioactive fallout. Professor Ansari's experiments have been yielding positive results. He and his team have been working closely with the Americans, Israelis and Germans. They are very close to cracking the process of generating fusion at an industrial scale. This technology will not only advance our nuclear weapons but also help us in generating cleaner fuel at an industrial scale for the country.'

Wasim Khan said, 'From what Vikram has overheard it seems the ISI will attempt to kidnap Professor Hamid Ansari and hand him over to Jahangir Niazi. What is their goal? Why is the ISI using an arms dealer? Whatever their motivations, we cannot allow the professor to be abducted, so we must intervene. We need to put a security detail on him.'

Sighing and pushing his hand through his hair, the secretary continued, 'Good work Vikram and Ranbir, but now you both need to come back.'

Vikram, who had been pacing the room, replied sharply, 'I'm sorry, sir, but I think tailing him would be a mistake. We have been after Jahangir Niazi for quite sometime now; he is a lot of things, but he has never been on the front line of the action. He has always acted as an enabler or a fixer, providing the manpower, guns and ammunition to various terrorist organizations. If Niazi is going to take delivery of our yet-to-be-kidnapped nuclear scientist, it would not be just for ransom money. It is only reasonable to assume that he plans to hand the scientist over to some other terrorist faction, which may require the old professor's expertise in arming a nuclear device.'

Ranbir piped up, 'What you are saying is plausible, but what can we do about it? We can put a tail on Niazi.'

Vikram shook his head. 'We can neither tail Niazi nor execute him here in Pakistan. He is too well protected. He is only going to Darjeeling because the professor is being kidnapped. If the kidnapping does not go through, he will never show up. And if he doesn't show up, we will never be able to expose his nexus or discover the ISI's latest plot against India.'

'Are you suggesting that we allow the ISI to kidnap Hamid Ansari?' Arvind Ghosh asked incredulously.

Vikram took a deep breath and replied, 'We don't have a choice. At this point we may be a step ahead of the ISI, but if they require a nuclear scientist, they can kidnap any one of our scientists. We will not be able to protect all of them all the time. Right now we have the upper hand, so we should be able to observe the events from afar and intervene at the right time. Lastly, if we show our hand and provide protection to Hamid Ansari, the ISI will be alerted and will likely alter their plans. We need to play our best with the hand that we have been dealt.'

Ranbir scowled and grumbled, 'Life is not a game of poker my friend, we cannot gamble away an innocent's life.'

Vikram responded calmly, 'No, life is a game of anticipation. The better you are at predicting the turn of events and the behaviour of your nemesis, the better are your chances of surviving the ordeal of life.'

Wasim Khan, who till now had been silently listening, said, 'Vikram has a strong point, but we cannot operate unilaterally on this. I will have to inform the prime minister. Till then we will put together a covert team to surveil the professor.

As Secretary Wasim Khan left to contact the Prime Minister's Office, Vikram continued his barrage of questions.

'What more do we know about Dr Hamid Ansari? What is his background?'

Since the man in question was one of the country's most respected nuclear scientists, R&AW already had a detailed dossier on him.

Flipping open the green file and scanning its pages with keen eyes, Arvind responded, 'Doctor Hamid Ansari was born in 1962 in Kanpur. His father was a physicist at the University of Delhi and his mother was a professor of mathematics there. He has no siblings. His parents passed away of old age about two decades ago. His wife, who was earlier a physics teacher, became a homemaker after the birth of their two children. He has been married for about thirty years. He has been cited over five thousand times in some very prominent research papers, and he himself has authored about three dozen papers all of which have been widely acclaimed. He has also authored a book titled *The Anatomy of the Electron*. There have been no known incidents of him criticizing the government or showing dissent or resentment towards India. As far as we know, Doctor Hamid Ansari is a patriot.'

Vikram absorbed these details about Hamid's life and began pondering over the current developments as Arvind cut the line.

3

Hunted for Sport

While the officers had been busy debating their strategy, a special ISI flight flew Jahangir from Peshawar to Lahore. In an hour he reached the eastern city that was not too far from its economically superior neighbour, Delhi. In Lahore Jahangir boarded a flight that was headed directly for New Delhi. This too was a special flight carrying a deputation of ambassadors. With the help of the ISI, Jahangir had obtained false paperwork that showed him to be one of the diplomats. In an hour he had landed in Delhi.

By this time R&AW had circulated Jahangir Niazi's identity across all ports of entry into India but had given specific instructions that he was to be allowed to pass through. Given the time period in which the events were to transpire, R&AW had anticipated that Jahangir would fly to Darjeeling via New Delhi. They had a team deputed there to tail him to his intended destination as soon as he arrived in the country.

When Jahangir got to the immigration counter at Delhi's international airport, the officer on duty flipped through his papers twice, and though his computer had flagged Jahangir, due to the instructions he had received from higher authorities, he did not raise an alarm and stamped his passport.

From Delhi, Jahangir took a local flight to Darjeeling. But this time a team of five R&AW agents were on the flight with him.

All this while Vikram and Ranbir, who were still in Peshawar, had been in discussions with the prime minister and his team of advisors. Vikram's plan had merit, but the risks were too great. If they lost track of Hamid, the ramifications could be perilous for the nation. But Vikram was adamant that a show of force now would alert the ISI and no one would then know how and when they would attack next. Therefore, he vehemently rejected the idea of someone impersonating the valuable scientist or even placing a tracking device on him; even when the ideas were pushed by Ranbir.

At about 11 p.m., the team of R&AW officers tailing Jahangir confirmed to Arvind Ghosh that the arms dealer had met with a group of ten people behind the Believers Church in Orange Valley, Darjeeling. The update was helpful, but the PMO was still undecided about the course of action that should be taken.

It was midnight, and it had started pouring in Darjeeling. Professor Hamid Ansari and his wife Mashal were fast asleep in a five-bedroom chalet located on one of the hills of the small, picturesque tea-growing town. The rain had caused the temperature to drop, and there was a slight frost on the French windows of the chalet.

Three teams of six of India's elite navy unit, the Marine Commandos or the MARCOS as they were more popularly known, had the chalet under observation. One unit was positioned below the chalet, hidden amongst the tea terraces; another was above the chalet, camouflaged amongst the trees, and the last unit was huddled in a hut located on the winding road that led down the hill. Snipers from each team had their night vision goggles on and despite the rain were able to view the chalet from different angles. The sky cracked with thunder, and the purple hue of lightning lit the sky and the hills every few minutes.

A while later three black sedans slowly rolled to a stop outside the chalet. The sky cracked and the multiple bouts of lightning highlighted the ten men, who were armed with silenced pistols, as they jumped out of the three vehicles. When the sky was illuminated again the MARCOS teams noticed that the drivers had stayed in the vehicles and kept the engines running.

The MARCOS team leader was on a direct line with the PMO, Secretary Wasim Khan and Joint Secretary Arvind Ghosh. Ranbir and Vikram were also patched in on the call.

As the ten men disembarked, the team leader's voice crackled over the phone, 'This is Alpha. I have a visual on ten bogies armed with small, silenced arms taking position outside the asset's residence. They are about to enter. Permission to engage?'

All eyes in the PMO were set on the commander-in-chief. The prime minister remained still as a statue. Only his chest heaved.

A few long seconds later, the voice on the phone crackled again, 'This is Alpha. The bogies have breached the chalet and have secured the asset. We are now in a hostage rescue situation. Three bogies are stationed outside, and there are three drivers, one in each car. About seven bogies are inside.

We can neutralize all six bogies outside and move in to force a surrender. Do we have permission to engage?'

Again, all eyes were on the prime minister.

When the ISI men had moved into Hamid Ansari's house, they had quietly crept into his bedroom, switched on the lights and woken the old couple. Amidst the thunder and the rain, their screams were not heard outside the chalet.

The scientist in his naivety pleaded, 'I will give you all the money we have. Take everything, but please do not harm us.'

But to his horror, the slim agent in front of him said, 'We are after the most valuable thing in the room, your brain and your capabilities. Please pack some clothes. You're coming with us, and you're going to help Pakistan.'

With a sense of pride, the professor retorted, 'I am not going to betray my country. You will have to kill me.'

'No, Professor, you are going to cooperate with us. Otherwise, we will first kill your wife and then your children. We know they are studying at Hansraj College and are staying on campus in dorm rooms seven and sixteen,' said the ISI agent with cold confidence.

Hearing the threat against his children weakened the scientist's resolve.

The agent then said, 'You better hurry, we are on the clock. And don't forget your blood pressure medicine.'

The startled look on the scientist's face did not escape the ISI agent, and he smugly said, 'Yes, we know all about you.'

Ten minutes later, the phone line in the PMO crackled again. 'This is Alpha. We have the asset in our sight. He is surrounded by ten bogies. We have a clear shot at seven of them. They are preparing to get into their cars. We can move in now and subdue them. Do we have permission to engage?'

Still there was no reply from the PMO.

A few seconds later, the voice came through on the phone again, piercing the prime minister's conscience and stinging like nettle leaves. 'The asset has been kidnapped and is in the middle car driving down through the tea gardens. Sir! Do we have permission to engage?'

Finally, the prime minister shifted in his seat and spoke with a sense of command, 'All teams, let the kidnapping go through. Do not engage. Pursue from a distance. Observe, but do not intervene.'

Then continuing, so everyone could hear, he addressed Vikram, 'Vikram, if there is a nuclear blast in our country, there will be blood on your hands and on my conscience.'

After the kidnapping, the MARCOS had entered Hamid Ansari's house to calm his shaken wife and prevent her from alerting the local authorities. They told her that they had the situation under control and would bring the professor back in no time.

Thirty minutes later, the ISI agents handed over the nuclear scientist to Jahangir Niazi. The exchange happened at the Believers Church. The ingenious scientist's face was covered with a black cloth, and he had no clue what was going on. The five officers of R&AW who had been tailing Jahangir along with the three MARCOS teams observed the exchange from afar. The authorities believed that the situation was still under their control.

4

Broken Wings

Five minutes later, Niazi and the ten ISI agents drove off in their dilapidated white SUVs. R&AW had the area covered via satellite and an unmanned aerial vehicle, or UAV, equipped with a precision high-definition multispectral camera, which was following the vehicles from a height of eighteen thousand feet. These technological advancements would allow MARCOS and R&AW officers to follow Niazi and his men from a distance of ten kilometres.

After about thirty minutes, the voice of a young analyst from the command centre of R&AW crackled on the wireless headsets of the agents in the field. 'Alpha, this is Eagle, we have eyes in the sky. The bogies have just reached the Senchal forest. Begin your pursuit. We will guide you along the way.'

The agents, who had camouflaged themselves in the tea gardens on the hill slopes above the Believers Church, emerged from their hideouts and swiftly moved into their vehicles parked nearby. They took off at full speed, not wanting to put any more distance between them and the perpetrators than was necessary.

The next six hours rolled by without much incident. The UAV and the satellites had performed their jobs immaculately and had allowed the field agents to pursue their target inconspicuously.

The circuitous mountain drive culminated at Nathang Valley in Sikkim. If not for the tense situation everyone was driving under, the drive from Darjeeling to Nathang Valley would have been an utterly beautiful one, starting with the lush tea gardens then moving through alpine meadows and forests laden with wildflowers, passing Buddhist monasteries dotting the hillsides and finally coming upon the snow-capped mountains that could be spotted from the valley. But alas, the appreciation of this beauty would have to wait for these war fighters.

Finally, Jahangir along with his prized asset reached the main road of the snow-clad valley. All around, huts and half-timber houses with colourful gable tin roofs were visible. Jahangir and his men ignored these clusters and headed straight for a large chalet built into a mountain side.

At 7.30 a.m., Wasim Khan and Arvind Ghosh were on the operations floor of R&AW's New Delhi office. No one had gone home since Jahangir's arrival in the country the previous day. A large screen in front of them showed Jahangir along with the ISI agents and the kidnapped scientist Hamid Ansari enter the large chalet, which sprawled across a mountain ledge. A cluster of five smaller screens on the right side of the room showed images being captured by the UAV. It was transmitting footage of the men taking up defensive positions on the terraces and verandas of the chalet.

A group of analysts was fervently typing away, trying to analyse the images and retrieve any information possible. The faces of all the men were covered with balaclavas, so only their eyes were visible. Each time the UAV captured someone's face, the digital demons behind the computer screens would run the set of eyes through various databases in an attempt to establish the identity of the men helping Jahangir.

Parth Sinha, the newly appointed additional secretary for R&AW, confidently walked into the operations room, carrying a grande cup of Starbucks mocha. A dynamic officer of fifty-five years with an illustrious military service behind him, Parth was the bureaucracy's blue-eyed boy. He had a salt and pepper goatee and wore rimless glasses.

Approaching Wasim Khan and Arvind Ghosh, he introduced himself. 'Good morning gentlemen, I am Parth Sinha and have been appointed as the new additional secretary.'

Everyone heard him, but none of the analysts raised their heads, they just kept working. Although Arvind was not pleased that he had been bypassed for this position, he understood that today was not the day to drag a colleague through the mud because of office politics and bureaucratic intricacies.

So, putting his feelings aside he replied, 'Good morning, sir. I'm Arvind Ghosh, joint secretary for the Pakistan Desk. I hope you have been briefed about the ongoing operation?'

'Yes, I received the details this morning and read the file about the operation on my way here,' replied Parth, draining the last of his coffee and ditching the cup in a nearby bin.

'Great. So, as you can see on the big screen, Jahangir Niazi, his men and our asset have just arrived at this chalet on the mountain ridge.'

Wasim Khan was relieved by Arvind's professional manner and the lack of hostility between the two senior officers, which is typically rampant through the government offices of the nation.

'Do we know who the chalet is registered to?' Parth enquired.

A young analyst, Shobha Dey, her hair tied back tightly in a bun, swiftly spun around in her chair and answered, 'No sir! We have checked the local land records, but there is no trace of this building or of its ownership. It seems to be an illegal construction as there are no records of any permits having been granted for the construction of the chalet. These mountain ranges have several old and abandoned mining sites.'

'Is our team in position?' Wasim asked. He was getting tired of this charade and wanted to secure the scientist as soon as possible.

'Yes sir! They reached the valley five minutes ago and have split into four teams. Our field agents are staying in the valley, which is to the south of the chalet, to cover the exit, while the MARCOS are camouflaged on the east, west and north sides of the chalet.'

'Good. Now let's get Vikram and Ranbir online so that all the players are in play.'

At 8 a.m. IST, everyone was online and connected with the agents in the field.

One of the MARCOS snipers, who had made his nest in a treetop about seven hundred metres above the chalet, had a direct view into one of the rooms. As luck would have it, Professor Hamid Ansari had been bound and strapped to a chair in that room itself. Everyone, especially Vikram, on whose shrewd calculation this grand scheme was being played out, was relieved.

The next three hours went by idly. Three of the guards kept rotating their positions, while the other seven and Jahangir had not been spotted yet. But thermal sweeps by the satellite up in the clouds confirmed the presence of twelve people inside the chalet. Everyone thought that the hand over of the prisoner would take place soon. And at that point the next player in this nefarious plot of the ISI would be revealed. The authorities were prepared to intervene at that moment, and after securing the scientist, they would either kill or capture the rest of the players.

Just before noon, one of the snipers observed Niazi pacing the veranda outside his room, which was on the eastern side of the chalet, and talking on his mobile phone. The view of the UAV and the satellite was blocked by the chalet's roof and a thicket of pine trees.

Technology cannot replace human presence, thought Arvind as he said to the fleet of analysts who were frantically typing away on their computers, 'We need to hear what he is saying and find out who he is talking to.'

The young analyst responded, 'Sir, we are trying to hack into the nearest cell tower.'

Another analyst on the floor claimed, 'I am trying to triangulate the call to trace its origin.'

Fifteen seconds later Shobha leapt with joy and exclaimed, 'Got it.'

As soon as Shobha patched the call to the main line, the sniper confirmed over the wireless that Jahangir had disconnected the call.

Dejected, Shobha said, 'If he makes or receives another call, we will be able to hear it. We are prepared.'

Arvind merely muttered under his breath, 'If there is another call.'

Then he told the team controlling the UAV to check the surrounding area for any inbound vehicles. None were observed for kilometres around.

All of a sudden, the lights in the chalet were switched off, and the windows were shuttered. The team lost the limited visuals they had of the chalet. A few minutes went by and there was no sign of any life or movement from within.

The analyst who had been trying to triangulate the call spun around in her chair and fearfully said, 'Sir, the call originated from the High Commission of Pakistan in New Delhi.'

As the analyst's words reverberated around the room, Parth Sinha, his years of experience with the army kicking in, said, 'Conduct a thermal sweep of the chalet immediately.'

Within ten seconds the satellite made a sweep and to everyone's horror, did not pick up any heat signatures from inside the structure.

At this point Wasim Khan lost his nerve and ordered the MARCOS to breach the chalet on his authority.

The team leader's voice crackled on the wireless, 'This is Alpha, all teams, we are a go. Secure professor Hamid Ansari. Kill all bogies. We are going in hot.'

The satellite, UAV and head cameras of the commandos showed them converging on the chalet from three sides. They went in announcing themselves, as it is the ethos of the armed forces to allow the enemy one last chance to surrender. One by one the rooms were cleared. There were five bedrooms with attached bathrooms spread across the property, with a living room and a kitchen in the centre. Ten minutes from the time Secretary Wasim Khan gave the order, the MARCOS had secured the premises, but there was no sign of Jahangir Niazi, his ten men or of India's top nuclear scientist Hamid Ansari.

Vikram was stupefied and felt the rug being swept from under his feet. Shaking, he sat down on the sofa in his hotel room in Peshawar.

Arvind ordered the MARCOS to conduct a room-by-room search and to take apart every piece of furniture. About twenty minutes later, one of the teams reported that they had found a trapdoor under a rug. The voice on the wireless crackled again, 'This is Alpha, we have found a tunnel under the chalet. We are going in.'

The images coming in from the head cameras of the MARCOS team showed that this was not a recently dug tunnel but an old passageway that had probably been built to facilitate mining operations on the mountain.

After a circuitous hike of about fifteen minutes, the team leader's voice crackled again, 'This is Alpha, this tunnel opens onto an array of tunnels that have been built inside the mountain. We are going to continue the pursuit by splitting into nine teams of two each, but we may not be able to cover all the rat holes. Send backup.'

After about two hours, the teams had made their way to the other side of the mountain, and the team leader's voice came over the wireless again, 'We have found no trace of the bogies or the asset. We have lost them. We seem to be lost ourselves.'

The Sikkim Scouts, the regiment of the Indian army stationed at the Sikkim border, had been sent as backup. Some of them had gone into the tunnels, others had linked up with the MARCOS commandos as they emerged through the various tunnel openings in the mountain on which the chalet was built and its surrounding hills. The army regiment even carried out air sorties and recces via their helicopters but could spot no sign of Jahangir or the captured scientist.

5

Daytime Nightmares

A little before 4 p.m., observing the overcast sky from his Delhi office, Secretary Wasim Khan called the PMO. Within seconds the prime minister came on the line, clearly upset by the disastrous news his personal secretary had just relayed. He ordered Vikram, Ranbir and all the key players to be patched in on the call.

As soon as everyone was on the line, the angry voice of the nation's commander-in-chief bellowed, 'Vikram, your plan has backfired miserably! Against everyone's advice I went ahead with your strategy, believing that you and the R&AW officers would have the situation under control. This is an utter mess. Professor Hamid Ansari will not be able to withstand torture by Niazi and his men. Who knows what they will compel him to do? I want Professor Ansari back before it's too late. I want results soon. Do we have any leads on their escape?'

Arvind quickly responded, 'Yes sir, just before the perpetrators left, Jahangir received a call from the High Commission of Pakistan. The call was triangulated to the high commissioner's office in the building. So, either the high commissioner himself or someone close to him made that call.'

'Is that the only clue we have?' the prime minister asked anxiously.

'Yes sir. At the moment, this is the only actionable intel we have on our hands,' Arvind replied.

The prime minister considered the situation then asked, 'Should I confront the high commissioner directly? I can put pressure on him and threaten him with dire consequences should a nuclear blast happen on our soil.'

Wasim Khan leaned forward in his chair and responded, 'Sir, this was a well-crafted plan by the ISI. If the high commissioner is involved, he would have had prior knowledge of the plan. We need to do this covertly.'

The prime minister considered, hummed in agreement then said bitterly, 'Get Vikram and Ranbir back here so they can clean up this mess.'

'Yes sir,' replied Wasim Khan.

The PMO then disconnected from the call.

Wasim Khan said, 'Ranbir, I am sending you all the details, including the habits and daily routine, of the high commissioner of Pakistan Humayun Haq. Leave Peshawar immediately, and by the time your plane touches down in Delhi, I expect to see a concrete plan of action for retrieving intel from the high commission.'

From Peshawar, Ranbir and Vikram flew to Lahore. During the one-hour journey the duo thoroughly read the file on Humayun Haq. The dossier highlighted his personal habits—he was a smoker, a teetotaller and was fond of chewing betel leaves with tobacco and areca nuts.

After a layover of just over an hour, the duo boarded their hour-long flight to New Delhi. By the time they landed, the two had formulated a plan to eavesdrop on every conversation of Humayun Haq.

6

A Crack in the Glass

At 10 p.m., Ranbir and Vikram reported at R&AW's Delhi office. Secretary Wasim Khan along with Parth Sinha and Arvind Ghosh were discussing their options in the conference room when the duo entered. After exchanging greetings, everyone settled in.

Ranbir opened the conversation by stating, 'We have gone over Haq's habits thoroughly and have found a way to bug his office.'

Then looking at Arvind Ghosh he continued, 'Sir, you need to register us with the company hired to undertake plumbing maintenance at the Pakistani high commission.'

After explaining their plan of action, Ranbir and Vikram left, while Arvind made arrangements to have his agents registered with the plumbing company.

Late that night Vikram and Ranbir drove to the Pakistani high commission and parked their vehicle near the rear entrance of the building, which opened up onto Niti Marg. They slept in turns so they could keep the high commission under continuous observation. There were no developments through the night, but at about 7 a.m. the following morning, a lanky fellow, who looked like he was one of the high commission staff, emerged from the rear gate and cycled his way down the road. Vikram, who had been on watch, woke Ranbir up, and the two followed the cyclist down the road. After ten minutes he stopped at a paan shop situated not very far from the Chanakyapuri post office. From there he purchased a few loose cigarettes and several paan. After he rode away, the duo approached the shop owner and showed him their credentials.

Looking at the R&AW badges, the plump owner, who was wearing a tight white vest and a lungi, seemed impressed.

Smiling and raising his eyebrows with a sense of self-importance he asked Vikram, 'How can I help?'

'Do you know who that man was?' enquired Vikram.

'Yes, his name is Yousef Lehri. He is the high commissioner's manservant. He comes here twice a day to collect paan and cigarettes.'

'Why does he buy loose cigarettes and not a full pack?' asked Vikram as he lit a cigarette of his own.

'Oh! The high commissioner's wife doesn't approve of his smoking. She regularly finds his hidden stash of cigarette packs, so he sends his staff to buy a few loose ones twice a day.'

'We have hit our jackpot,' said Ranbir. 'I'm calling for the backup team, you brief this fellow on what is going to happen.'

Vikram nodded, his face grim. 'We are going to lace some of your betel leaves and cigarettes with a mild dose of Shiga toxin, better known as Stx. It's a potent toxin produced by certain types of bacteria, but we have mutated this one to ensure that the high commissioner only gets an acute case of food poisoning and nothing more. We need you to cooperate. Our agents will have you under surveillance. If you try to inform the high commissioner or his manservant, they will arrest you,' explained Vikram.

The owner was excited about being part of the covert operation and was more than happy to cooperate.

Fifteen minutes later the backup team comprising two men and a woman arrived, dressed in plain clothes, and positioned themselves around the paan shop. On checking with the owner, they found out that the manservant would likely arrive sometime post lunch.

While Vikram laced a batch of betel leaves and several cigarettes with the toxin, Ranbir released three matchbox-sized robots into the sewage pipes outside the high commission. The remote-controlled bots speedily made their way into the draining system of the complex. The robots were equipped with palm-sized vacuum cups and by sticking to the walls of the pipes the cups would ensure that the sewage pipes were blocked. By 9 a.m. the robots were in place and Ranbir, with a single push of a button on a remote, caused the three vacuum cups to stick to the walls of the pipes, blocking the flow of sewage.

At 9.15 a.m., Clean and Clear Limited, the plumbing company that held the high commission's annual maintenance contract, received a complaint about three toilets in the building overflowing with sewage. One of these toilets was in the office of the high commissioner.

Following the complaint, a team of three R&AW officers who had embedded themselves in the maintenance team of the plumbing company arrived at the embassy at 10.30 a.m. The CEO and the maintenance crew of the company had been briefed beforehand. The workers were to go into the bathrooms and clean up the mess, while the spies would plant the bugs in and around the office.

When the maintenance crew arrived, their tool boxes and equipment were put through a scanner. Each member was also frisked thoroughly, but nothing out of the ordinary was found.

The team of seven quietly yet confidently strode into the compound. The architecture of the complex was beautiful with intricate carvings on the walls and pillars and blue-domed minarets, but none of the new entrants had the time to enjoy the ornate architecture. The pressures created by humanity more often than not deprive the species the luxury of enjoying the fruits of their own creative labour.

At 11 a.m., Lehri, the high commissioner's lanky manservant cycled to the paan shop again. The officers stationed around the shop, including Vikram, eyed him carefully.

The shop owner asked Lehri casually, 'How come you're here early today?'

Annoyed by the unnecessary question, Vikram cursed him under his breath but did not make a move yet.

'The boss wants more paan. He finished what I had got packed in the morning. He's been a bit tense for the past few days.'

Smiling, the shop owner said, 'I'll pack some more.'

Meanwhile, the R&AW agents were all working in the toilets. The agents were assembling the surveillance equipment while the cleaners sprayed the room with air freshener and started to clean up the mess.

High Commissioner Humayun Haq was pacing in his office. He had to be put out of play before the agents could make their move. Despite all their efforts, their plan was still only partially successful. The final execution depended upon the manservant being on time.

Fifteen minutes later the manservant softly walked into the high commissioner's office and delivered the tobacco-filled betel leaves to him. Humayun immediately put two in his mouth and tossed the rest on his desk. He had been very tense for the past few days, and the nicotine helped calm his nerves.

Ten minutes later, Humayun rushed to one of the working bathrooms. The toxin had taken effect. After thirty minutes and three rounds of passing loose stool, the high commissioner collapsed and was hurriedly carried to his car. Accompanied by his wife, manservant and two security guards, Humayun left in his motorcade for Aashlok Hospital situated in Safdarjung Enclave, a ten-minute drive from the high commission.

The office was now clear for the R&AW agents to start planting their bugs. The three officers instantly got to work. A listening device was placed under the sofa and a few more were concealed inside the LED lights in the ceiling. The landline was tapped, and another listening device was drilled into the wall behind the huge painting that hung behind the high commissioner's desk. Removing the gigantic eighteen-square-foot painting, depicting the victory of a general mounted on a white horse over his foes, had proved to be a daunting task. Next, the agents placed tiny cameras around the room. One was placed on the branch of an ornate bonsai tree that adorned a bright corner of the room. Another device, the size of a pinhead, was placed on the frame of the painting behind the desk so the agents could also monitor anyone who met the high commissioner. The last camera was concealed in the ceiling within the light fixtures, to give an overview of the room. By this time the staff of the plumbing company had cleaned up the mess. When the R&AW agents confirmed the success of their operation to Ranbir, he quickly disengaged the vacuum cups. Then with a push of a button he ignited the small charges that had been set inside the three robots, and the minute blast caused the machines to rupture. The broken pieces of the ingenious technology then flowed down the drain with ease.

But the team's work was not done yet.

After Humayun Haq was stabilized and given steroids to fight the infection, he was sedated and put to sleep. That was when a R&AW operative disguised as a nurse implanted a microchip in the high commissioner's arm. This would allow the spy agency to monitor Humayun's movements in real time.

At 2 p.m., as the R&AW agents were moving out of the Pakistani high commission, Wasim Khan received a disturbing phone call.

7

Good Morning! You Are Going to Die

Seven hours ago, at 7 a.m., Sarthak Jain, chief technology officer of Bellator Defence Systems Limited, entered his state-of-the-art office building located in Katraj, near the Rajiv Gandhi Zoological Park and Wildlife Research Centre in Pune. The head office of the company was situated right next to their first production facility, which had opened in 1964, where it manufactured propulsion systems for missiles. Over the years the company had grown manifold and had diversified into various fields of defence technology, from making torpedoes for submarines to microchips for thermal satellites.

The head office opened at 9 a.m. and the workforce would pour in slowly till 9.30.

But Sarthak had come in early for a specific purpose. Briskly walking into the eerily silent office, where only his footsteps could be heard, he took the elevator up to the thirteenth floor where his office was located. From his office safe he retrieved a large shiny black cuboid that was a little larger than an iPhone. Placing the object in a small, silver aluminium briefcase, he secured the case to his right wrist with a pair of handcuffs. This was the standard procedure that most defence companies followed when moving sensitive and secretive technology.

By 7.15, Sarthak was down in the lobby and his chauffeur was waiting at the wheel of his bulletproof Audi S7 at the main porch. For this journey, an armed bodyguard carrying a 9mm Beretta and a Sterling submachine gun would be accompanying him.

By 7.20 a.m., the car rolled out of the company gates for its three-hour journey to the Indian Space Research Organisation's (ISRO) office in Antariksh Bhavan located in Khar West, Mumbai. A meeting between ISRO, Bellator Limited and the country's premiere defence organization—Defence Research and Development Organisation (DRDO)—had been organized at ISRO's office.

Since Bellator Limited worked in the defence sector, all its innovations and day-to-day operations such as production and sale of technology and equipment, whether to the Indian government or to other countries, were closely monitored by the defence ministry. And DRDO was under the direct purview of the defence ministry.

The first thing that Sarthak did after sitting in the car was to log the journey on his company's central server. This would allow his colleagues to track his whereabouts and more importantly, the whereabouts of their latest innovation. The car was locked, and there would be no stops for the entirety of the journey.

A light rain shower during the night had made the trees and bushes along the six-lane expressway come alive. The first hour of the journey went by smoothly. Sarthak was making notes about the technology for his presentation to DRDO and ISRO. If this technology was approved by DRDO, Bellator could potentially become one of the most valuable companies in the country. This success would allow him to garner more swaps and equity in the company. This venture could even allow him to retire before he turned forty. Sarthak grinned at the thought and looked out at the lush greenery passing by.

That's when a huge eighteen-wheeler truck swerved in front of his car. The chauffeur braked in time and slowed down.

'Maybe the truck driver is getting drowsy,' commented Sarthak.

The chauffeur didn't reply but maintained a considerable distance behind the truck. Five minutes later the truck swerved again.

Not wanting to slow down, Sarthak said, 'Let's overtake him. I don't want to be late.'

The chauffeur sped up and using a combination of the horn and dipper lights, aggressively wove his way through traffic and overtook the truck. The journey again became smooth. They passed a few caves along the way, and as Sarthak watched the scenery flash by, he became drowsy, especially with the morning sun warming the car to just the right temperature. He drifted into a light slumber.

Twenty minutes later, as the Audi glided past another large truck and comfortably positioned itself in front of it, the lorry purposely rammed into the car at top speed. The bulletproof car skidded off the expressway into the shrub-laden ditch alongside and somersaulted before it hit a large tree. The car was totalled. The occupants were all hurt and disoriented. The airbags had prevented any loss of life, but everyone was bleeding from their injuries. The bodyguard, paying no heed to his injuries, kicked open his door and dragged Sarthak and the chauffeur to safety. Sarthak's briefcase was still secured to his wrist.

With his head still swirling and his vision blurred, the bodyguard saw two men descending from the side of the road into the ditch. Maybe someone driving down the expressway had decided to stop and help. Nonetheless, the bodyguard was on alert, gripping the gun holstered at his hip, as such behaviour is not often seen in the country. The two men approached, exclaiming about careless and drunk truck drivers. While the bodyguard was trained to neutralize any threat, hearing the men's words and seeing their helpful demeanour, he relaxed. Maybe this was not a conspiracy after all but just a bout of bad luck owing to a drunk truck driver.

But as the two men neared the bodyguard, they deftly took out their silenced pistols and shot the three survivors in under five seconds. The scene unfolded in such a flash that the poor souls did not even get a chance to contemplate their last few seconds on earth. The two men then shot at the handcuffs on Sarthak's wrist, freeing the briefcase from its now dead owner. Before anyone else could stop their cars and come down to help, the two scurried back up to the expressway and drove away in their red Honda Civic.

The accident had taken place at 9.05 a.m. By the time passers-by stopped at the site and called for the police after seeing the gunshot wounds, it was 9.30 a.m. The police secured the crash site and loaded the bodies into an ambulance. While the forensic team got down to their analysis, the investigating officer called up Bellator Limited's office.

For the past hour, the security team monitoring Sarthak's motorcade had been under considerable stress. The signal from the transponders on both the vehicle and the briefcase had been stagnant for a while. Since it had been decided that Sarthak wouldn't stop anywhere on the journey, the stagnant transponder signal had the team worried. Mobile phone signals were not great along the expressway, especially on an overcast day with heavy cloud cover. The security team had been trying desperately to reach the three occupants of the car, but their phones seemed to be out of network coverage.

When the police called to inform the company about the crash, the receptionist, without much stress, though with a sense of childlike excitement, put the call through to the company's head of security Bhim Singh. The security officer immediately reported the incident to the CEO Shiv Narayanan. As the news broke, pandemonium ensued.

Shiv spoke to the police team on the ground and fearfully asked, 'Did you retrieve a briefcase from the crash site?'

The police officer found it strange that the company cared more for their goods than the lives of its men and responded, 'No, we haven't found any briefcase yet. Your men survived the accident but were later shot in the head. Your employee who probably had the briefcase cuffed to him had his handcuffs shot at. It seems like the killers stole the briefcase.'

Horror stricken, Shiv sat down in his chair and mumbled, 'The transponder beacon is showing that the briefcase is still at the crash site.'

'Then the killers must have removed the transponder. We have searched everywhere and haven't found anything. I suggest sending some members of your security team here right away. It will help us with our investigation,' the police officer said coldly.

Numbly, Shiv cut the call and called Bhim Singh.

Bellator's security team, led by the muscular Bhim Singh, arrived at the crash site by 11.45 a.m.

They showed their IDs to the police on site. Bhim Singh explained to the investigating officer, 'Our company official, Sarthak Jain, was going for a classified meeting with ISRO and DRDO officials to present a novel and top secret device. Very few people knew about this meeting. It seems someone betrayed us.'

The officer exclaimed, 'This is a matter way beyond my authority; I need to contact my seniors.'

Bhim Singh shook his head and said, 'Our CEO, Mr Narayanan, whom you spoke to earlier, will have to speak to R&AW if that briefcase is not found. Do you mind if I take a quick look around?'

The officer felt that the muscular man knew what he was doing so he allowed him to look around the crash site.

Within the next thirty minutes, Bhim Singh and his team located the microscopic transponder that had been planted on the surface of the briefcase. They used a tracker locator to narrow down the area from where the signal was beeping. Only someone with knowledge about the workings of the company would have known where to look for this tracker, which was invisible to the naked eye. Most tracker locators would not even have detected this state-of-the-art device.

At 12.30 p.m., Bhim Singh called Shiv. The CEO had his worst fears confirmed. Badly shaken, he then called ISRO's chief Satya Kulkarni, who at the time was sitting with DRDO's research and development secretary, Dev Burman. Both of them knew what Bellator's new device was and had been anxiously waiting for Sarthak to demonstrate it. They had been involved since the inception of the idea and understood the ramifications of the technology getting into the wrong hands. So, while everyone was sorry for the dead, the concern was for the device that had now gone missing.

ISRO's chief, Satya, asked, 'Can we not hack into the device and shut it down remotely? That way it would become useless.'

'Our IT team says it cannot be done; it was built to hack into things and prevent anyone from hacking it,' replied Shiv. 'But we are trying to work through the device's code mechanism and figure out a back channel to remotely trigger a signal the moment it is connected to any electronic device. If we are able to do that, we may be able to pinpoint its location the moment someone tries to use the device. But the chances of us cracking the code are slim. Sarthak was one of the key players who helped us develop the technology and now without him, we are not so confident about breaking the coding of this monster that we have created,' finished Shiv, sounding defeated.

Listening to the conversation, R&D Secretary Dev said, 'I will have to inform the defence ministry about this. We need to alert the authorities.'

He then quickly dialled the defence minister's secretary and requested to speak to the minister urgently. The minister was informed, and he was deeply concerned about the developments. Following the appropriate chain of command, the defence minister, who also knew about the technology that Bellator Limited had been developing, informed the PMO about the crisis. Finally, after the prime minister had been briefed, Wasim Khan received a call from Bellator's CEO who informed him about the crisis that had unfolded earlier in the day.

The general explanation given by Shiv was not enough for Wasim.

Agitated, he asked the CEO, 'Shiv, tell me, what exactly is this device? Why such paranoia around it?'

Sighing, Shiv replied, 'It's a prototype of a novel overriding device that we created and named Vita. Once attached to a laptop, Vita allows the user to hack into any electronic medium within a radius of fifty kilometres.'

'So the thieves could potentially hack into our phones, obtain our personal information and take money from our bank accounts?' Wasim asked.

'Sir, what you are suggesting is possible, but the threat here is greater. This device would allow the user to even hack into our nuclear power plants and shut down the coolant pressures in the reactors, causing them to melt down. The user can practically play God with this device.'

As the CEO's words sank in, Wasim Khan felt petrified.

8

The Gathering of the Clouds

By 3 p.m., Vikram and Ranbir had returned to R&AW's Delhi headquarters and were being briefed on the overriding device called Vita and its potential threat to the nation. While everyone was trying to wrap their heads around the mayhem, Joint Secretary Arvind Ghosh got a call from one of his deeply embedded assets in Pakistan. Captain Akbar Moeen, a young officer of twenty-five years of age, had been turned by Arvind to work against Pakistan.

As soon as Arvind answered the call, he heard Akbar's scared voice saying, 'I think my cover has been blown. Major Usman Mallik and his men seem to have had me under surveillance for some time. I am being followed. I don't know what gave me away. I have been very careful.'

Hearing the distressed young man, Arvind attempted to calm him. 'Don't worry, we can arrange a safe passage for you. We can move you and your family to India. We can give you a new identity and no one will be the wiser.'

Agitated, Akbar replied, 'I am not doing this for your country. I turned spy for the benefit of the people of Pakistan and because our corrupt politicians are driving this impoverished country further into the ditch.'

Arvind couldn't help but think that the acronym 'MICE' was well suited for spies—only Money, Ideology, Coercion or Ego could motivate a person to turn against one's country, and this was a classic example of someone following their ideology.

But Akbar's next comment snapped him out of his thoughts.

He frantically exclaimed, 'Listen to me carefully, the ISI have turned one of your top people in the country. Here, in the ISI circle, the spy is known as Top Hat. They claim that Top Hat will be invincible, almost like a divinity.'

Just as Akbar finished, Arvind heard a loud crash from the other end of the line. The door of Akbar's apartment had been broken down.

Akbar's panic-stricken voice exclaimed, 'You have thirty days. Go to Myanmar.'

Before the call was disconnected, Arvind heard a man's voice yelling, 'Who have you been talking to, traitor? Your cover has been blown. We know all about you.'

As soon as Akbar heard the voice, he quickly fired three shots in the direction of his apartment's front door. The soldiers ducked for cover, and Akbar ran into his bedroom, firing at the soldiers who were huddled at the entry. Major Usman was yelling that he wanted the traitor alive, but the soldiers, in the frenzy of protecting themselves, returned fire and accidently killed Akbar.

Arvind heard the gunshots and sorrowfully disconnected the call.

He slowly walked back to the conference room and sat down in silence. He leaned his head back in his chair and massaged his temples. Finally collecting himself, he narrated what he had just learnt to Wasim Khan, Parth Sinha, Ranbir and Vikram.

Hearing this latest development, Vikram, who followed a meticulous approach, pulled out three whiteboards to jot down the key points of their discussion.

Parth took out his diary, hastily scribbled a few notes then said, 'Akbar stated that the turncoat Top Hat will be like divinity, and Bellator's CEO Shiv said that Vita would allow its user to play god, so it seems that whoever stole Vita or orchestrated its theft could be the traitor.'

Arvind nodded in agreement. His expression pensive, he said, 'Yes, what you are saying seems plausible.'

With a sudden sense of realization, Ranbir said, 'The device Vita can only hack into a medium that is within a fifty-kilometre radius of it. This means that if the device is misused in New Delhi, the perpetrator cannot be outside the National Capital Region. This limitation of the device will allow us to pinpoint a rough area or the city where the device may be located. Also, it's possible that the thieves or the user don't know about this limitation of the device just yet.'

'So based on which city is attacked, we can get an idea of where the device is,' said Vikram. Then raising his right eyebrow, he probed, 'Why did Akbar mention Myanmar? Why are we supposed to go there?'

Arvind shook his head and said, 'I have no clue. Five days ago, when Ranbir and you had flown to Peshawar, Myanmar's General Soe Min had carried out a coup. His armed forces, riding in jeeps, trucks and tanks, drove up to the elected leader's palace of residence and put him and his associates under house arrest. The general declared that the elections held last year were not fair and the results had been tampered with. We believe that China not only instigated General Soe to carry out the coup d'état but also supported him by assuring him protection against any sanctions imposed by western countries and international persecution. Presently, Myanmar is in a state of chaos with a large faction of civilians protesting the military coup.'

Hearing this, Vikram rose and paced the room. He had heard about the coup when he was in Peshawar and had also read about it in the papers but had not paid the news much attention. However, the present situation gave rise to a bizarre thought, and Vikram started smiling.

Looking at him, Parth asked, 'What's the matter? What have you realized?'

Continuing to smile, Vikram said, 'Chaos is the best camouflage.'

'What do you mean?' asked Wasim Khan.

'I suspect that China may have just used our two neighbours to carry out a devious plan against us. I think China, in cahoots with Pakistan, had our nuclear scientist kidnapped. But due to international pressure and fallout, neither could have risked keeping Professor Hamid Ansari in their country. That is why China pushed General Soe to carry out the coup, and they are now using the chaos in Myanmar to hide Professor Hamid. If my theory is correct then it seems like China is planning something devious against us, and maybe that is why Akbar pointed us towards Myanmar.'

Wasim Khan replied thoughtfully, 'We don't know whether or not you are correct, but in any case, we need to visit Myanmar. You and Ranbir shall leave for Yangon early tomorrow morning. I will activate our field agent there and he will guide you.'

Then looking over at Arvind, the secretary said, 'Meanwhile, you and Parth search for Vita, keep an eye on Humayun Haq and find out who blew Akbar Moeen's cover.'

Everyone stood up, collected their notes and as they prepared to leave, Parth said, 'We should also put Bellator's CEO Shiv Narayanan, ISRO's chief Satya Kulkarni and the DRDO's R&D secretary Dev Burman under surveillance. They have been involved in the development of this technology since its inception and could be behind its theft.'

Wasim Khan nodded in agreement and left the room.

The meeting culminated at 5 p.m. on Thursday, the fourth day of March.

9

A Thief in the Night

Two hours later, at 7 p.m., a slim man of dark complexion, wearing a white polo T-shirt, pink shorts and a black cotton fedora hat, was sitting alone on one of the benches of Lodhi Gardens in Delhi. He had just finished his chocolate chip ice cream. Now, as the last remnants of daylight bathed the garden in a golden hue and the elite of Delhi were completing the last few rounds of their evening walk, he took out his laptop and connected Vita to it. Next, he logged onto the server of the country's largest public sector bank. Within minutes, his fingers feverishly typed away on the laptop, and he had hacked into the bank's automated teller machine software system. With a single command, he directed the dispensing sensors of about three hundred of those machines, spread across New Delhi, Gurugram, Noida and Faridabad, to dispense all the cash in the machine at one go. Next, he targeted another public sector bank in a similar fashion. By 8 p.m., four banks had been targeted, and the sudden outpouring of money had caused hysterical excitement and pandemonium amongst the public. Despite knowing that all the ATMs were under camera surveillance, a lot of people helped themselves to the jackpot they had just received. At a few places, fights broke out between those attempting to collect the extra cash and the guards stationed at the ATMs. The country's media had a good time covering the situation, which seemed to be a case of a hacker playing naughty.

After he was recruited by R&AW, Vikram, along with his family, had moved to Noida from Mumbai. Vikram's father was a freelance cartoon artist and was happy to move to the capital, as most of the political drama unfolded here. His mother, who worked for the ISRO, had been readily transferred to the organization's Delhi office; R&AW had its ways of accommodating the needs of its officers.

The family had sold their flat in Mumbai and purchased a spacious three-bedroom flat in Noida, where Vikram and his wife Sanyukta lived with his parents. Sanyukta was an English teacher in a private school nearby.

Late that night, as he was packing for his trip to Myanmar, Sanyukta called out to him to join her and his parents in their living room where the TV was tuned to a news channel. A sari-clad news anchor was presenting the evening news and informing the gossip-hungry public about the ATM fiasco that was developing around the nation. As he watched the news, Vikram couldn't help but think it was funny that while the news anchors and cameramen of various channels were covering the incident and the theft on camera, none were interested in stopping anyone from getting away with the money. Rather, they were busy trying to get the best possible footage of the incident.

As Vikram watched the events unfurl, his father commented, 'Such incidents provide cartoon artists like me with ready content. We don't need to make up anything at all.'

Just then Vikram got a call from Ranbir, 'Are you watching the news?' he asked.

'Yes. Do you think someone has just tried Vita's capabilities?' Vikram questioned, tension evident in his tone.

'Yes. And this means that Vita is in the National Capital Region. I have informed Arvind, and he is handling the matter. Our trip to Myanmar stands. I'll pick you up at 7 a.m.,' Ranbir replied, sounding unruffled as always.

'Okay,' said Vikram before hanging up.

After he was recruited by R&AW, Ranbir too had moved to the National Capital Region from Mumbai and had bought a nice large flat in Noida. His flat was a few blocks away from Vikram's. Over the past few years, the duo had experienced some close calls with death during the course of their duty, and since they always operated together, their families had become close. When the two travelled, their wives would hang out together. Vikram's parents had grown fond of Ranbir's daughters, and they would gladly babysit them when their mother, Mousumi, went out with Sanyukta.

Arvind stayed at a government-issued farmhouse in Chattarpur. Unlike Vikram, who had greatly reduced his cigarette consumption, Arvind still enjoyed his cigarettes, and he now also occasionally smoked a pipe. On the days he could, Arvind preferred to eat his dinner by 7 p.m. and retire to bed by 9 p.m. He smoked his last cigarette for the day just after dinner.

At 9 p.m., just as he had settled into bed, his phone vibrated, indicating an incoming call from Ranbir Roy.

Arvind answered and said sarcastically, 'Having travel anxiety, are we?'

Ranbir snorted and replied, 'Switch on your television. The ATMs of four banks have been hacked across the National Capital Region. The hacker triggered the dispensing mechanisms of twelve hundred ATMs, causing all the money stored in the machines to be spit out at once. The public went berserk. Anyone who was near those machines tried to get their hands on the dispensed cash. By my rough estimate, the banks collectively lost about a hundred and forty crore rupees, and the hacker just distributed this money as if it were pocket change.'

As Ranbir was updating him, Arvind got out of bed and dressed. He then switched on the TV and saw the scenes unfolding on various media channels.

Lighting another cigarette, he said, 'Vita was stolen this morning on the Mumbai-Pune Expressway. If it was used to hack the ATM systems, then someone travelled to Delhi with the device. And given the time frame of events, the only possible way for the device to have arrived in Delhi so quickly is via a flight. Moreover, the accident took place at roughly 9 a.m.; the Pune airport is about an hour and a half away from the crash site, while Mumbai's airport is about two hours away from the site. So, we need to check the flights leaving Pune after 11 a.m. and those leaving Mumbai after noon. The news reports indicate that the first hack occurred around 7.15 p.m. It's possible that the perpetrator did not leave Delhi airport and triggered the machines from the airport itself and then took a flight to another city. Or, he may have left the airport and could be anywhere by now.'

'Precisely,' Ranbir agreed with Arvind's astute calculations.

'I will alert the authorities and get the city borders manned. Meanwhile, Parth and I will delve into the airport logs and surveillance feeds; maybe the cameras captured the person who arrived here with the device.' Taking a long puff of his cigarette he said, 'Carry on with your trip to Myanmar. We will investigate here.'

By 10 p.m., Parth and Arvind had reached the airport. For Arvind, the day did not seem to end. After briefing the security chief of the airport, Parth and Arvind began meticulously going through the arrival details and passenger manifests of the day's flights from Pune and Mumbai.

10

The Not So Grand Entrance

The following morning Vikram got up early and went for a jog. The first rays of dawn were bathing the city in a golden hue. With each stride he thought about his cover in Myanmar. R&AW's local asset had made some back-dated entries to accommodate Ranbir and Vikram's cover story, but there was no way to know if the Burmese army would accept their fiction. Vikram tried to sweat out his anxiety by jogging as rigorously as he could. After his jog, he took a cold shower. Next, he sat down and in silence ate a bowl of mixed fruits, some curd and muesli and finished his scrumptious meal with a toast.

By 6.30 a.m. he was ready to leave, but he knew he still had about thirty minutes before Ranbir arrived. So he woke up Sanyukta to chat and ease his anxiety. Sanyukta knew Vikram had joined R&AW, but she did not know the exact nature of his work.

While preparing her morning cup of ginger tea, Sanyukta casually asked Vikram, 'Are you happy joining the spy agency?'

'Absolutely,' came Vikram's instant reply, which made her glad. The raise in his salary was an added bonus for the family. Sanyukta poured her tea into an earthen cup. She liked the aroma of the clay mixed with her hot tea.

As Sanyukta took her first sip with a slight slurp, Vikram asked, 'Are you enjoying your new position as an English teacher? Although with your proficiency in Arabic, you could have continued with your translation work as a freelancer.'

'I wanted a change, and this job pays better. We need to increase our savings as I want us to start a family, but we'll talk about that later,' explained Sanyukta.

Humming in agreement, Vikram realized that talking to his wife calmed him. Her pragmatic nature gave him a feeling of reassurance and tranquillity. Vikram hated unwanted surprises.

Ranbir arrived at five minutes to seven, and the duo left for the airport. Before their flight, Vikram finally gave in and smoked a cigarette to curb his anxiety.

At 1 p.m., the duo landed at Yangon's international airport after a three-hour, forty-minute flight. After the coup d'état, the Burmese military was cross-checking the credentials of all incoming passengers against various databases. Each immigration counter had military personnel sitting along with the immigration officer.

Upon their turn, Ranbir and Vikram walked up to the immigration counter together, something that only families or couples generally did.

Smirking at the duo, the immigration officer tauntingly said, 'Your honeymoon seems to be in jeopardy, the general does not approve of such alliances.'

The soldiers nearby all broke into laughter.

Smiling, Ranbir replied, 'We are here as security consultants for Myanmar Oil and Gas Enterprise, or MOGE as you probably know it.'

Swiftly taking out two sheets of paper, he handed them over the counter and continued, 'This is the letter of invitation from the company.'

Hearing the words 'security consultants,' several soldiers huddled around the immigration counter. While one of them read the invitation letter, another asked Ranbir, 'What do you mean by security consultants?'

'We work for Gradient Limited. Our company provides personnel and cyber security consultancy to firms around the world. We educate companies on how to keep themselves secure from outside threats.'

The senior soldier who was reading the letter called up MOGE to enquire about the invitation and confirm that it was not falsified.

Meanwhile, a lanky soldier exuding confidence and power said, 'This is Myanmar. Now everything belongs to General Min. No need for your expert advice. You can go back to your country.'

Ranbir did not react and stayed silent. There was no point in irking these young boys.

The senior soldier returned, displeasure clearly reflected on his face. The invite had turned out to be genuine and had been generated a week before the coup. So, in an attempt to find some flaw, he checked the credibility of Gradient Limited online. Finally, when the authorities could find nothing out of order, they allowed Vikram and Ranbir to go through. They did, however, note down that the duo was staying at Inya Lake Hotel in Yangon city.

As soon as they sat in a taxi, Vikram lit a cigarette. Ranbir smiled at his friend's anxiety and quipped, 'We've chosen a dangerous location for our honeymoon.'

Vikram smirked but didn't respond.

En route to the hotel, which was a twenty-minute drive from the international airport, Vikram noticed that the city of Yangon was eerily silent despite it being a Friday. Shops and establishments were closed, and military checkpoints and armed guards were stationed every few hundred metres. All the civil unrest between the pro-democracy faction of citizens and the general's army that the media had been fervently reporting on was happening in cities other than Yangon. The capital had become the military's stronghold, with no sense of chaos visible.

As the taxi turned left onto Parami Road, Ranbir, who was looking out the window, noticed a street dog lying dispiritedly on the pavement. He lifted his head, and for a few fleeting seconds Ranbir and the dog looked at each other, but animals are not interested when humans are out to hunt each other, and so the dog calmly lay his head down on the pavement again.

11

Let's Disappoint Each Other

At the hotel, Vikram was surprised when he found that they had been booked into two separate suites. It seemed their local contact Tin Tun was being frivolous with the government's resources.

A while after they had checked in, Vikram's doorbell rang. He opened the door to find an old Burmese man of about seventy years, wearing a loose white linen shirt paired with white cotton pants, standing there. The bald man, who had large eyes that were evenly spaced under pencil-thin eyebrows, calmly said, 'I am Tin Tun, your contact in Burma. Call your partner, we have a lot to discuss.'

Vikram stepped aside, and the man silently walked in and settled on the sofa in the large suite.

Vikram followed him and called Ranbir on the intercom. Eyeing the bald gentleman, he said, 'Our contact is here.'

Without replying, Ranbir hung up and soon walked into Vikram's room.

As the two R&AW agents settled into their seats, Tin said, 'I was briefed by Secretary Wasim Khan. You think the general is harbouring your nuclear scientist. But this coup is not like the last one; the situation on the ground is quite complicated. There are roughly twenty ethnic militias in the country fighting for autonomy. The civilians are waging a guerrilla war on the general's army. They're using home-made weapons after being trained by local militias and instigated by local politicians who lost their power after the coup. Many civil servants have resigned en masse, but the military is threatening to punish peaceful protesters, and with the lost wages and limited monetary backup, their resolve might just falter. If a solution is not reached soon, anarchy will drive Myanmar to become a failed state.'

With an air of confidence Vikram replied, 'We can use the chaos to our advantage and find out if Professor Hamid Ansari is here.'

Shaking his head in disapproval, Tin raised his thick left thumb as he replied, 'Firstly, no one will talk to two outsiders. There is an acute sense of distrust and fear prevalent amongst the masses.'

Then raising his index finger, he continued, 'Secondly, your cover here is only for seven days and the general's lieutenants may have you under observation. Yangon is tightly controlled by the army. Even if the scientist is here, I doubt you will be able to look for him or rescue him.'

'And lastly,' he finished, now raising his thick middle finger, 'none of my sources have heard of a nuclear scientist being smuggled into Myanmar or being held by the general.'

Ranbir stood up, irritation boiling inside him, but not wishing to show it, he calmly yet assertively said, 'Sir, you probably don't comprehend the seriousness of the situation. But cover or not, we will only leave Myanmar after establishing whether or not Professor Hamid Ansari is being held captive here. Right now, we are not here to rescue the professor but only to ascertain his presence and to understand the motive behind his kidnapping.'

Vikram looked hopefully at the grumpy old man and said, 'Sir, you must help us. We somehow need to make the general show his hand.'

Clicking his tongue, the bald man got up and said, 'What you are asking for is dangerous. It could cost me my life. Tell Secretary Khan that my fee for this assignment has doubled.'

Sighing, Vikram said, 'I will arrange for your payment, but please carve out a strategy.'

Nodding, Tin left the R&AW agents and strolled out of Vikram's room.

After Tin left, Ranbir stated, 'Money is the easiest yet the most dangerous incentive in the spy world. A person working solely for money is more often than not a coward and will always put his own livelihood and interests first. Such people are usually the first to backstab. However, our only choice is to rely on the sly old man.'

Agreeing with Ranbir's assessment, Vikram said, 'I fear that our contact may double-cross us. We should come up with a plan of our own.'

12

In the Dark

In Delhi, Parth and Arvind had not found any clues about who had activated Vita. None of R&AW's three suspects—Bellator's CEO Shiv Narayanan, ISRO's chief Satya Kulkarni and DRDO's R&D secretary Dev Burman—had taken a flight for Delhi. The agents had not found anything peculiar or out of place when they went through the footage from the airport's surveillance cameras. Not a single person had shied away from the authorities while exiting the airport or cast furtive glances at the police officers. Nothing stood out. Consequently, Parth and Arvind had spent the better part of the night going through the passenger details and surveillance feeds multiple times.

The following morning, after Ranbir and Vikram had flown to Yangon, Arvind got an update on the high commissioner from a team member.

'Good morning, sir!' he exclaimed. 'High Commissioner Humayun Haq is stable and is recovering well. His fever and stomach cramps have subsided. The hospital has confirmed that in all likelihood, he will be discharged tomorrow.'

Arvind hummed an acknowledgement and cut the phone. He was glad. Once the high commissioner was back in his office, R&AW would have the chance of finding out about Jahangir Niazi's whereabouts and his nefarious plans.

By the time Ranbir and Vikram had settled into their rooms, a junior analyst, who had been tasked with analysing all of Pune's traffic camera footage from the day of the theft, had observed a red Honda Civic that seemed to have tailed Sarthak's car. The junior analyst took the findings to Arvind's team of officers. They in turn cross-checked the car against witness statements, and at 4.27 p.m., Arvind received another call from his team.

The analyst informed him, 'Sir, we may have had a breakthrough. A red Honda Civic is seen on various traffic cameras in Pune and on the expressway, maintaining considerable distance behind Sarthak's car on the day of the theft. We cross-checked it with witness statements and a few people did report seeing a red Honda Civic stop right near the ditch where Sarthak's car tumbled over. The reports highlight that two people got out of the car and ran down into the ditch. They seem to be our guys. No one saw their faces though. Lastly, sir, we also checked the main gate surveillance camera at Bellator. When Sarthak's car was inside waiting for him, a Honda Civic parked on the opposite side of the road was captured on the surveillance feed.'

Arvind was relieved on hearing the update and with a tinge of excitement he replied, 'Good work. Do we have the number plate of the car?'

Sighing, the analyst replied, 'Sir, the car did not have any number plates. But we are trying to search for the vehicle in Mumbai and Pune.'

Disappointed, Arvind simply stated, 'Keep searching. Alert the local authorities. I need that vehicle found immediately.'

'Yes sir,' came the crisp reply.

With no other leads in hand, Arvind decided to put his energies back into Vita and figuring out how the device had got from the Mumbai-Pune Expressway to Delhi in about ten hours. Roughly twenty-four hundred passengers had landed in Delhi in that time frame. Arvind would have to dedicate a team to cross-check everyone who had arrived in town. He set up a team of five analysts in a conference room and told them to go through the details of each person who had arrived in town, cross-check their facials with the government-issued identity cards, carry out a thorough background check and flag any phoney ones.

It was a Friday evening, and by 7 p.m., most people leave their offices for their journey back home. The Indian economy is growing on the backs of the enormous yet crucial middle class, who work tirelessly to feed their families and provide their children with a secure future. A lot of them commute via the extensive Delhi Metro.

At exactly 7.20 p.m., all ten lines of the Metro came to a sudden halt. The metro trains stopped dead in their tracks. The drivers of a few of the trains did manage to revive the engines via a manual override, but every time they did that, the engines would stall again, as if all the energy were being drained from them. For over two hours Delhi Metro Rail Corporation (DMRC), the public sector company tasked with managing the operations of Delhi Metro, tried its best to solve the issue. The company has a fleet of engineers at its disposal, but no one was able to understand what was happening. A few of the computer engineers tried to hack into the system from an external source but found themselves to be blocked out. Then at 10.20 p.m., the trains unexpectedly came to life. Hesitantly, the drivers gained speed to reach the nearest station. As the various trains across the different lines neared the next station on their lines, an announcement was made in each train, a crisp female voice stating, 'We regret the delay and inconvenience. All further services are cancelled for the day. This will be the final stop. Please disembark. Please mind the gap.'

More often than not, the middle class of the country faces such hurdles in their lives. And unfortunately, they have become so accustomed to it that they have stopped complaining; instead, they let the irritation pile up. So across the various metro stations, a frustrated and defeated crowd could be seen walking back home in silence.

In a café in Khan Market, a slim man of dark complexion, wearing white chino shorts and a pink polo, was finishing his second scoop of double choco-chip ice cream. It was not the sugar rush but a sense of sadistic pleasure that made him beam and glow.

A little before midnight, Arvind got a call from his team informing him of the developments of the catastrophe that had engulfed the Delhi Metro. Ready to retire for the day, the call had initially irritated him only to later become the cause of his distress.

He got out of bed then and while lighting a cigarette called Parth.

Parth answered on the second ring and said, 'What happened?'

Arvind briefed him about the incident. 'The fact that the trains were halted and not made to crash, which the hacker could very well have done, gives me a bad feeling. It seems as if someone is challenging us. The incident is more like a taunt than an actual attack. The perpetrator is subtly telling us that he is still in Delhi and is still in control.'

Parth shut his eyes tightly and his forehead furrowed as he listened to Arvind. Shaking his head, he replied, 'Or it could just be someone who hasn't realized Vita's full potential yet.'

Inhaling a drag, Arvind replied, 'Or it could be that someone is trying to get the attention of international buyers for Vita.'

Again shaking his head Parth replied, 'If someone wanted to grab the attention of terrorists, he would have wreaked havoc. We need to trace the events after the accident on the expressway and get hold of the Honda Civic.'

Arvind hummed in agreement and said, 'Okay, I just hope that Vita hasn't fallen into the hands of a mad man. Terrorists are predictable. Sadists are not.'

After the ATM hacks, R&AW had circulated an image of Vita to all security agencies and police stations in the National Capital Region. The city borders and all train stations, bus terminals and the airport were being heavily manned. Cars were being checked on the highways. A team of R&AW's computer engineers was sitting with Bellator's team to try and open a back channel into Vita that would pinpoint its location. But the two best hopes for R&AW now seemed to be locating the Honda Civic and High Commissioner Humayun Haq quickly resuming his duties.

With nothing more to do or discuss at the moment, Arvind and Parth decided to catch a few hours of sleep and convene at their office in the morning to work through the situation with fresh minds.

13

Who Cares if They Die?

On Saturday morning, their second day in Myanmar, Vikram and Ranbir woke up early and went for a swim in the hotel's odd balloon-shaped swimming pool. Vikram reckoned that the adrenaline boost from the rigorous cardio would boost their brain cells into conjuring a much-needed plan. By his thirteenth lap Vikram had a rough idea on what they had to do. Stopping Ranbir in the shallow end, he discussed his scheme with him. Though dangerous, it seemed to be the only way ahead. So, after breakfast, Ranbir called Tin for a meeting.

Tin arrived at Ranbir's tidy suite at 10 a.m. and settled on the sofa.

Without wasting time Ranbir said, 'We want you to introduce us to the various militia heads of the country. We have a proposal for them.'

Tin looked at Ranbir, then laughed for a minute, indicating his thoughts on Ranbir's suggestion.

When he saw that the two spies were serious, his expression became sombre and he said, 'Have you both lost your minds? If the general or his lieutenants find out that you are meeting with the rebel leaders, both of you will be executed.'

Vikram replied coldly, 'No one will find out, and it's a risk we are willing to take. Will you help us?'

'Pray tell, what ingenious proposal do you have for the rebel leaders? Why would they entertain you?' asked the bald Burmese man, his tone dismissive.

'We will ask the rebel leaders to look for Professor Hamid Ansari. With their extensive network across the country, they will be able to ascertain if the professor is being hidden here, and if so, in which part of the country. Then, with the help of the rebel leaders, we will kidnap the general's daughter. This will not only give the rebels a huge bargaining chip but will also allow us to force the general's hand in revealing the presence of Professor Ansari. For their help, we will provide the rebels with arms and ammunition, free of cost.'

Tin was flabbergasted. He jumped up, and throwing his hands in the air he yelled, 'This is preposterous. Are you both insane or do you have a death wish? If anyone from the rebel camps tells the general of your plans and intentions, all three of us will die.' Then looking at Vikram he said, 'It's not a risk I am willing to take.'

'Do you have a better plan?' Vikram asked coldly.

'No. But that does not mean I don't value my life. All the money that you pay me will be useless if I die.'

Ranbir stood up, placed a hand on Tin's shoulder and stated, 'We will triple your pay. But we do need your help.'

Tin shook his head and said, 'I also want a guaranteed safe passage to Thailand, once this mission is over.'

Vikram asked curiously, 'Wasn't your mother from India?'

'She was, but Thailand's climate suits me better,' replied Tin with a scowl. He did not like the fact that Vikram knew his family history.

The grumpy Burmese then slowly walked towards the door, and as he was leaving, muttered, 'I will arrange for the first meeting tonight. Be prepared.'

As soon as Tin left, Vikram turned to Ranbir and said in a hushed voice, 'I think he is going to rat us out to the general. But seeing his greed, I think he will only do so after he has set up our meetings with a few militia leaders. Once he has a considerable pool to bargain with, he will sell us out for a handsome reward.'

Sighing, Ranbir replied, 'What more can we do to lure him?'

Vikram paused thoughtfully before replying, 'Nothing. We rat him out before he does. We will burn his cover and the location of all the militia leaders to the general. The general is hungry for power, and I have just the right plan that will compel him to show his hand.'

'You're playing a dangerous game, Vikram. Playing both sides could be lethal for us.'

'Alexander the Great invaded India in 326 BC and was challenged by King Porus at Hydaspes which today lies in Punjab (Pakistan) between the Jhelum and Beas rivers. Porus knew that to attack, Alexander's forces would have to cross the river. But Alexander was shrewd; he kept moving his army up and down the river. Porus made his army shadow Alexander's forces. This went on for days, with Alexander's forces initiating a few false attacks; they would routinely advance only to fall back. This made Porus overconfident. One night when the tide was high and everyone in King Porus's camp believed that no one would cross during the high tide, Alexander's army deftly crossed the river and defeated their unprepared enemy. Thus, my friend, life is a series of calculations. We must always keep our enemies occupied with our bluffs. Never let them realize when and how we shall strike.'

'When do you intend to meet the general?' asked Ranbir sounding a tad bit reassured.

'Now!' said Vikram with a sense of determination.

'And how do you plan to meet him?'

'We will waltz right into his villa.'

At 4 p.m., Ranbir and Vikram reached Pyigyi Zeyar Road. It had been a five-hour drive from their hotel. The taxi dropped them off just before the army barricade then sped away in the opposite direction. Taking a deep breath, the duo walked up to the barricade. The soldiers looked at them suspiciously as they neared and surrounded them as soon as they reached the first fortified open bunker.

A fit, lean soldier walked up to them and said, 'This is no place for tourists. Turn around and go back.'

Vikram slowly took out his identification card and said, 'We have some information for the general. We need to meet him now.'

The soldier was taken aback. He had not anticipated this. He radioed the information to his senior. Five minutes later a captain in the general's army arrived in a jeep. Without giving the spies a second look, he went through their papers and identification. Then he cross-checked their arrival details with the immigration office.

Stepping out from the bunker the captain said, 'You are in Myanmar to advise on security for MOGE. What are you doing here? Give me the message and if I find it to be relevant, I will pass it on to the general.'

Vikram shook his head and said, 'My information is for the general's ears only. We will talk to him and no one else.'

The captain gave them a long stare before walking away to radio the developments to his commanding officer. A few seconds later he came back, and pointing his bony finger at the spies he ordered, 'Arrest them.'

Instantly, soldiers surrounded Vikram and Ranbir, put them in handcuffs and shoved them in a jeep. As the jeep was about to drive away, Ranbir yelled at the top of his voice, 'We have sensitive intelligence regarding the militias revolting against the general. If you do not let us speak to him, you will be responsible for the general's failure at the hands of the rebels.'

The captain considered his position, then radioed his commanding officer again. For the next thirty minutes, Vikram and Ranbir sat in uncertainty about their future as the soldiers radioed back and forth, speaking in their local language. Finally, the captain snapped his fingers and indicated to the driver to turn the jeep around.

Glaring at the duo, he hissed, 'You have five minutes with the general. If you utter any nonsense, I will shoot both of you.'

The ten-minute drive up Pyigyi Zeyar Road led to Pyidaungsu Hluttaw, the Burmese Parliament. A huge villa in a secluded part of the compound, east of the Parliament, near the Nigalaik Creek, served as the general's residence. Security was intense throughout the route, with multiple barricades manned by heavily armed soldiers.

The jeep drove up to the side of the intricately constructed wooden villa. Swarms of officers with a lot of medals pinned to their chests, indicating that they were of senior ranks, could be seen moving around.

The jeep stopped and Vikram and Ranbir were hurriedly escorted into a large conference room, situated on one side of the ground floor.

Fifteen minutes later the general, accompanied by five colonels, entered the room.

Vikram and Ranbir stood up as a mark of respect. The general eyed them closely as he plonked himself at the head of the table. He looked more like a schoolteacher than an authoritarian figure with his salt-and-pepper hair, thick gold-rimmed glasses and piercing gaze. As the colonels seated themselves, the general said, irritation clear in his voice, 'You have five minutes.'

Vikram hastily replied, 'Sir, thank you for taking the time to listen to our proposal. We are from Gradient Limited. Our company provides personnel and cyber security to firms around the world. We are here to provide security consultancy services to Myanmar Oil and Gas Limited. However, last evening, one of the rebel leaders, Aung Su, contacted our office in Delhi with a request to provide them with weapons and training for his rebel group. Our company wishes to make the following proposal, sir,' taking a deep breath Vikram nervously continued, 'We want you to allow us to meet the rebel leaders with the promise of providing them with weapons and training.'

The colonels and the general stared at Vikram as if he had lost his mind.

'We will meet them over the next couple of days and gain their trust. On the day of the final meeting, my partner and I will inform your soldiers of our location. Your soldiers can swarm in and wipe out all the rebel leaders at once.'

The general continued to stare at Vikram. Then he got up and walked up to him and said softly, his tone terrifying, 'And what does your company want in return for this generosity?'

'An opportunity to keep you in power and form a long-term business alliance. Our company would prefer to back you and not the rebels. We believe in siding with the stronger force.'

The general frowned and said, 'What happens when I am no longer the stronger force in the playground?'

'We will ensure that you remain the strongest. Our company is on the verge of developing a novel fusion warhead. It will guarantee you become the greatest general in the southeast,' explained Vikram with a gleam in his eyes.

The general thought for a moment then said, 'Fine. If you hold up your end of the bargain, I will give your company a chance. But before I commit any financial resources to your novel device, I would like to have it inspected by my own experts.'

Vikram and Ranbir knew that General Soe did not have any Burmese nuclear scientists in his team, so the fact that he confidently spoke about inspecting their proposed warhead indicated that he may be harbouring Professor Hamid Ansari. But probing any further could blow their cover, so Vikram just thanked the general for his confidence in their company, and the spies were allowed to leave peacefully.

After they returned to their hotel, Ranbir, while looking out of the window in his suite, said, 'We almost got ourselves killed today. Do you think he is hiding Hamid Ansari?'

'We won't know unless we execute our plan,' replied Vikram.

'If we rat out the rebel leaders to the general, Myanmar will be doomed forever. Who knows what he will do,' mused Ranbir, his conscience pricking him.

'We don't have a choice. For now, Myanmar will have to suffer the loss. If we survive this ordeal, then we might be able to help the local population. Besides, if we don't rescue Professor Hamid from their clutches, they might use him to arm a nuclear device. So right now, even for the people of Myanmar, we are the best choice they have.'

Ranbir gazed out of the window pensively without replying.

14

Riddles in the Dark

Vikram and Ranbir had returned to their hotel at 9.30 p.m. Thankfully Tin had not contacted them yet.

So after reviewing the day's events, the two settled in Ranbir's room and ordered a tea leaf salad, thick udon noodles served with a bowl of fish-and-shallot broth on the side and a portion of deep-fried spring rolls. For the two of them this was a light meal.

After they ate, as Vikram was leaving for his room, they heard a soft knock. Vikram, who had already walked up to the door, opened it and found Tin standing there with two slim men dressed in the red robes worn by the monks in the country. The three of them entered silently and sat on the sofa in the living room of the suite.

Without wasting time Tin got straight to the point. 'These two gentlemen are affiliated with Aung Su's group. They are here to hear your proposal.'

Vikram eyed them carefully. 'Why are they wearing monk's robes?'

'Because they really are monks. They are from the Maha Bodhi Ta Htaung Monastery. They have unofficially allied themselves with Aung Su and other local rebel factions,' explained Tin.

Nodding, Vikram then told the two young monks about their need to locate Professor Hamid Ansari and the support that R&AW could provide to the rebel groups.

The monks heard Vikram's proposal in silence. They sat poker-faced and gave no hint of their thoughts on Vikram's grand scheme.

The monks were aware that four of India's eastern states—Manipur, Mizoram, Nagaland and Arunachal Pradesh—shared their borders with Myanmar; so if R&AW intended, it could easily smuggle in the said weapons and ammunition to the various rebel groups. Vikram's proposal could be practically executed.

As soon as Vikram finished explaining his plan, the two monks stood up and without saying a word, left the room.

A bit astonished at their behaviour, Ranbir looked at Tin sceptically.

Understanding his bewilderment Tin replied, 'They have heard your proposal. They will now discuss it with their seniors and the rebel leaders. If they find it worthwhile, they will contact us for a meeting to take things forward.'

'Fair enough,' replied Ranbir.

'Not quite. I am the link between you and the rebel leaders. So I expect a percentage of my payment tomorrow morning. Also, I suggest that you speak to Secretary Khan and start mobilizing your weapons cache. The rebels might ask for a token payment as a sign of good faith and commitment from your side.'

The bald Burmese man then heaved himself up and left.

In India, Saturday remained largely uneventful. Arvind and Parth were nowhere close to solving any of the clues they had been working on. Arvind's team was diligently sifting through the twenty-four hundred passengers, but carrying out the daunting task of a thorough background check on each of them was proving to be time-consuming.

Another group of analysts was going through the various traffic camera feeds from Pune again to see if the car's number plate or any other distinctive mark was visible, which would make their search for it easy.

R&AW's analysts who were sitting in Pune with Bellator's team had still not been able to crack the code for Vita.

High Commissioner Humayun Haq had been discharged, but he had decided to resume work from Monday, after resting through the weekend. The spies would have to wait till he returned to the office to get any leads from him.

Parth and Arvind were sitting later than usual in the R&AW headquarters, trying to wrap their heads around the developments that had occurred so far. A timeline of events was made, the list of suspects was put up on a whiteboard and a variety of possibilities were being discussed. The spy agency had activated all its local assets in the NCR to establish eyes and ears on the ground and gather firsthand intelligence.

As the clock struck seven in the evening, the bars that indicate the strength of a cellular network in an area vanished from the phones of all personnel in the building. No one noticed the lack of signal at the time but about fifteen minutes later, people started huddling in groups and looking at each other's mobile phones. Several confirmed that their mobile phones were not receiving any signal at all. The news quickly circulated throughout the building and reached Arvind and Parth, who were busy strategizing in the conference room. Upon hearing of the bizarre issue, both checked their phones and found the signal gone. Only the landline which transmits voice and data via copper wires through electric pulses and not via cell towers was working. A few of the analysts called their family members on their landline numbers. They too confirmed that their mobile phone signals were down.

Arvind massaged his temples, lit a cigarette and said, 'Our perpetrator is using Vita again. It is astonishing that all three attacks have been mild, without any loss of life.'

Parth was pedantic by nature so ignoring Arvind's comment he first said, 'Smoking inside the building is not allowed.'

Taking a long drag, Arvind stubbed the cigarette in a glass filled with water in front of him.

After this Parth continued, 'I've also noticed another pattern; all attacks occur around 7 p.m. and the disruptions are stopped after an hour or so. Vita should allow the user to inflict permanent damage, yet this person only inflicts controlled chaos. Why would anyone do that?'

'Maybe he is showing off the power of the device to some international buyers?' replied Arvind.

'But if that were the case, then this perpetrator's point would have been proven after the first two attacks. Typically, someone yielding such powers makes certain demands. Yet this person hasn't made any contact,' said Parth, sounding worried and perplexed.

'All the attacks have occurred in Delhi, which indicates that this person is in the NCR and is therefore confident about his strategy and antics,' Parth continued as he made a list of clues relating to the mysterious user of Vita.

The continuous roadblocks were frustrating Arvind. To calm his nerves, he lit another cigarette, ignoring Parth's earlier comment about not smoking on the premises.

Two hours later, the slim man with a dark complexion, wearing a red polo T-shirt with denim shorts and a pair of brown suede shoes, was enjoying his chocolate sundae at a diner in Greater Kailash market. After he licked the last of the chocolate from the bowl, he typed out a few lines of code on his laptop, and mobile service was restored in and around the National Capital Region. Smiling like a child at the success of his endeavour, he quietly paid the bill and left the diner.

Late that night, Vikram called Secretary Wasim Khan and explained the developments that had transpired in Myanmar. The secretary was furious at Vikram for firstly offering weapons to the rebel groups and then planning to betray them to the autocratic and ruthless general.

In a fit of anger and irritation, the otherwise calm secretary said, 'You had no authority to make such a deal on behalf of R&AW. You have been sent there to ascertain the presence of the professor, who I might remind you, we lost due to your ingenious plan. Your macabre scheme will not only doom Myanmar, it will also lead to the creation of a highly unstable neighbour for us, especially one that will be under China's control.'

Patiently, Vikram reiterated to the secretary that the said plan was the best course of action. His tone sombre, he said, 'I regret losing the professor, but at least we know who we are rescuing. I need your help. Please arrange to send a weapons cache and the research papers on nuclear fusion from Professor Hamid Ansari's lab.'

'The moment the general sees the professor's name on the research notes, he will understand your ruse,' replied Wasim Khan, his voice tired.

'No, I will copy the notes and make certain omissions and errors, which hopefully only Professor Ansari will realize. This way we will be able to ascertain his presence in Myanmar.'

While sceptical about the ruse, Wasim Khan realized they didn't have many choices, so he grudgingly agreed to the plan before cutting the call.

15

A Walk in the Woods

On Sunday morning, ISRO's chief Satya Kulkarni was having an omelette along with a buttered toast and a chilled glass of canned watermelon juice. This was his staple breakfast, which he prepared for himself every day. Satya came from modest means. He had worked hard and earned a doctorate degree in aerospace engineering. Till his parents were alive, he would regularly send them money. After their deaths, he had found solace in his work. However, he was meek by nature and had never married for the fear of bearing the extra responsibility.

The morning news broadcast, which he was watching on the television in the dining room, was showcasing the three hacks which the news anchor called 'glitches'. Clearly, the media had neither linked the three events, nor did they suspect foul play. The government too had not bothered to clear up their misunderstanding for fear of pandemonium amongst the masses.

But Satya realized what was going on, and as he downed the last bit of his buttered toast with a big gulp of the juice, he decided to call the DRDO's R&D secretary, Dev Burman.

Dev was a stout man with a receding hairline and lampshade moustache. As the R&D secretary for the DRDO, Dev was privy to the latest technological innovations happening across the nation, especially in the fields of defence and espionage. Although not corrupt in his dealings and practices, Dev, by virtue of his position, received a lot of gifts from various private companies that manufactured defence components and materials. Keeping aside his scruples, Dev received the gifts quite readily.

When his mobile vibrated, he was busy playing solitaire on his laptop.

Leaving his game, Dev answered the call. 'Hello, Satya. How are you?'

'Have you been watching the news?' Satya asked anxiously, ignoring the courtesies.

'Yes, the media has labelled these instances as some sort of technical glitch.'

'I fear Vita has landed in the wrong hands. I have been sceptical about this technology since its inception. Now look where the scientific progress of Sarthak Jain has landed us.'

'I'm sure the authorities are doing everything they can to get the device back. Scientific progress always has an element of risk. And anyway, why do you worry? The liability of the misuse of this technology will fall on Bellator and not on us,' replied Dev casually.

'The user can wreak havoc on our nation; all our satellites and defence technologies are at risk. A misguided fool could doom us all. The loss of human life would be unimaginable. This is not a casual matter, Dev.'

'But what can we do?' asked Dev, not wanting to be burdened with tension on a Sunday morning.

'I think we should speak to Shiv and hire a private investigator to look into the theft of Vita. If we find any clues, we can hand them over to the investigating authorities.'

'It is not our place to start an investigation. If we do, we could be held liable. I don't want to be caught up in this mess. You can speak to Shiv about this matter, but I am out of it,' replied Dev and hung up before Satya could reply.

Shaking his head in disbelief, Satya decided to call Shiv.

Shiv Narayanan lived in a posh penthouse on Boat Club Road, near Koregaon Park, in Pune. He was a first-generation entrepreneur and had started Bellator Limited after working for fifteen years in the mergers and acquisitions divisions of various prestigious investment banks. He stayed with his parents and wife, Devasree. Bellator's success had catapulted Shiv into the elite crowd of the city. Before the project to create Vita, Shiv's company had seen steady growth. Recruiting Sarthak Jain, who at the time had been working in Germany, had proved to be a favourable decision for Shiv. Sarthak had brought with him innumerable innovations and ideas. A few initial successes, such as creating an efficient laser guiding mechanism for torpedoes, had allowed Shiv to garner greater clout with DRDO. This in turn had allowed him to get funding for the research and development of Vita. Devasree liked her new lifestyle and her ambitions had pushed Shiv to grow the company faster and take extraordinary risks. The creation of Vita had been a risk, and now its theft was proving to be an even bigger liability. The government could hold Shiv responsible for being negligent and allowing the misuse of Vita and for any deaths that may be caused by it.

On weekends, Devasree and Shiv would do an hour of yoga in their terrace garden, followed by some strong hot filter coffee, which they enjoyed slowly.

But since Sarthak's death, Shiv's caffeine intake had increased while the yoga and the disciplined lifestyle that he generally followed, even during the tough early days of his company, had gone out the window. Shiv had not been sleeping well and had become a recluse. Moreover, the news reports from the past three days had sent jitters down his spine. Consequently, he spent long hours in the office and arrived home at odd hours.

When Satya called, a dishevelled Shiv answered the phone in a daze, 'Hello?'

'Shiv? How have you been? Have you been following the news? Who do you think has taken Vita?' Satya shot the questions at him.

The last question jolted Shiv, then looking at the caller ID, he regained his composure, took a deep breath and said, 'The authorities are working on it. Some officers are also working with our engineers to open a back channel to pinpoint the location of the device.'

'You sound tired. Can I be of any help?' asked Satya, genuine concern in his voice.

'No, Bhim Singh has gone to Delhi to try and locate the device.' As soon as Shiv said this, he regretted his statement. Fatigue had clouded his mind and he had unthinkingly replied to Satya, who did not need to know the details of the investigation at this point.

'Do the authorities know that your security chief is hunting for the device?' enquired the ISRO chief.

'I don't know, and I don't care. I have to secure that device with or without R&AW's help. I will speak to you later, Satya,' replied Shiv, irritated, and cut the call.

After the harrowing experience of the past few days, Shiv did not want to trust anyone.

R&AW's analysts had tapped the phones of Satya Kulkarni, Shiv Narayanan and Dev Burman as they were all persons of interest in this vital investigation. The Sunday morning calls from Satya to Dev and Shiv had been overheard by Arvind's team.

As Arvind's team was briefing him and Parth about these calls, Shiv made a call to Bhim Singh, but this time he used a different cell and number, one that he had purchased under a phoney name and address.

'Have you found any leads?' enquired Shiv.

'No, I haven't been able to locate the men yet. Though I can confirm that they are in South Delhi. But I haven't been able to pinpoint their exact location. Have they made any demands?'

'No! I also fear that R&AW is tapping my cell. No one knows about this number, but I think R&AW will soon realize that you are in Delhi, hunting for the device. If they come questioning, I will have to admit that I have sent you to Delhi, as it is our company's moral responsibility to secure the device. Time is of the essence. Find them quickly and get hold of Vita.'

'Understood,' replied Bhim Singh and cut the call.

Despite it being the weekend, Shiv was in his office. After speaking to Bhim Singh, he went to prepare some filter coffee. He was particular about his coffee and liked to make it himself. Shiv spent the next fifteen minutes enjoying his hot coffee. A while later he got a call from Arvind Ghosh.

The joint secretary came straight to the point. 'My local assets tell me that your security chief, Bhim Singh, is in Delhi trying to locate Vita. Is this true? Are you running a parallel investigation?'

Sighing, Shiv replied wearily, 'Yes, he is in Delhi trying to locate Vita. It is my moral responsibility to locate the device. It is not my lack of confidence in you, but rather my own guilt, shame and sense of duty that pushed me to send Bhim to look for the device. You must understand, sir, I cannot and will not sit idly by while this madman strikes terror through our country.'

'I see. Very well, in that case, tell Bhim Singh to report to me. We must pool our resources and work together,' replied Arvind, much to Shiv's surprise.

Masking his excitement, Shiv responded, 'Thank you, sir, I will tell him to report to you right away.'

Five minutes later, Shiv dialled Bhim Singh using his regular phone and instructed him to report to Arvind's team and share all the information he had amassed so far.

Arvind's analysts, who had tapped Shiv's regular phone, confirmed that Bellator's CEO had not conveyed any coded message to his security chief.

16

The Pit of Despair

The slim man with a dark complexion was wearing a yellow polo T-shirt and dark blue shorts and was sitting with his brother in room number thirteen of the Ambassador Hotel, situated on Subramania Bharti Marg, New Delhi. His name was Akhilesh, and he was a tech genius who suffered from mild schizophrenia which ignited sudden bouts of the need to fulfil his sadistic desires. Sweets and chocolates helped calm him down.

His older brother, Ayush, was mentally balanced and extremely shrewd. In the world of black marketeering they were known as 'the couriers' for their ingenious ability to steal and deliver almost anything their client wished for. From prestigious art to innovative technologies, they stole anything for the right price. If a company wanted to know about a rival's new product, the couriers could be used to steal the relevant data. The brothers were masters at infiltrating an organization and hacking their software. Ayush could be approached via the dark web or word of mouth. Payments were generally made up front, partly in bitcoin, partly in dollars and the balance in the local currency of the country where the theft was to take place.

Ayush had received his payment in full, but this was the first time he had decided to betray his paymaster. The device they had stolen was one of a kind. It was an ingenious technology and his brother had successfully used it for three days in a row. For Ayush, this device was his ticket to retirement and out of this dangerous lifestyle. He had decided to settle down in Indonesia with his brother after selling Vita on the open market.

At noon, as Ayush was chatting over the dark web with a prospective buyer while his brother was enjoying his cookie dough ice cream, a tall, broad man smashed in the door of their room and shot Akhilesh in the head with a silenced pistol. Petrified by the sudden butchery, Ayush raised his shaking hands and fell to the floor. As he uttered the word 'mercy', the man shot him at point blank range. In under a minute the brothers known as 'the couriers' were pitilessly executed. The Brobdingnagian man collected Vita and stealthily left the hotel via its rear exit, which was connected to the emergency staircase that served as a fire escape.

Per Shiv's instructions, Bhim Singh had spoken to Arvind Ghosh and had been instructed by the spy to report outside R&AW's Delhi office at 2 p.m. When Bhim notified Arvind of his arrival, the latter came out of the building to meet him. Bhim Singh wasn't important enough to be seated inside the country's top spy office.

In the parking lot, Bhim handed over the details of his Delhi contact, a hacker who went by the name of 'Astra'.

Looking over at the details, Arvind asked, 'Who is Astra? And how is he linked to Vita?'

'No one knows his true identity. He never meets anyone in person. He contacted me earlier today and said that he had a lead on who stole Vita and where the perpetrators were hiding, but he wants a hundred million dollars deposited in a numbered account before he gives us any further leads,' replied Bhim.

He then took out his phone and showed Arvind the message from the hacker.

'How do we know Astra exists? And how do we know he is not sending us on a wild goose chase?'

'That is for Mr Shiv and the authorities to find out. I have told you everything I know. These decisions are above my pay grade.'

'Even if what you are saying is true, we cannot give him a hundred million dollars without first apprehending the culprits and securing Vita,' said Arvind.

'I suggest you start a dialogue with Astra, then,' replied Bhim.

Arvind thought for a moment, then led Bhim inside the building into a small seminar room on his floor. This was the room where agents met to discuss tactics before embarking on any mission. Arvind sat Bhim there with the analyst who had put Bhim's number under surveillance. Using the number, the analyst would try and triangulate Astra's location the next time the hacker made contact.

Bhim updated Shiv about the developments.

After the room was set up with a call monitoring device attached to Bhim's phone, Arvind came in to oversee the operation. It was 4 p.m., and he was sipping his afternoon cup of black coffee to get his midday kick of caffeine.

While inspecting the set-up Arvind asked Bhim, 'How does the hacker know the location of Vita?' Then answering his own question he continued, 'Either the hacker was involved in the theft or he has successfully opened a back channel into Vita, which has allowed him to pinpoint the device's location.'

'If our experts along with your IT team haven't been able to crack Vita's coding then I doubt a street hacker would have been able to achieve such a feat. I think he was involved in the theft,' declared Bhim.

Arvind probed further, 'But if he was involved in the theft, then the hacker and his gang could have secured more money by selling Vita on the open market. A piece of a bigger pie would make more sense than getting a smaller pie for himself. Why would the hacker backstab his allies? Is this a bluff?'

Realizing the insinuation, Bhim smiled and without breaking a sweat retorted, 'I am just the security chief of a company. I am not Astra, nor do I have an ulterior motive. If I had, this would be the last place on earth where you would find me.'

Arvind stared silently at Bhim. He had not expected the prosaic man to get the subtle hint. If he were guilty, he would surely have been nervous, thought Arvind.

Rubbing his hands together and slowly nodding Arvind said, 'I agree with you. If either Shiv or you were involved, then those attacks, however restrained they might have been, would not have happened as everyone involved in Vita's development knows what this novel technology is capable of. Besides, you wouldn't have risked using the technology on home turf. So it seems there was a leak from somewhere. Someone realized the value of the technology and stole it. The attacks were then carried out to ensure the device worked and to showcase the same to international buyers.'

'I am not a strategist. I am here because the device was lost on my watch, and I intend to get it back for Bellator Limited.'

Bhim's phone beeped, indicating that a message had been received. It was from Astra. Bhim read the message aloud, 'Are you willing to pay?'

Without a second thought Bhim typed, 'Yes.'

A second ping came and Bhim read out loud, 'CH007007999007, under the account name "Cello". These are the details of my numbered account. Do not try to trace or hack it. The account is in a Swiss bank. Once the funds are transferred, I shall send you the location of Vita.'

Arvind took the phone from Bhim and typed, 'Call me.'

Ten minutes went by. Time moved at a snail's pace. Finally, the call came in.

Arvind answered and said, 'I am not interested in knowing your identity. But unless you can show us some proof that you know the location of Vita, how can I initiate the transfer of funds? Working on just "good faith" is not enough. You need to show your hand.'

On the other end Astra listened patiently, while Arvind's analyst was desperately trying to triangulate the call's source.

The analyst rotated his hand, indicating to Arvind that he needed more time and that he should keep Astra engaged in conversation. Arvind nodded.

After careful consideration, Astra replied, 'If I give you the location, I will lose my bargaining chip, and you will have no incentive to pay me. It seems that we are in a deadlock.' The hacker was using a voice mask, which distorted his voice, making it sound robotic.

'What should we do then?' asked Arvind and then cupped his hand over the phone's speaker as he whispered to the analyst, 'Any luck?'

The analyst whispered back, 'No sir. He is using a multiple tracer and routing his calls via a computer system that is allowing him to bounce his calls to different locations without disconnecting the ongoing call. I will have to hack into his system to trace his location.'

'Do it immediately,' Arvind whispered back.

Then Arvind quickly said, 'Astra, I have a solution to our stalemate. Let us meet in person. When you give me the location of Vita, my officers will go there and secure the device. Till then you can hold me as a hostage. I will come alone. Once the device is secured, I will wire the money to your account.'

'I am not a terrorist or a criminal. I am a hacker. I don't want to hold you as a hostage,' came the reply.

'If the device is sold or moved, you will lose your chance of earning a hundred million dollars. Time is of the essence. Do you have a better plan?' asked Arvind, trying to keep the conversation going.

Astra thought for a moment then replied, 'The device hasn't been moved since late last night. But I don't have a better plan. I will send you location for a meeting in fifteen minutes. Come alone. If I spot anyone else, I will disappear,' replied Astra before disconnecting the call.

As soon as Astra disconnected, the analyst swivelled around in his chair and said to Arvind, 'I wasn't able to get his exact location, but the calls kept bouncing back to towers in South Delhi. It is my assumption that he is somewhere in that area.'

Fifteen minutes later, true to his word, Astra sent the location of the proposed meeting. They were to meet at Jahanpanah City Forest located in Chirag Delhi.

As Arvind was preparing to leave, Bhim Singh approached him and requested, 'I would like to go with the field agents to retrieve Vita. Once secured, your officers can keep it in their custody till you decide to officially hand it over to Bellator. I will not interfere with their operations, but please allow me to go with them.'

Bhim's request seemed reasonable, so Arvind readily agreed. 'Fine, but you will observe from afar and not be part of the assault team.'

A team of ten R&AW field agents prepared their weapons and gadgets. Armed with silenced pistols, they, along with Bhim Singh, got into their cars and waited for Astra to reveal Vita's location.

Meanwhile, Arvind drove to Jahanpanah City Forest. It was a fifteen-minute drive.

The forest is spread over eight hundred acres of land. Local residents generally go to the lush, emerald-green lungs of the city to jog, walk, practise yoga or attend one of the laughter therapy sessions held there.

As Arvind entered, his laptop slung over his shoulder, he could hear a variety of chirps at various decibel levels from the diverse congregation of birds that were singing out their presence to nature.

He stopped and called Astra.

The hacker answered on the fourth ring and said, 'Keep walking. I need to make sure that you are alone.'

Arvind had expected this, so he did not fight this customary practice, which is generally followed by dubious, jittery characters who work on the wrong side of the law and have no faith in the government and its authorities.

Astra made him walk for thirty minutes. Then a call came through on Arvind's phone, and as soon as he answered, the voice on the other end said, 'Ditch the jogging track. Take a left and go deeper into the forest.'

A while later the hacker's voice came from the surrounding thicket, 'That's far enough. Open your laptop and log in using the dongle lying in front of you.'

Arvind obeyed. He logged on to Bellator's online banking system. The government was not going to pay for a private company losing its fancy toy.

Once Arvind had logged in, he looked up from the screen and spoke to the trees in front of him, 'I now need the location of Vita.'

From his left came a voice, 'Hotel Ambassador, room thirteen.'

Instantly, Arvind dialled the field agents and told them the location.

The next fifteen minutes passed in silence.

Then Astra said, 'Put your phone on loudspeaker, I want to hear your agents' confirmation.'

Arvind silently obeyed. He was too anxious to initiate small talk with the hacker. As soon as the field agents confirmed that they had reached the hotel, Arvind lit a cigarette to calm his nerves.

As per standard operating procedure, two agents stood in the lobby to cover the main entry, two others went via the kitchens to cover the rear exit, while the remaining six, along with Bhim Singh, proceeded to the first floor to room thirteen. The manager on the floor had been taken into confidence. He had handed over the master key to the commanding officer. As the lift pinged its arrival on the first floor and the doors slid open, the officers rushed out and took up defensive positions. Bhim Singh and the manager were told to stay put by the lift while the officers proceeded towards the room.

Two officers stood on either side of the door, while another inserted the key card. As soon as the door unlocked, the commander breached the entry, followed by his officers. The officers of the armed forces of the country lead by example and generally lead their team from the front.

As soon as they went in, the officers saw two dead bodies sprawled on the ground in a pool of blood.

It had been a clean execution. Two single shots to their heads had killed the duo. The room was filled with the stench of death. When the commanding officer called Bhim to see if the security chief could identify the dead, he puked at the sight and left the room.

It took R&AW just under ten minutes to trace the arrival details of the two dead men. The facial recognition software corroborated the fact that the two thieves had arrived in Delhi via Mumbai on the day the ATMs were hacked. The time frame of the sequence of events proved that these were the culprits who had shot Sarthak on the Mumbai-Pune Expressway and stolen Vita.

A few kilometres away in the middle of the City Forest, the commanding officer's voice crackled over the loudspeaker of Arvind's phone, 'Two bogies have been found dead. No sign of Vita.'

Hearing this, Arvind shut the laptop and turned. The veteran spy, following the hacker's voice, had known exactly where he was amongst the bushes but had played along till now. But the situation had taken a grim turn, so Arvind, looking towards Astra, said in a commanding voice, 'Someone got to the thieves before us. They are dead. Please tell me how you located them. We can still work together, and if you help us, I will make sure you are compensated for your efforts.'

The field commander's words had numbed the geek. The thin, hooded fellow was visibly shaking.

Without looking at Arvind he said, 'I have been used. I have been betrayed. They will kill me too. What a fool I have been!'

'Who used you? Who contacted you? How did you locate Vita? Who killed the two men at the hotel? Help me identify them, and I will protect you.'

Shaking his head, the hacker took a few steps back and said, 'No, I need to disappear. I need to go underground. I am leaving.'

He then turned and ran towards the nearest exit. He knew where it was, since he had set the meeting up. Arvind quickly gathered the laptop and the dongle and chased after him.

One of the exits of the City Park opened onto Alaknanda Road. Astra took that exit.

As he reached the road, Arvind called out to him, 'Astra, wait! I can help you. We need your help!'

The hacker turned to respond but kept running, his brain signalling his legs to keep moving to maintain distance between himself and Arvind. 'No one can help...' he uttered just before a bus rammed into him, killing him on the spot.

Helplessly, Arvind witnessed the macabre scene unfold in front of him. Upset by the turn of events, he called his team and instructed them to secure the hacker's body. The only option for Arvind now was to delve into the hacker's life and join the dots from him to the deaths in the hotel.

As dusk fell over the city, a dark red hue was visible in the sky. Suddenly, Arvind found nature to be very morbid.

17

Delusions of Happiness

Twelve hours ago, in Myanmar, on Sunday morning, Ranbir had received Professor Hamid Ansari's notes via email. R&AW had sequestered these notes after the physicist's kidnapping.

Ranbir had also received a text from Secretary Wasim Khan saying, 'The milkmen shall arrive at Khampat tonight.'

When Ranbir told Vikram of the morning's developments, the latter asked, 'Where is Khampat?'

'It's a small village near Manipur's border. The border there is quite porous. Send the pick-up details to the monks and their rebel leaders. It looks like your plan is in motion.'

After sending the information, Vikram started reading the professor's notes. Referring to Google to better understand the complex formulas and chemical equations and their detailed explanations, he grasped the gist of the professor's theory.

To create a believable bluff, Vikram took the help of a physicist hired by R&AW. He spent several hours talking to the physicist on the phone to understand the research. Then, after a light lunch, which the duo ordered in their room, Vikram made slight changes to some of the equations. In some places he replaced hydrogen with helium, elsewhere he added or deleted a few compounds and thus altered the equations, all in accordance with the guidance provided by the physicist and Google.

Late that afternoon, Vikram informed the general as well as Tin Tun about the weapons drop that was to take place that evening. The general reassured Vikram of his cooperation and confirmed that he would remove his troops from Khampat.

That night, five monks along with fifteen armed militiamen reached Khampat.

In India, R&AW agents assembled in the border village of Laijang in Manipur. Amidst the cowpea fields that spread across both sides of the border, the chirping of crickets and croaking of frogs could be heard in an otherwise silent night.

At 11 p.m., an agent cupped a hand over his mouth and cooed into the pitch darkness. The sound travelled over the vast expanse of the field. The call was reciprocated from the other side. Slowly, the parties emerged from their hiding places and met at the border. Five chests filled with guns, ammunition, knives and bombs were handed over. No payments were made. While the monks thanked the Indian agents and enquired about the next shipment, the militiamen quickly loaded the chests into their vehicles. The transaction was completed in under twenty minutes.

Now, at the end of seventy-two hours in Myanmar, Vikram and Ranbir had made substantial progress towards winning the general's trust and had successfully completed the first phase of their treacherous plan.

While this drop was being executed, Ranbir received another text informing him of the location of the next drop. This time the location was the border town of Behiang, again in Manipur. The town was twenty minutes away from Cikha village in north-western Myanmar. Ranbir passed on the information to the rebels and then to the general.

By 6 a.m. on Monday morning, a total of five such drops had been made. All of them were successful. The rebels were happy.

While Ranbir and Vikram were having their breakfast by the poolside, the two monks, dressed in their traditional red robes and accompanied by Tin Tun, arrived to meet the duo.

Once everyone was seated, Tin ordered some coffee and a bread basket before saying, 'Your plan went smoothly. The drops were successful. You have given this country a strong ray of hope. The rebels will now start striking hard at the general and his forces. Aung Su has told his followers to start searching for your scientist. Although we are not certain of the professor's presence in Myanmar, a rumour amongst the locals is that a high-profile guest was flown into Yangon a few days after the coup. Some say the flight arrived from China. The said guest appears to be a close ally of the general and stays with him at all times.'

Hearing this, Vikram looked at the monks, who were enjoying their coffee, for a sign of confirmation.

The two looked up silently and nodded.

Feigning ignorance, Vikram enquired, 'Where does the general stay?'

'In the compound of Pyidaungsu Hluttaw, the Burmese Parliament. He has converted the entire area into a fortress, and to effectively administer, he stays in a wooden chalet in the compound,' replied Tin.

'So if this guest of his is our scientist, we would find him in this chalet inside the parliament compound?' asked Ranbir, continuing the ruse.

'Yes, but you cannot just waltz in there and rescue him. The security is very tight. Penetrating the compound is impossible.'

'Could a united effort by the rebel forces overwhelm the security at the Parliament?' enquired Vikram.

'No, the general has a strong force along with air support. The rebels will have to go district by district. Once they are able to corral the general's forces, then surrounding the city and attacking from all sides would work. If the rebels attack right now and are defeated, then their morale will be crushed, and the rebellion will be squashed.'

Vikram digested the information in silence. Then he looked at the monks and said, 'I have a plan, but for it to succeed we will have to meet all the rebel leaders together. Can you organize such a meeting?'

The monks looked at each other. Tin was silent. It was not his place to object; the decision had to be of the rebels.

The monks whispered to one another, then breaking silence one of them said, 'You have helped us and our cause. So we will try and arrange this meeting for you.'

The monks then silently got up and left.

Tin Tun quickly and quietly polished off the bread basket and then left without discussing the matter any further.

After everyone left, Vikram dejectedly lit a cigarette and said, 'I gave them a chance to overthrow the general. But the rebels are not ready yet, and we cannot lose anymore time. We will have to push forward with our plan. Unless the rebels can confirm Professor Hamid Ansari's presence and agree to help us extract him, we will have to betray them.'

By late afternoon the rebels had distributed their newly acquired weapons and ammunition. The general, on the other hand, anticipating the repercussions of Vikram's audacious plan, had left only junior soldiers and fresh recruits to guard the various outposts around the country and patrol the cities. Most of his well-trained war fighters had been pushed back to the reserve bunkers. The general wanted to lose this battle to make the rebels feel overconfident about their abilities. This was his way of winning the war.

By that evening, skirmishes between the various rebel factions and the general's army had started across the country. The rebels formed themselves into groups of seven. Each group was assigned three outposts and a patrolling party to attack. In each group, four members carried guns while three carried only home-made weapons and kitchen knives. The idea was that if any one of the gun-carrying members were killed, then one of the other three would replace him or her. The skirmishes lasted through the night and continued into the wee hours of the following day. A lot of rebels were killed, but they had managed to kill a lot more soldiers. Following the principles of guerrilla warfare, the small units of the rebels were able to launch quick surprise attacks and then disappear into the surrounding villages or forests.

18

The Whispering Room

On Tuesday morning, Vikram got a call from the general.

Almost like an excited child, he said, 'Hello, my friend, your plan seems to be working. Last evening's skirmishes will have given the rebels a false sense of hope. They must now be overconfident. Although we killed about two hundred and fifty rebels, I too lost an equal number of soldiers. I have paid a steep price, so I hope you are meeting the rebel leaders soon.'

The rebel leaders had told Vikram that the skirmishes had cost them the lives of about two hundred and fifty of their comrades, but they reported having killed at least four hundred of the general's soldiers. No general would highlight his losses accurately. But Vikram wasn't going to debate numbers with the present commander-in-chief of the country, so he simply said, 'I have sent them a proposal. I expect their reply soon.' Then with a heavy voice he added, 'I am sorry for the loss of your men, General.'

'It is a small price to pay for the greater good of this country. All that matters is the end game. And you must make sure that ours is the hand that wins,' responded the general, with no sense of regret at the loss in his voice.

Just as Vikram cut the call, Ranbir received one from Secretary Wasim Khan.

Twenty-four hours ago, on Monday morning, R&AW had been grappling with the hacker Astra's death. The items found on him after his untimely death—his mobile phone, wallet, a few pen drives and a key—were being investigated. The driving licence in the wallet identified the hacker as Monish Razdan. Raiding the address, R&AW found that Monish was a college dropout and had been a professional hacker for some time now. Bundles of cash amounting to around thirty thousand dollars in various currencies were found in the house. The officers learnt that the modest two-bedroom flat in Punjabi Bagh was not owned by Monish but was rented by him. As per the landlord, the young boy of twenty-eight had been living there for nearly three years. He always paid the rent in cash and on time. The officers had found the apartment to be fairly tidy, with no rotting food or pizza boxes or takeout lying about the floor and around the house. The fridge was well stocked with chocolates and beer and some energy drinks. Some more pen drives, a few laptops and a few grams of weed were also found. Most of the pen drives had hacking tools like Wireshark, Intruder and Aircrack. A few had the bank account numbers of some MNCs and high net worth individuals.

By afternoon, it was apparent to the officers that nothing in Astra's apartment or on his pen drives pointed towards Vita or its theft. The only unanswered question that remained was of the key found in his wallet. The engraving on the key read IRCTC, which stands for Indian Railway Catering and Tourism Corporation, indicating that the key was to a locker on a railway platform.

While Parth led a team to investigate the railway lockers, Arvind and his team kept a close watch on High Commissioner Humayun Haq who had resumed his duties after his sudden bout of illness.

The first half of the day went by without much activity for Arvind's team. The high commissioner was back to smoking his cigarettes and chewing betel leaves. He answered calls from his friends and colleagues, who were enquiring about his health. Post lunch, the excitement and anticipation went up when he received a call from Bangladesh, but the build-up fizzled out quickly when all that the two high commissioners spoke about was their health and routine work. Within the hour, the mood in R&AW's office was once again tense when a call came from Pakistan. But this too proved to be a mere enquiry about the high commissioner's health and nothing more.

Late in the afternoon, a tall, fair man walked into the high commissioner's office. He did not sit across from him at the desk but walked straight to the window and stood by it. One of the analysts in Arvind's team quickly displayed all the camera feeds from the high commissioner's office on the screens of the operations floor. Since the window was at one end of the large room, the camera did not clearly capture the face of the new entrant. Yet the team could see that he was wearing a black suit and a red fez, which sat nicely on his egg-shaped head.

Without looking up from her monitor the analyst said, 'Sir, we have hacked into the security feed of the high commission, but surprisingly none of the cameras caught this man entering the facility. We don't know who he is.'

'He must have used the back entrance. Increase the volume and record his voice. I want you to run his voice through our database to see if we can match it to any known criminals,' replied Arvind.

Just as he uttered these words there was a blackout inside the Pakistani high commission. The faint light in the room made it impossible for the cameras to capture any visuals. The voices from the high commissioner's office, however, could still be heard.

The tall man, who was still standing by the window, said in a stern voice, 'You have been sloppy Mr High Commissioner. R&AW delivered multiple weapons and ammunition consignments in the early hours of the day to the rebel groups of Myanmar. Our plan and package maybe disrupted, especially if the general is overthrown. I think we should send in Jahangir Niazi for additional security.'

The comment was not missed by anyone on Arvind's team. A surge of excitement passed through everybody in the room. Finally, a breakthrough. This comment at the very least proved that the Pakistani high commissioner to India, Humayun Haq, was involved in Professor Hamid Ansari's abduction. R&AW now at least had a target in its sight.

'I was ill,' replied Humayun defensively.

'Excuses don't solve anything,' retorted the tall man.

'Should we inform our asset?'

'No. First send Jahangir there and then speak to Soe Min. How could he have been so careless? The Indians handed over the weapons to the rebels right under his nose. Remind him that this is much bigger than his country, and if he cannot keep his area under control, we will find someone who will,' said the man, now fiddling with his lighter.

Arvind noted that the man had addressed the general by name, without his designation.

Humayun did not reply. After a brief period of silence, the man walked out of the room and left via the rear exit of the building. The high commissioner's manservant Yousef Lehri escorted him out of the complex.

Fifteen minutes later the high commissioner called General Soe Min and said in a tone mimicking that used by his visitor on him earlier, 'You have been sloppy. The Indians armed the rebels earlier today. They did it right under your nose. What are your forces doing?'

General Soe Min was a tough man and unlike the high commissioner, was not easily intimidated. He replied in an equally stern tone, 'Do not preach war tactics to me. I know what I am doing. Besides, have you forgotten that you are speaking to the head of a state?'

'We helped you become the head of Myanmar. Now what is your game plan? How is our guest doing? Have you made any progress with him?'

'I am not answerable to you,' said the general furiously.

'Without our help, there will be international intervention in the country. I suggest you cooperate,' said Haq, his voice cold.

Taking a deep breath, but with a hint of irritation still in his voice, the general said, 'The rebels will be crushed soon. It's all a part of my master plan. Your guest is safe but hasn't made any progress yet.'

'We are sending Jahangir Niazi there for extra protection. Please cooperate with him,' the high commissioner said before hanging up.

Since R&AW had bugged the high commissioner's landline, they were able to hear both sides of this conversation.

It was now clear that the high commissioner was guilty. But if the authorities made an official move against him, he would protect himself through diplomatic immunity. If they made an arrest, the Pakistanis would simply recall him and state that they would run an inquiry against him in Pakistan. Moreover, they would know that his cover was blown. So, for now, everyone at R&AW agreed to let Humayun Haq remain in play. Secondly, the high commissioner's conversations with both his visitor and the general implied that the said guest could be Professor Hamid Ansari. There was no mention of a 'Top Hat', so no one knew who this turncoat could be. Lastly, everyone agreed that Vikram should be informed that Jahangir Niazi would soon be arriving in Myanmar as an additional layer of protection for the said guest.

Over a conference call with the Ministry of External Affairs and the PMO, R&AW presented its findings and recommended that Humayun Haq's passport be flagged so the authorities would be notified if he tried to leave the country and would have the option of apprehending him. The suggestion was well received and accordingly implemented.

While Arvind had been overseeing the surveillance of the high commissioner, Parth and his team were hunting for the railway locker whose key had been found on Astra. As per government rules, IRCTC lockers can be hired for a maximum of seven days. Additionally, a ticket to or from the station where the locker is hired is required, and the journey must take place within a month's time. So, while one team analysed the security feeds from all the railway stations in Delhi for the seven days prior to Astra's death, another team looked for tickets booked under the name of 'Astra' or 'Monish Razdan'.

As Parth's team meticulously searched for clues, Bhim Singh slipped out of the R&AW office and dialled a number using his secret burner phone.

When the recipient answered the call, Bhim said, 'R&AW may soon find a lead. I think it is time for us to meet.'

The man, who till now had just been an observer of the chaos surrounding Vita, replied, 'Tomorrow morning in Varanasi.'

19

The Plot Thickens

On Tuesday morning, while Vikram was speaking to the general over the phone, Parth's team finally had a breakthrough when one of the analysts observed the hacker entering the New Delhi railway station. The time stamp on the footage from the station's surveillance camera showed that Astra had arrived at the station at noon, two days before his death.

While Parth's team left for the train station to secure the hacker's locker, about eight hundred and fifty kilometres away in Varanasi, Bhim Singh was on his way to meet his confederate. After Astra's untimely death, he had taken a risk and waited to see what the investigative agency found out. He had an ace up his sleeve, which allowed him to brave the risk. However, when the agents had found a key to a locker at the railway station, Bhim was worried. He had contacted the observer who to his relief had agreed to meet with him. So, after a drive of over twelve hours, Bhim

Singh reached the ancient and sacred city of Banaras, now known as Varanasi.

As the R&AW agents cut through the crowd to reach the security office at the railway station, Bhim Singh calmly strolled through the lobby of a plush five-star hotel in Varanasi.

By the time the R&AW agents got hold of the security chief, showed him their credentials and started moving towards the lockers, Bhim had sat down across his host by the poolside. The host had ordered a lavish breakfast.

Taking a few bites of a croissant, Bhim said in a rush, 'The authorities will soon link the disappearance of Vita, the deaths of the thieves who stole it from Sarthak Jain and Astra's role in this game to my employer, Shiv Narayanan, and me. It's time I jump ship. Shiv is rich and can hire a team of lawyers to protect himself, but I intend to get rich. Anyway, Shiv has already been backstabbed once by those thieves; I think he can handle another betrayal.'

As Bhim was speaking, his host had been munching on bread and reading emails on his laptop. Multitasking was his way of tackling the anxious thoughts that raced through his mind. A few minutes after Bhim fell silent, his host, taking a sip of his black tea garnished with a large slice of lemon, calmly and softly asked, 'What do you want from me?'

By then, the R&AW agents in Delhi had successfully retrieved a pen drive from Astra's locker.

Twenty minutes later the agents, including Parth, Arvind and Wasim Khan, were all huddled around a laptop in a conference room on the third floor of the agency's office. The pen drive was plugged in, and to everyone's relief, it was not password protected. It seemed the hacker had intended for this pen drive to be found and easily accessed. It contained a single folder with an audio clip. The agents played the recording.

'Hello! Who is this and how did you get my number?' Astra's voice came through the laptop's speakers.

'We know all about you, Mr Razdan, or should we address you by your hacking handle, Astra?' came Bhim Singh's voice from the other end.

'Who are you and what do you want?' said the hacker, his tone unruffled.

It seemed he was not one to be intimidated easily.

'We have proof of your illicit activities, especially of the funds that you have embezzled over the years from various government funds and bank accounts,' replied Bhim. 'So I suggest you take us seriously.'

'Even if I do believe you, it is clear that you want me to do something for you. If you wanted to expose me, you would have done it already. So I ask again, what do you want?' came Astra's cold response.

'We want to give you the opportunity to earn a hundred million dollars. Have you heard about Bellator Limited's latest innovation, Vita? We want you to hack into it and find its location,' said Bhim Singh.

'I have heard about Vita. I also know that it has been stolen. According to the rumours I have heard, the device can only be hacked into if a back channel for it is opened up, and that can only be opened by the user. Unless the thieves who stole the device do not know the true value of Vita and unknowingly open the channel, there is no way the device can be hacked into. If the thieves are even remotely smart, they will never make the device vulnerable to hacking.'

'What if we told you that there was another way to locate the device?' came Shiv Narayanan's voice.

The authorities were shocked. Everyone in the room wondered why the esteemed CEO hadn't shared this knowledge with the authorities. Was he ashamed about losing the device or was he involved in its theft?

'How can I locate it?' asked Astra curiously.

'We installed a secondary micro transmitter in the device. The activation code for the transmitter is PVS0079. Once you locate the device you will inform us of its location. Then, for the benefit of the authorities, you will contact us again and demand a hundred million dollars in exchange for the location. The funds will be transferred in front of the authorities, so it will be a legitimate transaction, and when the authorities reach the designated place, they will find Vita along with the two thieves,' explained Shiv, his voice bitter.

'If you have the activation code of the secondary transmitter, why don't you hack into it and locate the device? Why pay me a hundred million dollars?' asked the hacker.

'I am Bellator Limited, Mr Razdan. In a moment of weakness, I committed a heinous crime by orchestrating the theft of my own device. My greed led me to believe that I could sell Vita on the black market and park the money from its sale abroad. However, its creator, Sarthak Jain, was not supposed to die that day. The thieves known as "the couriers" betrayed me and started using the technology. Now I want to clean up my mess and a hundred million dollars is a small amount to pay for that. Once the authorities seize the device, I will be able to retrieve it from them. Then, through proper government channels, I will sell this technology in the international market,' explained Shiv.

'What if I decide to double-cross you and keep Vita for myself? How can you trust me?' asked the hacker.

'You don't have the capability to steal or to kill the thieves who have Vita. Also, from what we have found out about you, you prefer to make money with the least amount of effort and minimum risk. So we don't think you will make the effort to betray us,' said Bhim Singh.

'You're right. I won't take unnecessary risk. Okay. I agree with your plan and am on board,' Astra replied.

The conversation was compelling evidence against Shiv Narayanan and Bhim Singh. Arvind immediately ordered an arrest warrant to be issued against the two culprits.

That evening, R&AW agents flooded into Shiv Narayanan's house and office buildings. All activities were halted, files and accounts were seized and senior company officers apprehended.

When the police and agents arrived at Shiv's penthouse, he was swimming in his infinity pool on the terrace. A mug of Duvel beer with a thick layer of froth was placed by the poolside. Looking at the swarm of officers that had rushed into his house, Shiv got out of the pool, wore a fluffy cotton robe, took a large swig of his beer and then approached the authorities.

Addressing one of the officers in plain clothes he said, 'To what do I owe the pleasure?'

'I suggest you get dressed. We have a warrant for your arrest. We have conclusive evidence that you orchestrated the theft of Vita by using the couriers,' replied the officer coldly.

Shiv instantly understood that either Bhim had betrayed him or Astra had recorded the conversation they had had earlier. Still maintaining his cool, the astute CEO set down his beer and said, 'I was coerced at gunpoint by my security chief Bhim Singh. He is the culprit. You need to arrest him.'

'Our officers are looking for him. But whatever you have to say or present in your defence, you must now do at the police station. We are going to take you into custody.'

Twenty minutes later, Shiv was escorted to the local police station. From there, R&AW officers, who had already got the transfer approved, took Shiv into their custody and flew him to New Delhi.

By 9 p.m. on Tuesday night, as Shiv Narayanan's interrogation began in Delhi, Bhim Singh, along with Vita, which he had stolen earlier after killing the couriers, was on his way to the ancient Buddhist city of Kapilavastu in Nepal.

20

I Spy from the Corner of My Eye

About eleven hours before, Ranbir had received a call from Secretary Wasim Khan to inform him about Jahangir Niazi's possible visit to Myanmar and to discuss the likelihood that Professor Hamid Ansari was in the country.

That night Ranbir called the secretary again to update him on the skirmishes and developments in Myanmar. The duo was also informed about Shiv Narayanan's involvement in the theft of Vita and his subsequent arrest.

As the second day of the week came to a close, Tin Tun, who had received 75 percent of his payment from R&AW, was installing a small spy camera in his pen. He planned to take a photograph of Vikram and Ranbir as they met the rebel leaders and then show it to the general. The bald old man confidently thought this would enable him to earn some more money before finally retiring to Thailand. He was done with India and its problems. He felt the nation had been thankless towards him, and he had earned the right to retire early after playing his hand right. Tin believed his allegiance was only to himself and did not feel any guilt about his planned betrayal. At some stage in life, every individual starts to make selfish plans for their future, and for Tin that stage had arrived. So after testing the camera thrice and carefully going over his plan, Tin decided to retire for the night and wait for events to unfold. He knew he must tread with patience and care.

At 10 a.m. on Wednesday morning, Parth, Arvind and Wasim Khan were standing on the other side of the one-way mirror observing Shiv's interrogation. The senior spies all had coffee cups in their hands and were sipping the hot liquid as the questioning progressed. Shiv had been grilled since late the previous night and had been allowed only two hours of sleep. This was a form of passive torture that the agency followed to enervate a suspect.

Shiv could not see who was on the other side of the mirror observing him, yet when the interrogator bellowed at him demanding, 'Where is Vita? Where is Bhim Singh? Who else is involved with you?' he turned towards the mirror and calmly replied, 'I have already stated that Bhim Singh coerced me into speaking to Astra at gunpoint. Also, you cannot prove that those attacks were carried out under my instructions or were caused by Vita at all. The recording you have in your possession is not enough to get me convicted. I demand to see my lawyer.'

'You will get your lawyer once you confess to your crime and tell us where Bhim Singh and Vita are. If there is another attack, then the blood will be on your hands, and you will be charged as a terrorist.'

On the other side of the glass, Arvind muttered, 'Technically, what he is saying is true. We cannot yet prove in court his involvement in this fiasco, especially if he uses the phoney coercion excuse as his defence.'

'Yes, there's no point wasting time on him. He will keep stalling, and he is not a petty criminal on whom we can inflict physical torture,' replied Parth as he drained his cup of black coffee. 'Let's have a talk with him; we can offer to release him in exchange for his help, and then maybe later, with a pool of compelling evidence we can arrest him again.'

Taking a deep breath, Secretary Wasim Khan silently nodded.

Parth strolled into the interrogation room and nodded at the interrogator, signalling that he could leave. He then sat down across from Shiv.

Parth began, 'Okay, we accept your theory that Bhim Singh coerced you, but then why did you not inform the police or us, especially when Bhim was here in Delhi with us?'

'Bhim did not have the resources to pull this off on his own. I was scared and didn't know who else was in cahoots with him. They could have killed my family,' lied Shiv.

'What do you want?' asked Parth plainly.

'I want you to release me. As you already know from that recording, I intended to retrieve Vita and was back-stabbed by Bhim,' said Shiv, a sense of urgency in his voice. 'I genuinely don't know where Bhim is. Or what his plans are. I wish I could help you, but sadly I cannot. I am sorry for my actions and for my greed, but I cannot help you any further.'

After carefully considering the situation Parth said, 'If you cannot help us, then we will continue to detain you. R&AW is not your normal police, Mr Shiv; we have the authority to detain you indefinitely.'

Then passing him a bottle of water, Parth continued, 'Maybe you can help us.' He paused deliberately then said,

'Have you heard of Top Hat, Humayun Haq or Professor Hamid Ansari?'

At this point there was a light tap on the one-way mirror, indicating to Parth to step out of the room.

As Parth stepped out, Secretary Wasim, frowning deeply, asked irritably, 'Why are you discussing an unrelated investigation with him?'

'I just had a brainwave—we can use him as a patsy to help us investigate High Commissioner Humayun. Since he cannot help us with Vita, and we are unable to make any headway with the high commissioner, why not use him to lure Haq into a trap? His greed has caused enough of a fiasco for the country, why not let him pay for it?'

'I cannot officially sanction this. We cannot legally use an under-trial for our missions. But I agree with your reasoning. Let's go ahead,' exclaimed the secretary.

Parth returned to the interrogation room and explained his plan to Shiv. The cornered CEO had no choice but to agree.

Meanwhile, in Myanmar, on that Wednesday, skirmishes between the rebel forces and the general's army had increased. The news of the rebels overpowering army units spread like wildfire. The unexpected victory gave the locals newfound hope. Many died and many more joined the movement. The army had started booby-trapping bunkers and cars with improvised explosive devices or IEDs with the aim of trapping the rebels and catching them off guard. In the eyes of the international media, Myanmar was a failed state. There was talk of the United Nations sending a contingent of peacekeeping troops to re-establish law and order in the nation.

The rebels, happy with their success, decided to meet their guardian angels, Vikram and Ranbir, on Friday morning.

That night for the first time since the fiascos began, Top Hat received a call from Pakistan. Till now he had been a silent observer.

The handler from Pakistan asked, 'Updates?'

'I met our local source. He has become sloppy after his illness. I think it's time to cut loose ends and strike while chaos and confusion reign.'

'We trust your judgement. May God be with you,' replied the handler and cut the call.

21

Killing Time

On the following day, Parth and his team dropped Shiv off near the Pakistani high commission. Since R&AW had already bugged the high commissioner's office, they did not plant any wires on Shiv. Anyway, he was a CEO-turned-patsy, not a trained spy.

Shiv walked from the drop-off point to the high commission's gate. Generally, one would require an appointment letter to meet the high commissioner. It was not a building one could merely waltz into. But when Shiv declared that he had sensitive information for the high commissioner pertaining to Pakistan's security, the guards let him in. They checked his identification papers and cross-checked his social media accounts and then allowed the novice spy in.

Shiv was jittery and nervous, so he went to the restroom to relieve himself and wash his face. While he was refreshing himself, a lean man in a black suit, who looked like he was a staff member of the high commission, was openly watching him. As Shiv stared at himself in the mirror and thought about his meeting with the high commissioner, the man quietly came and stood near him. Shiv saw the man's reflection in the mirror and as he wiped his hands, the man leaned close and whispered into Shiv's ear.

A few moments later, Shiv exited the restroom and walked to the lobby where he waited, his right foot tapping with anxiety. Fifteen minutes later, Shiv was escorted to the high commissioner's office.

Seating himself across Humayun Haq, Shiv handed over a file and said, 'I am Bellator Limited's CEO. My company created the novel device, Vita. I orchestrated its theft, and the authorities of this country are now after me. If you help me recover this device, I will not only sell this technology to Pakistan but also move my company to your country with all its technical know-how. It would be a big boost for your country's defence systems.'

Humayun read through the file. He had heard rumours about a novel defence technology going missing, but as he read the file he learnt exactly what the device was and its capabilities.

Shiv waited while Humayun read the literature provided. He found it irritating that each time the high commissioner turned a page, he would lick his thumb to wet the corner of the page to make it easier to flip.

After understanding what Shiv was proposing, Humayun casually asked, 'Is there anything else that you want from us?'

'I want to be part of the core group and I want a slice of the bigger game. I want to know who Top Hat is, where Professor Hamid Ansari is and what your plans are,' said Shiv, his face sombre.

Hearing this, the high commissioner stood up and said, 'Mr Shiv, I don't know who you are, what you know and how you have come across this information. Presently I am not at liberty to discuss any of these matters with you. Whether you will be allowed to be a part of the core group, only time will tell. For now, I want you to stay in a hotel nearby. We shall meet again on Saturday morning. Till then I will delve into your background and check the authenticity of Vita. If your device can indeed do what your dossier suggests, then we will do everything in our power to locate it.'

'Thank you,' said Shiv, feeling relieved.

'Don't thank me just yet. If any of your information turns out to be false, then we will kill you, for the sole reason that you seem to know about our activities and agents. So, I hope you won't mind if my manservant Yousef Lehri also stays with you at the hotel.'

'Everything will check out,' replied Shiv nervously and continued, 'but please hurry, the authorities have released me due to lack of evidence. If they find anything new against me, they will arrest me.'

'Understood,' replied Humayun Haq as he once again flipped through the dossier on Vita.

Shiv was irked by the fact that the pages of the dossier were stained red with the high commissioner's betel juice-laden saliva. Consequently, he did not bother to ask for the dossier back.

R&AW had heard the conversation, and everything had gone according to plan.

Pleased, Arvind exclaimed, 'If Humayun agrees to help Shiv, then there's a chance Vita can be located, especially given Haq's black market sources and the people backing him. And if he confides in Shiv and includes him in his core group, then we will finally make headway in our investigation into Professor Hamid's kidnapping and in stopping the possible misuse of his skills.'

Nodding, Wasim replied, 'Finally, we have found our joker, someone who can embed himself in the opponent's team and pass on valuable information. Generally, it takes years for a spy agency to develop and implant such a deep asset, but sometimes in life, circumstances open unique windows of opportunity.'

Heaving a huge sigh of relief, Arvind, Parth and Wasim now waited patiently for their game to begin.

The following day was uneventful for the spies at R&AW. They patiently waited for Humayun to conduct his background search into Vita and Shiv Narayanan. The fact that the High Commission of Pakistan approached the Pune police station where Shiv's arrest was initially recorded gave the spies the confidence that their well thought out plan would work.

For Vikram and Ranbir in Myanmar, it too was a day of waiting in patience. While the skirmishes played out, Vikram finalized the research paper that he was going to present to the general.

At some point in history, nature had decided to enforce a sadistic law that when people anxiously wait for something, time will move at a snail's pace. For the geniuses around the world, this is simply relativity at play, but for more common minds, it is God's way of testing one's patience.

22

T Is for Trauma

On Saturday morning, Arvind and Parth both planned to be present in the hotel lobby before Shiv and Yousef Lehri departed for the high commission.

As soon as they arrived, the spies were greeted with the sight of a swarm of police officers in and around the building. Flashing their credentials to the investigating officer on site, when the spies asked what the matter was, they were informed that two people had been found murdered in a room. Within seconds it was clear that Shiv and Yousef were the victims.

A tight knot formed in Arvind's stomach as he felt an overwhelming sense of nausea. Parth closed his eyes and cursed under his breath. Their best laid plan, for which they had worked so hard, had gone down the drain.

Fifteen minutes later, Secretary Wasim Khan received the news that High Commissioner Humayun Haq had been found dead in his bed.

As R&AW grappled with this bad news, Vikram and Ranbir approached Thanlyin, a major port city by the Bago River in Myanmar. Leaders of seven different rebel groups were coming to meet them. The meeting was scheduled to take place on the penultimate floor of an old building by the river, next to a temple complex. Vikram and Ranbir were the last to arrive. Tin Tun had organized the meet and had been the first to arrive.

As the leaders entered, Vikram noticed that they were all similarly dressed in blue jeans, white shirts and sports shoes. Except for the colour of their shirts, the leaders were dressed like the rebels, in comfortable clothes that would allow them to move around easily and mix in a crowd. These rebel leaders were not like politicians, who more often than not only speak from a pedestal; they were actually working hand-in-hand with the rebel forces under them. The leaders were young and exuded a sense of righteousness mingled with ambition about their purpose and their right to rebel. They saw themselves as the future leaders of the country.

While the leaders greeted each other and sat down, Vikram purposely took a seat next to Tin. With one look at his pen, which was neatly placed in his shirt pocket, Vikram knew that the stout bald fellow intended to take photographs of the meeting and betray them to the general. It was an old trick in the spy textbook. But it did not matter now, as Vikram was already a step ahead of Tin. Poor Tin had relied on backstabbing after the event, while Vikram had already turned traitor and executed his plan.

Over the course of his spy training Vikram had learnt how to observe a situation. He noticed that to not attract attention, each leader had come with only two bodyguards and a driver. Of the fourteen guards, three were stationed on the roof to act as lookouts and over watchers, two were stationed outside the room where the meeting was to take place, three were positioned at the building entrance, two were by the riverside and the remaining four had gone into the nearby streets around the building. The seven drivers had all parked their cars outside the building and kept the engine running. This modus operandi was generally followed by armies, mercenaries and defence contractors around the world. It seemed to Vikram that the rebels had acquired the knowledge by going through videos on the internet.

The meeting began, and the leaders started discussing where the rebel forces would attack next and who would gain power once the general was overthrown. They agreed that each would activate the forces under them at the same time. This would compel the general to firefight on multiple fronts and as his forces would thin out, overthrowing him would be easier. One of the leaders then suggested that he would lead a direct action team to the airport to bomb the runways to prevent the general's fighter planes from providing air support.

After over three hours of deliberation, an overall action plan was agreed upon. Then the youngest leader boasted that once the general was surrounded, he himself would shoot him in the head and that his fellow comrades would drag his body through Yangon, just like the Italians had done with their ousted leader Mussolini. As the others laughed at the boastful remark, the young leader, who could almost taste victory and feel its glory, banged a fist on the table as he declared that he would establish a leftist democracy in Myanmar. His remark instantly led to a fight breaking out over who would seize power once the general was overthrown and what course the country would be put on. Everybody wanted a democracy, but everyone had their own notions about the form it should take.

Vikram silently observed their behaviour and thought that simply overthrowing the general would not solve Myanmar's problems. They needed one strong leader with a concrete plan.

Finally, diverting everyone's attention to their own requirements, Ranbir enquired about the status of their missing scientist. Vikram's trepidation was eased as the leaders unanimously confirmed that a foreign dignitary had been flown in after the coup, but no one knew for sure if it was the scientist Vikram was looking for. Ranbir confirmed that the next cache of weapons and ammunition would arrive soon and that the rebels should be ready to collect the consignment at a moment's notice.

Despite the loud talking in the room, Vikram could hear the archaic camera clicking away in Tin's shirt pocket.

After he had left the hotel earlier, Vikram had messaged the general the location of the meeting, so he expected his soldiers to storm in at any moment. Time passed by quickly, but nothing happened.

The meeting ended after another hour. No one wanted to stay more than was necessary. As the leaders got up to leave, one of them received a message that his forces had killed an army major in Mandalay who went by the nickname 'the hangman of Mandalay' as he regularly hung rebels from the city's trees and buildings. All the leaders leapt with joy and banged on the table as a show of force and belief in their cause. They believed this to be an auspicious sign from the cosmos signalling their victory.

Finally, as the leaders prepared to leave, they all thanked Vikram and Ranbir for their support, and the duo gave no hint of their anxiety.

Despite their differences on how to take the country forward, the rebel leaders all believed that their plan was going to work and that they would be able to defeat the general's forces. They knew that their forces were not trained like the army, but they had strength in numbers and in their guerrilla strategy.

Just as the first leader approached the door, Vikram received a text saying, 'Do not leave the building.'

Vikram pulled Ranbir aside. 'We need to arrange the next cache fast. We should speak to the command right now,' he said in an audible whisper, emphasizing the last two words and nodding his head slightly.

Hearing Vikram's words, the leaders nodded in appreciation as they left the building. The bodyguards, who had spread themselves in and around the old building, had collected at the entrance and were quickly huddling into the cars with their respective bosses. Unfortunately, one of the leaders had dragged Ranbir along with him to discuss the final details of the weapons drop and whether R&AW would play a role in establishing a secure democracy in Myanmar.

Vikram was irritated by the turn of events but knew that he could neither stop the attack nor signal Ranbir without blowing their cover. Even Vikram did not know the general's exact attack plan as the latter had not trusted him with the details.

In desperation, Vikram ran down the steps and yelled out, 'Ranbir! I need my lighter.'

Understanding the signal that his friend was trying to give him, Ranbir smiled and told the young leader, 'My friend is a hopeless addict. Please excuse me.'

As Ranbir hurried away, the leader confidently said, 'Don't worry, we shall have this conversation soon.'

Vikram purposely flicked his own lighter and shook it, to show that it was faulty. As the leader got into his car, Ranbir took the lighter from Vikram and helped him light his cigarette.

As the cars rolled out and approached Thanlyin Bridge, the highway that connected the port city to Yangon, a soft whooshing sound was heard and seconds later the first car was struck by a rocket-propelled grenade or RPG, killing everyone inside on the spot. Before the other cars could turn back, another RPG, this time from the opposite end, struck the last car of the procession. In a sweeping move, the general's army had blocked the bridge from both sides and slaughtered the rebel leaders and their bodyguards. In under five minutes, the country's fate had changed.

Tin Tun, who had stayed back with Vikram and Ranbir, watched in horror as the events unfolded a few hundred metres down the road. As the last explosion reverberated through the port town, Tin, realizing that his bargaining chip lay pulped to pieces, said angrily, 'Your plan has failed. All the rebels are dead. It seems like the army followed you here. We are now doomed.'

Vikram calmly said, 'No, we are not doomed. The army did not follow us here, rather, we brought them here. I gave them the address for this meeting. I know you took photographs of us attending this meeting and intend to sell us out to the general. But sadly for you, I am a step ahead and have already cut a deal with the general.'

Tin was visibly shaken by Vikram's revelation. He did not like being outfoxed. In a spurt of anger, he declared, 'I will tell the general that you are R&AW agents. I shall still make my money and retire.'

Shaking his head Vikram replied, 'I suspected you would say this,' and then pulling out his handgun, he shot the dubious spy thrice. Vikram then walked up to the dead man, took out the spy camera and destroyed it.

Fifteen minutes later, the duo were being escorted by the army to meet their new-found friend General Soe Min.

The thirty-minute drive to Yangon passed quickly. From there, a helicopter flew them to the parliament compound. News of the success of the operation had been shared immediately with the general, so the duo was received with much pride and pomp.

A troupe of traditionally dressed dancers performed the Yein dance to the resonating sound of drums to welcome the now esteemed guests. Everyone was enthralled by the burst of sound and colour as the graceful ladies, their longyi wrapped around their delicate waist, flirted with the ground on which their soft feet danced.

At the doorstep of the wooden chalet, the general, as a token of their friendship, gave Vikram and Ranbir silk scarves woven from Myanmar's indigenous lotus stems.

'It's a painstaking process to extract fibre from the lotus stems,' explained the general. 'At times it can take up to two months to extract a kilogram of fibre, which is required to weave a single scarf. These scarves are not just a token of appreciation, they are also a reminder of your efforts that helped my forces and me achieve a great victory. Without your help it would have taken us months to overrun these rebels, but we have now achieved this arduous feat in under a week.'

The general then clicked his fingers, and two maids walked up to him, handing him two small, intricately carved and well-polished wooden boxes which the general presented to the duo.

'These boxes contain two moonstones each, extracted from our local mines. Again, these are not simple gifts. A moonstone is composed of the compound sodium potassium aluminium silicate. Individually, these elements have little value, but when nature combines them, they transform into a beautiful, semi-precious stone. The value of a person is determined by the company that he keeps and the circumstance he chooses to dwell in. We must all make choices in our lives, which determine our journey and our fate. Let these gifts remind you that your astute calculations allowed us to form a strong alliance, one that will determine the fate of Southeast Asia for years to come.'

This was the first time Vikram and Ranbir had heard the general speak at length. As was reported, he indeed was an effective orator.

'Oratorical skills are probably a prerequisite for politics, especially if semi-literate masses are to be influenced to march for one man's ambition,' Vikram thought to himself as the two were escorted to an open-air dining area on the other side of the chalet.

Ranbir observed a chicken and a swine being slowly roasted over a fire in the middle of the dining courtyard.

Lunch was served along with ice-cold, locally brewed beer, the poison of choice given the tropical climate of the country. The meal and the festivities lasted for three hours. At the end, General Min ordered his associates to leave and prepare the army to start retaking their lost territories over the coming days. Then he held Vikram's hand and escorted the duo to his office on the first floor.

As they entered, the general said, 'I want to introduce you both to some other friends of mine.'

The general settled himself in the leather chair behind his opulent, polished teak table while the duo settled in the simple wooden chairs across from him. He pressed a buzzer and a minute later Jahangir Niazi was escorted into the office by one of the general's stewardesses. Since the spies knew of the arms dealer's presence in Myanmar, thanks to the intercepted communique between the high commissioner and the general, his entrance did not come as a rude shock. Niazi didn't recognize either of the two and introduced himself as a consultant.

After some small talk, Vikram asked the general, 'Is he going to scrutinize our research papers? Should we show him our calculations?'

'Oh no. We have an expert in that field with us here. Let me call him,' replied the general and pressed the buzzer for a second time.

This time the stewardess walked in and stood in silence, awaiting further instructions.

The general glanced at her and said, 'Bring my esteemed guest here please. Tell him we require his expert opinion on an urgent matter.'

The stewardess silently departed and returned ten minutes later, escorting the said guest.

As the man walked in, the sun's evening rays falling upon his face, Vikram slowly got up from his chair. As the man settled into the sofa placed on one side of the room, next to Niazi, Vikram couldn't take his eyes off him. He looked to be in his late fifties. He had a paunch, a long white beard and bushy white moustache. Vikram wasn't yet sure if he was Professor Hamid Ansari, for the long beard, the moustache and the thick-rimmed glasses made it difficult for him to identify the man. Although the man did look shorter than what Vikram had envisaged from the photographs he had seen, and seemed quite well fed, unlike a prisoner, Vikram still hoped that it was Professor Ansari.

Vikram's uncertainty was finally put to rest when the man removed his specs and while cleaning them with his dominant left hand said, 'I am Doctor Zulfiqar Ali, physicist from Pakistan. The general has told me all about you and your ingenious plan to thwart the rebels. I am happy to look at your company's research paper regarding the nuclear bomb you had mentioned earlier to the general.'

Zulfiqar Ali's words, spoken in a strong Urdu accent, his facial features, his physique and his use of his left hand formed a deadly cocktail that gave Vikram a punch in his belly.

At an acute loss for words, Vikram excused himself and rushed to the toilet. Minutes later he was joined by Ranbir. Neither said anything but both read the horror in the other's eyes.

After washing his face, Vikram, accompanied by Ranbir, went back to the general's office.

Seating himself, Vikram took out a few folded sheets of paper from his coat pocket. Handing them over to Zulfiqar, Vikram calmly said, 'These are our research findings so far. Please be aware that this project is still under development and the research is an ongoing process. Nothing has been established yet nor have we tested this technology.'

'I understand. Please give me two days to go over this research. Maybe I can help your company to practically implement the technology. After all, we are now partners and our interests seem to be aligned,' replied the physicist.

As Zulfiqar flipped through the pages, Vikram lit a cigarette to calm his nerves.

Ranbir too was fearful as he thought to himself, 'If Professor Hamid Ansari is not here, then where is he? And did we just help a notorious general retain his hold on a country for a man who was never here and may very well be dead?'

For the first time since receiving their gifts, Ranbir noticed the colour of his scarf. It was blood-red. Looking at the expensive silk, he felt nauseated.

As the day drew to a close, Vikram and Ranbir sat mulling over what they should do to get a grip on the situation.

23

Dead Ends

In India, R&AW had lost its new-found patsy, CEO of Bellator Shiv Narayanan and the innocent bystander witnessing this chaos, Yousef Lehri, to gunshot wounds. Surprisingly, Humayun Haq, whom the agency was certain was at the centre of this chaos, had been found dead too earlier in the day. Even though there were no injury marks or oddities surrounding the death, R&AW had insisted that a post-mortem be carried out. Especially as the high commissioner was a key suspect in an ongoing investigation.

The Ministry of External Affairs had a rough time explaining to their counterparts in Pakistan the necessity of carrying out a post-mortem, especially as the ministry could not reveal that the high commissioner had been a prime suspect.

So, the minister, while talking to her counterpart, had astutely said, 'If the high commissioner was murdered, it would mean that a Pakistani national, who was a guest in our country, was killed under our watch. His untimely death is shocking. I want to launch an investigation into the matter to determine if there has been any foul play.'

'Madam, the high commissioner was inside the high commission. The high commission is considered Pakistani territory. You have no jurisdiction in Pakistan,' Sana Khan, the equally formidable minister for foreign affairs of the Islamic Republic of Pakistan, had countered.

'I understand, but if at a later stage someone points out that there was foul play, then this event could spiral out of control, and it could lead to an international incident. All I am asking for is a chance to inspect. We will transparently share the results with you. Presently, the situation can be controlled and resolved; later, we might not get a chance to control the chaos,' the minister had explained.

Sana Khan was aware of the brewing undercurrents in her country, about the powerful ISI wanting to take control of the government. There were talks that certain factions of the agency, in collusion with some ministers, wanted to disrupt peace in South Asia and use the war as a pretext to topple the existing government. Of course, none of this conjecture had been proven yet, but Sana Khan had a gut feeling that something was amiss.

So, she had finally relented. 'I cannot officially sanction a post-mortem without raising eyebrows in the Parliament here. You will need to do this discreetly. Conduct a post-mortem under Humayun's manservant Yousef Lehri's name. He was shot outside the high commission, so you are legally entitled to conduct an investigation.'

'Very well, madam, and thank you for your cooperation,' the minister had replied with a sense of relief.

Next, the minister's secretary had dialled Wasim Khan and when the old spy answered the call, the secretary had handed the phone over to the minister.

'Secretary Khan, send the doctor who is examining Yousef Lehri to the high commission. Under the garb of the investigation into his death, the doctor will carry out a post-mortem of the high commissioner's body. The staff and personnel at the high commission have been briefed by Pakistan's minister for foreign affairs. But the ruse won't last long, and before word spreads and the objections start coming in, let's get the job done.'

So, a squad of agents had quickly escorted the doctor and his team to the high commission and had asked to conduct a medical examination of the deceased high commissioner. Secretary Wasim Khan knew that a thorough autopsy would not be possible. Consequently, he had instructed the doctor to take the necessary blood, skin tissue and hair samples as these would indicate if any poison had been administered. Poisoning was not the only way in which the high commissioner could have been murdered. Someone could have suffocated him with a pillow or administered a lethal chemical compound via an injection. But unfortunately for R&AW, Wasim Khan did not have the luxury of time to delve into the details of the matter and had to select the most obvious ways of murder to be examined during post-mortem.

The frustration of hitting roadblocks and dead ends had begun mounting for everyone on the team.

24

The Cloudburst

The following day, on Sunday, Vikram and Ranbir, who were now staying in the general's chalet as his guests, were worried and upset about the turn of events. More so, as they were to leave for India in the next twenty-four hours. Since the previous evening they had been trying to figure out who Zulfiqar Ali was and if he had any connection with the now missing Professor Hamid Ansari. The duo had shared the developments with Secretary Wasim Khan and had asked the agency to conduct a background search on physicist Zulfiqar Ali.

As the sun rose and the rays filled the room with warmth, Vikram, while sipping his hot tea, said, 'R&AW hasn't been able to find any details on our esteemed new guest. But in any case, we cannot leave a physicist eager to work for the general alive.'

Ranbir shook his head. 'He is being protected by Jahangir Niazi and the general's guards. We cannot just kill the general or his guests and simply walk out of here. It would be a suicide mission—we would be killed by the numerous guards before we could kill them all. We need to find a discreet way of killing them.'

'If any of the three die before we leave, the general or his lieutenants will suspect us and detain us. We need to find a more subtle way,' agreed Vikram and opened his laptop to do some much-needed research.

Just then a sealed envelope was pushed under the door of their room. As Ranbir bent down to collect it, he heard footsteps hurrying away from the room.

After a quick examination, Ranbir hastily tore open the envelope and found a neatly folded sheet of paper inside. He opened the letter and read aloud, 'I know you are from R&AW. This conspiracy runs deep. Don't trust anyone. I don't want anyone else ensnared in my position. Your lives are in danger. Kill the general and leave.'

Then looking up at Vikram, he continued, 'The note is signed "H.A.". This means Zulfiqar Ali is Hamid Ansari. But how does he know we are from R&AW? And why hasn't he approached us for help? What does he mean by saying he doesn't want anyone else ensnared in his position? Why does he want us to kill the general?'

As Ranbir's barrage of questions ended, Vikram took the letter from him and examined it. He noticed that the message was hurriedly written in sloppy handwriting.

Then looking at Ranbir, he said, 'There seems to be a bigger ploy at play. We are not seeing the whole picture. Why is Hamid Ansari not obviously scared and grabbing the first opportunity to get himself to safety? Why does he look so calm and composed rather than behaving like a scaredy cat hanging on to its last life? However patriotic he may be, he has not been trained like a soldier or a spy, so why is he behaving less like a hostage and more like a spy? Has he been kidnapped or was it orchestrated by a puppeteer who is also controlling our esteemed scientist's actions?'

Ranbir mulled over Vikram's questions, his fingers drumming on the arms of his wooden chair.

After a few minutes of silence, he declared, 'We now have no choice but to assassinate the general and leave Myanmar. Then, while confusion reigns amongst the Burmese army, we can send our forces and extract Hamid Ansari from here.'

While the duo were grappling with this development, Doctor Zulfiqar Ali was pacing in his room. After reading the notes given to him by Vikram, he had had a sleepless night.

Jahangir came to his room and said, 'I have spoken to the ISI, and they haven't yet been able to establish a credible background for these two, who claim to be employed by Gradient Limited. They and their company appear legit, but it all seems too good to be true and superficial. A lot is at stake here. They are presently the general's blue-eyed boys, and without strong evidence, this ambitious general may not believe me if I point fingers at them.'

He paused before continuing, 'What about the research papers they gave you? Are they credible?'

Zulfiqar calmly replied, 'I haven't really read through their research. Also, we cannot risk exposing them for fear of my own cover getting blown in front of these two. After all, it hasn't been mere words; these two have delivered what they promised. No, it is time for us to leave Myanmar. If these men are credible, we will use them later. Make the preparations, we should leave immediately.'

'Okay,' replied Jahangir as he left the room.

Only Zulfiqar knew about his predicament and knew that he must tread very carefully else it would be more than his life that he would lose.

As soon as Jahangir left, Zulfiqar's stomach churned, and his face turned white. The esteemed scientist was walking a tightrope between the ISI and R&AW. Playing the two sides was becoming dangerous. A small mistake could put him in the crosshairs of the spies, and he could lose his life.

At noon, Vikram received another rude shock when the general informed him that Doctor Zulfiqar Ali and his accomplice Jahangir Niazi had left for Pakistan.

Bewildered, Vikram asked, 'But what about the analysis of our research?'

'He said that he shall get back to us in a few days,' the general told him, then continued with a large grin spread across his face, 'Since you both are also leaving in the next eighteen hours, why don't we celebrate our victory with a nice little party.'

The dictator's offer made Vikram's task much easier, and the duo enthusiastically agreed.

More than the food, it was the drinks that did the rounds. Initially, everybody started slow, lining their stomachs with cheese and food and pacing their drinks. But as the evening progressed, the drinks became larger and stronger. Ranbir observed that the general and his lieutenants drank like fish. As their buzz set in, the spies started mixing the sap of Asclepias, or milkweed as it is more commonly known, in the general's drinks.

During their training the spies had been taught how to make use of every resource in their environment and create poisons from naturally occurring substances. Milkweed is a common poisonous plant found in Southeast Asia and is easily identifiable by its elongated leaves that end in acute tips. All parts of the plant are poisonous, but the white sap secreted when the leaves are torn contains active glycosides and asclepiadins which when administered in sufficient quantity can cause paralysis of the heart. Such knowledge and ingredients in the hands of a trained asset can prove to be lethal.

Earlier that day, the duo had walked around the estate plucking the leaves of the milkweed plant and had spent the better part of their morning filling their small soap bottles with the sap of the leaves. Then they crushed the leaves and a few thin stems to make a paste. They were able to fill two 125 ml bottles with this deadly mixture.

When the buzz of the alcohol gripped the general, Vikram and Ranbir started to mix the poison into his drinks. By nightfall, all the poison had been administered, and the general reeked of alcohol.

In his intoxicated state he had been praising the two for their ingenious plan and their role in helping him secure a swift victory. He slurred and swayed as he spoke. He kept repeating himself along with the fact that with Gradient's support, their alliance would become a dominating force on the continent.

Ranbir was surprised that despite consuming so much alcohol, the general did not puke. Vikram, however, who always focused on his goal, was thinking of Jahangir Niazi and the physicist Zulfiqar Ali and said to the general, 'I wish Doctor Zulfiqar had given us his thoughts on our research.'

'You mean Professor Hamid Ansari?' enquired the general, his head tilted backwards.

'I'm sorry, I don't understand,' replied Vikram, suddenly sitting up straight, while trying to feign ignorance.

The general straightened and began fidgeting with his lighter in a desperate attempt to light a cigarette, then said,

'Doctor Zulfiqar and Professor Hamid Ansari are the same person. You don't know, but this cunning man, Hamid Ansari, who is also India's top nuclear scientist, orchestrated his own kidnapping with the ISI's help. Then they hid him here with us. Looks like India is no longer going to remain the dominant power in this part of the world, especially after it loses Siachen.'

Vikram and Ranbir heard the general, then silently waited for him to pass out. Then they requested the guards to immediately fly them to the airport. As the guards had been instructed earlier to escort the duo to Yangon airport, no one objected to their request.

It was 3 a.m. on Monday morning. Their flight out of Yangon was in three hours. They knew that by the time someone tried to wake the general up, they would be long gone.

At 10.30 a.m. on Monday morning, when Ranbir and Vikram landed in Delhi, the news of General Soe Min's death was being flashed across all news channels. While waiting for their bags, Ranbir heard the reporter on the TV say, 'The rebels and the pro-democracy forces of Myanmar have found a new ray of hope after the ruthless dictator General Soe Min was found dead a few hours earlier. Rumours suggest it was a heart attack, probably caused due to excessive drinking. Chaos now reigns within the ranks of the Burmese army as many try to gain control of the military. The rebels are taking full advantage of the situation and slowly regaining control over the country. It looks like the rebels might finally win...'

Ranbir had heard enough to ease his conscience, and after collecting his luggage, he walked towards the exit.

Vikram had never cared about the collateral damage caused by his actions because for him the end justified the means. His goal had been to locate Professor Hamid Ansari and rescue or eliminate him, as per the situation. For him, only the bigger picture mattered, and everything was justified by the goal. So the fact that the general was dead and the rebels had another chance to secure democracy in the country was inconsequential to Vikram. He had killed the general to ensure stability in the region, not to ease his conscience.

Now, Vikram was eager to head to R&AW headquarters and formalize a strategy for the way ahead.

Vikram's apathy had not gone unnoticed by his friend. As Vikram and Ranbir sat in the car that had come to pick them up, Ranbir casually said, 'Vikram, we are in the business of hunting monsters; but we must not become one ourselves in the process.'

With a forced smile Vikram replied, 'A secure future is a safe future and that is what we need to work towards. Everything else is just noise.'

'You cannot fight fate,' said Ranbir.

'No, I cannot. But if in the end the situation takes a turn for the worse, then at least I can say that I tried my best.'

By 11.30 a.m., all essential personnel had assembled in R&AW's conference room.

Addressing the head of the table, Secretary Wasim Khan, Ranbir began by saying, 'We now know for sure that Professor Hamid Ansari and Doctor Zulfiqar Ali are the same person. He orchestrated his own kidnapping and was hidden in Myanmar by his confrère. He was wearing a wig and beard extensions when he briefly met us in the general's office. Anyway, he has now flown to Pakistan along with his aide Jahangir Niazi. Our plan was to give him the research notes, with obvious flaws in it, to signal to him that we are from India and were there to rescue him. Professor Ansari must have understood or at the very least suspected that we are from the Indian government or have strong ties to it. So instead of taking the risk of blowing his cover by challenging us, he fled. Yet in a hurriedly scribbled note he instructed us to assassinate the general and claimed that this conspiracy runs deep into the higher echelons of the government. He also stated that he wouldn't wish his fate to befall anyone else. However, we believe that he is playing both sides and has an agenda of his own,' said Ranbir.

He paused and reached for the bottle of water placed in front of him and after taking a few sips, continued in a grim tone, 'It is possible that Hamid Ansari wanted us to assassinate the general as he no longer needed the dictator, and he and the ISI did not wish to fund the man any further. Or he wanted us to get killed while trying to assassinate General Soe Min, thereby removing us from his tail.'

As Ranbir's words sank in, the spies realized that the scientist was playing a dangerous game, and it was crucial to stop him before any more damage was inflicted.

Vikram opened his notes and continued, 'We had proved ourselves to the general, yet Professor Ansari did not attempt to confide in us. I thus suspect that whatever they are planning is extremely dangerous. I don't believe it's a game of mere misplaced beliefs; someone intends to make huge profits and has planned the game very carefully. Lastly, after the general's death, Hamid will surely be wary of us. As far as he is concerned, we may have blown our cover.'

Ranbir, playing with his pencil, pitched in saying, 'The general had declared that we will no longer be the dominant power in Southeast Asia and will also lose Siachen. Now, we don't know whether he was bragging and simply stating his own wishes or if he was privy to the professor's plans and had genuinely spilled the beans.'

Additional Secretary Parth now spoke, while sipping his hot coffee, 'I had put a pair of agents on the professor's family. They were keeping an eye on them. But to add to our misery, this morning, Professor Hamid's wife and children gave our agents the slip and boarded a bus to Nepal. Either they knew about Hamid's plan or have been coerced to go to Kathmandu. One of Arvind's agents is in pursuit, and I have also activated our local sources there.'

Arvind Ghosh finally stood up and said, as he wrote on the whiteboard, 'So far, facts state that Professor Hamid Ansari is one of the culprits. Secondly, his family is bound for Nepal, and we may be able to apprehend them there. Thirdly, there may be a nuclear attack on Siachen or its surrounding areas, especially if they intend to render the area useless for everyone. Fourthly and closer to home, we still don't know the identities of Top Hat and the strange tall man in the fez who visited Humayun Haq in his office. Fifth, the motive for Haq's and Shiv Narayanan's deaths is still not known. Although, our team has secured some samples and we may at least soon know how the high commissioner was killed. And lastly, we still don't know the location of Bhim Singh and Vita.'

Arvind was a methodical man and believed in a structured approach to working. The points he had jotted down highlighted all that R&AW had to figure out and where exactly the agency stood in its investigation.

Before the meeting ended, it was decided that if Hamid Ansari's family was spotted in Nepal, Vikram and Ranbir would fly there to either tail them or apprehend them, depending on how the situation developed. If, however, none of the family members were seen in the next seventy-two hours, then the duo would possibly have to go to Pakistan in search of Hamid Ansari and Jahangir Niazi.

Parth and Arvind, on the other hand, would concentrate on the local assignments of securing Siachen, flushing out Top Hat and figuring out the identity of the mysterious man in the fez, locating Bhim Singh and Vita, and lastly, determining the motive behind Humayun Haq's and Shiv Narayanan's deaths.

As everyone prepared to leave the boardroom and were gathering their papers and notes, Vikram asked the secretary, 'Is Siachen being targeted for its vital geographic advantages or is there a deeper agenda?'

Wasim Khan gave Vikram a piercing gaze as he replied, 'The Saltoro Ridge of the Siachen glacier prevents the direct linking of Pakistan-occupied Kashmir with China, stopping them from developing military linkages in the area. It also allows us to keep watch on the Gilgit and Baltistan regions of Pakistan. Additionally, we can monitor China's activity in the region, especially as they have greatly improved their infrastructure in the area. Besides, the fresh water from the region is vital. Not just for sustenance, but fresh water is becoming a crucial resource in the manufacturing industry. The production of semiconductors and microchips, which are used in almost all electronic media, industrial equipment and even in cars, requires about two to four million gallons of ultra-pure water every day. Siachen is an expensive yet a vital resource that we need to defend and maintain for our country to progress.'

Vikram pondered over the explanation and then slowly drifted out of the room while trying to establish his next move.

25

Be Still, Be Quiet

Roughly 855 km away, in Kapilavastu, Bhim Singh had been living a quiet life amongst the monks. It was his sixth day at the Sakya Tharig monastery. It was not that Bhim had turned a new leaf, he just wanted to lie low for a few days. At the monastery, Bhim worked and lived with the monks. He participated in cleaning, cooking, pruning shrubs and maintenance activities; in return, he was provided with clean robes, meals and a roof over his head.

He had kept Vita in his bedroom cupboard. Upon his arrival, when he was searched by the monks, lest he be a terrorist, he had presented Vita as a mere hard drive to them. His hosts had not given it a second look.

Bhim was not quite enjoying the pious lifestyle and was hungrily waiting for the money that would come his way when he sold Vita. After giving R&AW the slip, he had met a prominent man in Varanasi, who had advised him to run to

Nepal. He had told him to lie low and to wait for instructions. The days seemed to stretch endlessly for the distressed Bhim.

Satya was feeling anxious and scared and had been pacing around his room all morning. In fact, after the news of Shiv Narayanan's death broke on Saturday evening, the ISRO chief had been contemplating leaving to hide in another town. He had no family, so disappearing would be easier for him. He had enough savings to help him remain on the move for a few months. Plus, he could always operate remotely, via his secretary and staff. Pondering over what to do, he started spreading extra butter on his toast with a tinge of frustration, for he still did not have clarity about the path he should take. Adding to his irritation was the fact that his friend Dev Burman had probably switched off his phone as he had not been reachable for the past two days and consequently Satya did not know where he was.

Dev had been busy over the past week, attending numerous meetings all over the country. He had been to Mumbai, Pune, Kolkata, Delhi and Lucknow. As the head of the R&D department for the DRDO, he was required to regularly meet the heads of the various companies engaged in the manufacture and assembly of defence equipment.

It was Monday, and he had to drag himself to the remote town of Turtuk in Ladakh for a meeting between India, China and Pakistan.

The village of Turtuk was 2.5 km from the Line of Control between India and Pakistan. India's defence secretary, Shekhar Banerjee, who served as the administrative head of the country's defence ministry, along with the army chief, Govind Pratap Singh, were present with their counterparts from China and Pakistan. The agenda of the meeting included discussing the role each nation should play in stabilizing Myanmar, reducing tensions along the border, the possibilities and conditions of sharing the fresh waters of Siachen and the sharing of defence technologies with the aim of maintaining peace in Southeast Asia. Dev's presence at the meeting was primarily for the last part. He had no say in geopolitical matters but was expected to shrewdly answer questions pertaining to the sharing of technologies. Dev knew such meetings to be an eyewash. They were a political manoeuvre to de-escalate tensions amongst the three belligerent and cantankerous neighbours. More often than not, these meetings were held behind closed doors and in remote areas, away from the prying eyes of the media. The location also ensured controlled participation. But for Dev, this meeting was an irritating waste of time, especially as he was required to use the army's satellite phone to contact his home as there was no cellular reception in this pristine part of the country.

The Army Chief Govind Singh started the meeting by addressing the Pakistani delegation and saying, 'I am sorry to hear about the sudden demise of High Commissioner Humayun Haq. May his family find the strength to endure the loss and may he rest in peace.'

While the members of the delegation silently accepted the condolence, there were a few who scowled at the mention of the late high commissioner's name. So did the Indian defence secretary, Shekhar Banerjee.

Observing the members of the meeting, Dev started fidgeting with his pen and anything else that he could lay his hands on, for his mind had started drifting. Now he could not wait to get back to Mumbai.

Since the army chief's comment, Shekhar had been observing Dev and had not liked his body language.

26

Things to Come

The following day, on Tuesday morning, the tall man, now no longer wearing a fez, was walking barefoot on the wet grass in front of his villa in a resort in Nagarahole National Park in Karnataka. He had flown into the state in the wee hours of the morning and had decided to spend some time at the peaceful and luxurious resort. He had not slept through the night and a cup of strong filter coffee had given him the required caffeine hit to keep him alert for the next few hours.

A while later he called Jahangir Niazi and asked him to hand the phone over to Hamid Ansari. When the scientist came on the line, the man, plucking a few leaves as he walked, said, 'I have helped your family escape to Nepal. Our esteemed friend Bhim Singh is also there, along with Vita. Your family will have to steal Vita from him, kill him and then meet you in Pakistan. Do you think they will be able to carry out the task?'

'Yes. I have trained them well. But don't you think we should bring Bhim Singh to Pakistan and use his skills, or simply purchase Vita from him?' asked the scientist, sensing the possible danger in the mission chosen for his family.

'No! We have no further use for him. He is extra baggage, and his death will be the key to the chaos that we intend to unleash; besides, we cannot risk him getting caught. He needs to be terminated. I have already instructed him to meet your family in Kathmandu. Ensure that our goal is achieved.'

'Very well. It shall be done,' replied Ansari with firm resolve.

After the call disconnected, Top Hat crushed the leaves in his hand, whistled and walked on as the morning rays of the sun warmed his body.

Meanwhile, in Delhi, Vikram and Ranbir were in their respective homes. They had been told to take time off and recuperate till their next assignment came up. Mentally exhausted from their ordeals in Myanmar, both had chosen to sleep first.

Naina Narain, an old field agent under Joint Secretary Arvind Ghosh, was one of the agents tailing Ansari's family in Nepal.

Early on Tuesday morning she called Arvind and said, 'I have located Hamid's family. They are staying in a nice four-star hotel, located in the old town, called Kathmandu Guest House. I have also taken a room there. Send Vikram and Ranbir at the earliest.'

It had not been very difficult for Naina and her local fellow agent to track down the family. A word with the border forces and the local informers had pointed Naina straight to them.

Her fellow agent was R&AW's local contact in Kathmandu and after sharing the location where Hamid's family was staying, he had retired back into the shadows. Local assets were never encouraged to participate in field operations, for fear that their cover might be blown, or they may be killed. It takes years for local assets to credibly embed themselves in a country and they were therefore not risked unless absolutely necessary. Their main job remained to gather information and pass it on. Thus, Naina had requested for Vikram and Ranbir as back-up.

Twelve hours later, at 9 p.m., Vikram and Ranbir were on a flight to Kathmandu. While Ranbir gorged on the in-flight food and enjoyed the view of the clouds from his window seat, Vikram put on some Sufi music, leaned his head back against his headrest and relaxed. As the songs played, Vikram recalled the conversation he had had with his wife just before he had left home.

'I now think that your job as an inspector was much better; at least you would come home every night,' Sanyukta had said, the dejection clear in her voice.

'I am now playing a greater role in serving and protecting the nation,' Vikram had explained.

'There are many who can do this job. Why don't you quit and aim for a normal life? You even bring your work home now. Earlier, you were never tense when you returned from work. These days you are mostly lost in thought and have lost your carefree nature,' his wife had continued while handing him his small suitcase.

'I do get a high from stopping terrorists, you know, and I have been trained well to do it,' Vikram had said.

'Life is not about getting a high. The atmosphere in the house has started to get tense due to the pressures of your work. You need to seriously think about what your aim in life is, Vikram. Terrorists have operated in this world for centuries and shall continue to do so much after us. You cannot stop them all. Thinking about your safety gives me anxiety, and I certainly don't want to live the rest of my life in fear,' Sanyukta had finished, her tone firm.

'Let me see this catastrophe through and then we can talk about my career options,' Vikram had said while lovingly caressing his wife.

That same day, on Tuesday evening, at about 7 p.m., Bhim Singh reached Kathmandu. It had been an eight-hour drive and to his irritation, the taxi driver had talked to him throughout the journey. Even when he had tried or pretended to sleep by shutting his eyes, the driver's monologue had continued without a break.

Bhim had shaved his hair and worn a monk's robes as he believed that no one would trouble a monk, and he would be able to blend in better.

Bhim had instructed his driver to drop him off at Asan Tole, a residential, ceremonial and market centre in Kathmandu. Six streets merged into the central square, which made the place look like a bustling beehive of humans. Even at that late hour, the place was crowded. Bhim had booked himself into a modest hotel in the area, but he got off at a nearby traffic signal and chose to walk the remaining distance. He had had enough of the driver's talking, and it had given him a headache. The driver had shared his opinions on Indian politics, the performance of the Indian cricket team and the lack of vision of the Nepalese politicians with regard to ensuring the economic growth of the small mountainous country, amongst various other topics, which he changed every five minutes. Bhim could not care less for any of these things, and now his brain unwillingly stored information about the driver's children, which school they went to and their favourite subjects. Bhim continued to hear the vexing voice of the driver in his head as he crossed the various spice and bullion shops that lined the street. So, instead of going to his hotel, he first went to a quaint little tea shop and ordered some hot tea and steamed momos.

Bhim had been told to make contact with a lady called Mashal Ansari who was staying at the Kathmandu Guest House. But Bhim was tired from his journey and decided that he would contact the lady the following day.

27

Into the Tunnel

On Wednesday morning, Parth received a call from the doctor who had been tasked with conducting the autopsy of the late high commissioner.

The doctor plainly said, 'The blood and tissue samples we took from Humayun Haq have been tested, and there is clear evidence of arsenic poisoning. The dosage administered was such that the poison's effect would have kicked in after several hours and not immediately. To achieve this, the killer must not have directly injected the poison, but rather administered it via some substance that came into contact with the high commissioner. The tissue samples that I took from the fingers of his right hand along with the tissue cultures from inside his mouth are the only ones that show traces of arsenic. So, it is my conclusion that the arsenic was either in his food or in something that he chewed or ingested.'

Parth recalled the fateful day and then slowly said, 'Or on something that he repeatedly licked.'

'I'm sorry, I don't follow,' replied the unassuming doctor.

'That day, Shiv gave Haq a file on Vita in an attempt to lure him to spill the beans on their secret agenda. But someone who knew of his habit of licking his thumb before turning pages must have laced the pages of the file with arsenic.'

Parth realized that the only way to prove his theory was to retrieve the file from the high commissioner's office. Covertly breaking into the complex was an option, but it was a risky one. Taking a deep breath, Parth thought about how he could retrieve the file and while thinking, idly flipped through the daily newspaper. In it he noticed a quote that said, 'Life is really simple, but we insist on making it complicated.' As he read the quote, his path forward became clear.

Parth summoned two analysts from his team and sent them to the High Commission of Pakistan with a request to retrieve the file from the late high commissioner's office.

Humayun's wife would be returning to Pakistan within the next few days, after mourning and packing up all their belongings. The late high commissioner's replacement would arrive a day after Humayun's wife left. Parth resolved that if his simple request was not granted and his analysts failed, then he would plan a covert mission to retrieve the file.

The file was important, for if the pages were found to be laced with arsenic, then by tracing the file's journey, R&AW could identify where, when and by whom the pages had been poisoned.

As Parth's agents left for the high commission with a duly signed and stamped request letter, the situation was steaming up in Nepal.

28

Outfoxed

Vikram and Naina were jostling their way through the crowds in Asan Tole as they desperately tried to follow Mashal Ansari. She and her two children had been staying at the four-star Kathmandu Guest House.

After breakfast, Mashal had taken a taxi, and Vikram and Naina had followed her. The kids, Aqsa and Ali, had stayed back, and consequently Ranbir had remained at the hotel to keep an eye on them.

Ranbir, Vikram and Naina were all online with R&AW headquarters in Delhi, where Wasim Khan and Arvind Ghosh were closely monitoring the developments. R&AW had not yet established whether Mashal and her kids were Hamid's accomplices. The spies were still giving the family the benefit of the doubt and had decided to observe and monitor them from afar. The agency's decision was based on the fact that nothing about Hamid's family suggested that they had been radicalized. When the family had fled to Nepal, the agency had conducted a proper background search on all three of them. Not one instance of them attending any sermons of radical leaders, denigrating the nation or the government, posting vengeful rhetoric on social media or voicing any radical views had emerged.

So, the agents still believed that someone had contacted the family and made them go to Nepal with the aim of taking them to Hamid Ansari, and the family had complied in a desperate attempt to reunite with the patriarch. R&AW hoped that by tailing the family they would be able to nab the nefarious scientist.

Naina and Vikram each had a small camera attached to their shirt buttons and were trying not to lose sight of Mashal in the maze of hole-in-the-wall shops that lined both sides of the street. There were six such streets that culminated in the central square, but they were also interconnected via narrow alleys. One could easily get lost there.

Mashal was wearing a slightly oversized white shirt paired with comfortable black jeans, and her hair was tied in a bun held by a thin red silk scarf. That scarf allowed Vikram and Naina to keep track of her from afar.

A while later, Mashal crossed a shop that was selling brass and copperware items and turned into a spice shop to purchase some organic ground spices. Next, she walked up the road and quickly spoke to a shopkeeper. The shopkeeper gestured towards a small lane behind his shop, making a 'c' with his hand and then pointed ahead indicating that she should go straight. Vikram and Naina saw the shopkeeper's gestures and followed Mashal from a distance. Crossing a conch shop, Mashal arrived at her intended destination, a shop selling scented candles. She purchased a few then continued walking casually up the road. A man on a bicycle was selling nice yellow bananas. Mashal purchased one and ate it as she walked. With her energy restored, she entered a homeware store and purchased what she was looking for and left. After her varied shopping spree ended, she hailed a cab and headed back to her hotel.

Vikram and Naina did not have the time to check with the store what Mashal's last purchase had been. They did not want to risk losing her, so without further enquiry, they too hailed a cab and instructed the driver to follow Mashal's taxi from a distance.

At the hotel, Bhim Singh was waiting in the coffee shop for Mashal Ansari. He had been told by the receptionist that the lady he was looking for had stepped out earlier that day.

Finally, Mashal arrived and as she was collecting her key from the reception, she was informed that a gentleman was waiting for her in the coffee shop.

Vikram had told Ranbir to meet them in the lobby. When the trio heard the receptionist tell Mashal that a gentleman was waiting for her, their excitement increased as they all thought that Hamid had finally shown himself. They decided that if it was the scientist then they would apprehend the family instantly. However, if it was someone else, then they would only observe and intervene at the right moment.

Without giving the spies a second look, Mashal walked to the coffee shop. There the floor manager guided her to Bhim Singh's table.

The spies followed her soon after and sat at a table near the door, diagonally opposite her table.

Bhim did not recognize Vikram, Ranbir or Naina for he had never seen nor heard of them. The spies, however, were aware of Bhim's identity.

Vikram had a clear line of sight to the person sitting with Mashal. As his video camera transmitted the live footage to R&AW headquarters, his phone buzzed. As soon as he answered, he heard Arvind say, 'The man sitting with Mashal Ansari is Bhim Singh.'

'Yes, I know,' muttered Vikram and continued, 'He may be carrying Vita with him. But if we intervene now, we'll blow our cover.'

'Wait and see how the situation plays out. If Bhim leaves, I want one of you to tail him,' instructed Arvind.

'Understood,' said Vikram and cut the call.

R&AW could have apprehended them and tried to force a confession, but that could take days and the spy agency could lose time they did not have. Also, Mashal and Bhim were the proverbial small fish in the eyes of R&AW. The spy agency couldn't yet take the risk of alerting their actual targets.

So they decided to wait and watch.

About thirty feet away, Mashal was saying, 'We leave tonight after dinner. Get here at 9 p.m. sharp. Bring Vita with you.'

Then handing Bhim an envelope she continued, 'This contains your new passport and identity papers.'

Bhim took the packet and checked its contents then said, 'How can you trust me? What if I disappear with Vita? I could sell it on my own.'

'You have already betrayed your associates once; I don't think you would betray Top Hat. We are your only allies left. Besides, no one except us can help you get the right price for Vita. So then, we shall see you at nine?' asked Mashal with a soft smile.

'Yes, you shall,' replied Bhim, liking the smile on her face.

'Come straight to room 502, the key is in the envelope,' said Mashal as she got up, signed the bill and briskly walked away.

Bhim lingered in the coffee shop for a while, ordered another coffee and a pastry, ate heartily and then left.

Vikram tailed Bhim's taxi while Ranbir and Naina kept watch on Mashal and her children in the hotel.

The day went by quickly. Bhim had returned to his hotel in Asan Tole and slept. He woke up a little after six, had a shower and a hearty meal, packed his belongings, paid his bill and left for the Kathmandu Guest House.

Throughout the day, Ranbir and Naina had had it pretty easy as there had been no developments at the hotel. The Ansari family had ordered their dinner in their room and had not stepped out since the afternoon.

At 9 p.m., Bhim, tailed by Vikram, arrived at the hotel. Bhim headed straight to room 502. As he rang the bell, Vikram, who had now entered his own room down the hall, called Ranbir to ask him for an update.

Ranbir, who was in the opposite tower but had a clear view of Mashal's room from his balcony, said, 'I can see Bhim entering room 502. It's booked under Mashal's son's name and adjoins her room.'

'Her kids have a separate room?' enquired Vikram.

'Yes, the kids are in room 502, while Mashal is in 500,' replied Ranbir.

A few minutes later, Ranbir reported, 'Mashal and the kids just entered room 502 via the connecting door. Mashal has drawn the curtains of room 502. I have lost my view.'

'Okay, I'll go and stand by the lift. Where is Naina?' said Vikram.

'She is down in the lobby, sitting near the main entry.'

In room 502, Mashal was telling Bhim, who was sitting on the chair by the desk, their escape route. While handing out tickets to everyone, she explained, 'We will all leave together via Pakistan International Airlines and head straight to Karachi. From there we will each take a separate flight to Multan.'

Opening a bottle of water, Bhim enquired, 'When is our flight? And why are we taking three separate flights from Karachi to Multan?'

'Now!' said Mashal casually as Bhim tilted his head back and gulped the cold water down.

In a swift move, Ali grabbed Bhim's hair, wrenched his head back and slashed his throat with the French chef's knife that Mashal had bought earlier from the homeware store. As Bhim grasped his throat, the blood spurting from the clean slit, Aqsa and Mashal stabbed him repeatedly in the chest with their carving knives to puncture his lungs.

Mashal then tied oil-soaked cloths around the base of the candles she had bought and lit them. Tying the oily cloths any higher would have risked them slipping down the candles, ruining her plan. She placed the candles around the room. As they burned down, the cloths would catch fire and in turn, set the room on fire.

She then sprayed the organic ground spices in her kids' and her own room to mask their body odour and make it difficult for the police dogs to catch their scent.

Mashal had burnt the candles through the afternoon, so now it took a little over fifteen minutes for them to burn down to the oil-soaked cloths and set them alight. Once the fire caught, it spread with a rage. Within minutes thick black smoke could be seen coming out through the cracks around the room's windows and doors.

Vikram, Ranbir and Naina had been on the phone, keeping the communication channel open amongst them.

As soon as Ranbir saw smoke coming out of the room, the three of them rushed to room 502. As they opened the door, the smoke inside billowed into the corridor and fire alarms started blaring as the water sprinklers in the ceiling burst to life.

In the pandemonium, with a mist of smoke and water covering the hallway, Mashal and her kids stepped out of room 500, mingled with the crowd and went down the fire escape. Instead of assembling in the courtyard, they slyly slipped away into the darkness.

29

Race You

An hour later, Vikram, Ranbir and Naina were sitting outside the hotel with their heads throbbing from the soot and the smoke. When the spies had barged into room 502, they had found the mutilated and half burnt body of Bhim Singh and no sign of Mashal Ansari and her kids. They had immediately informed R&AW to activate all local assets in Nepal and to tighten the borders to prevent the Ansaris from leaving the country. Local assets had not been used earlier as no one wanted either Bhim or Mashal to get a hint that they were being observed. Had that happened, R&AW's operation would have failed. But the way the situation had unfolded now compelled R&AW to pursue Mashal with full force.

The home ministry and the army of Nepal had been briefed almost immediately and photos, fingerprints along with the Ansaris' Indian passport numbers were widely circulated. The National Investigation Department or NID, Nepal's primary intelligence agency, had also been briefed. They had sent their officers to the airport and train stations to help R&AW.

Even though the three Indian spies were now sitting on the pavement across the hotel with dejected looks on their faces, they had ensured that a nationwide manhunt was now underway for Mashal, Ali and Aqsa.

Sitting on the dusty pavement, a frustrated Ranbir wondered, 'Who led Bhim Singh to Mashal? Who is the common link between Vita and Hamid Ansari?'

'Top Hat is the common link. The turncoat is someone high up in the bureaucratic hierarchy,' replied Vikram.

'Why do you think Top Hat is at the epicentre of these events? Maybe Bhim approached him for help, instead of it being the other way round,' said Naina.

'Even if Bhim approached Top Hat, he would have had to know about Vita, its success and its potential, to agree to help him. Secondly, the murders of the high commissioner and Shiv Narayanan point towards someone who can track our investigation and has the resources to hamper our progress. And lastly, the Ansari family giving our agents the slip to come to Nepal and almost immediately orchestrating a murder highlights a certain sense of confidence, which would be possible only if the turncoat kept the Ansaris informed of our location and progress. Otherwise, a family that has just fled to another country would not have the confidence to commit murder. Even the most hardened criminals are scared of being caught. But the Ansaris knew that they were a step ahead of us. And let us not forget the fact that they are not looking to become martyrs, rather, they intend to reunite with Hamid, so ideally it would have been easier for them to slip away. Instead, they took a great risk in killing Bhim and stealing Vita,' explained Vikram.

'Okay, but if Hamid is in Pakistan and is being helped by the ISI, then why not take Bhim there, snatch Vita from him and shoot him in cold blood? It would have been easier for them to cover it up in Pakistan. Why did they go through the effort and the risk of murdering Bhim Singh here?' enquired Ranbir.

Vikram pondered over his friend's question and found his theory stymied. He had no logical explanation for Mashal's actions. He wondered about the chaos that was unfolding and the probable end game of Hamid Ansari.

After Mashal and her kids had left the hotel, they set off for their destination, Rinchenling Gompa, an ancient Buddhist monastery in Nepal's Limi Valley. It would take them nine hours to reach the remote valley situated in north-western Nepal.

Although geographically situated in Nepal, the valley had a heavy Tibetan influence in terms of its culture. A direct road connected the valley to the Tibetan Autonomous Region and China. Thus, most shops there sold Chinese items. Using trade and commerce as a tool, China had shrewdly involved itself in this secluded part of the world; the valley's other neighbour, India, had failed to do so.

Surrounded by mountains, Limi Valley was home to only about two hundred families, and they were isolated from the morbid affairs of the world. That was why this location had been chosen for Mashal and her children. They would hide here before travelling onwards to Tibet.

30

On the Doorstep

Twelve hours earlier, at 11 a.m. on Wednesday, in Delhi, Parth's team had reached the High Commission of Pakistan. Showing their papers at the gate, the agents requested entry and were granted the same without any fuss. They went straight to Humayun's office, which was being cleaned by the staff.

Before the agents could start looking for the file, Humayun's wife Amina Haq entered the room and asked, 'Can I help you?'

'Yes, we are looking for a file that was handed over to the late high commissioner before he died,' replied one of the agents.

'All his files and papers have been kept in the adjoining room. We will pack them up shortly. But you may look at them,' said Amina politely.

'We may have to retrieve one of the files. We have a written letter from our agency requesting you to relinquish that file to us. However, we would prefer it if you could hand it over to us without any documentation or notary,' replied the agent.

'Will this help you find my husband's killer?' enquired Amina.

'Yes,' said the agent confidently.

Amina stared at the agent for several seconds, then said, 'Okay. You may retrieve the file and we won't make a note of its existence in our catalogue.'

'Thank you, ma'am,' replied the agent, a hint of surprise in his voice. He had not expected the lady to cooperate so easily.

'I can understand your surprise, officer,' said Amina, picking up on the officer's tone. 'I realize that more often than not there is tension between our two nations. Yet, I would like you to promise me that you will catch the killer and bring him to justice.'

'We will do everything in our power, ma'am, and thank you for your cooperation.'

The agents then sifted through the files and found the one that Shiv Narayanan had presented to Humayun Haq during their meeting. After wearing a pair of gloves, the agent retrieved the file, and the team left the high commission.

By noon Parth received confirmation that the file had been successfully retrieved and had been submitted for forensic analysis.

Within the hour, Parth's conjecture had been confirmed. The file had been laced with arsenic. Now, he had to work out who all had had access to the file before Shiv's meeting with the high commissioner.

31

Never Trust the Silent Ones

A few days ago, the ISRO chief Satya Kulkarni had informed his team that he would be on leave for the next twenty days and was to be contacted only in case of an emergency. He had instructed his secretary to give him daily updates, via email, about work at the office. Satya had not informed anyone where he was headed. He had left with the intention of not being found easily, and the wildlife sanctuaries of south India were the perfect place for him to find solitude. They were free of crowds and had low network connectivity, which allowed him to switch off his phone intentionally.

On Tuesday evening, Dev Burman had returned from his string of meetings and had taken the following day off. He was soundly asleep on Wednesday morning when his expergefactor, the milkman, rang the bell. Waking from his slumber, Dev collected the milk bottles and dragged his feet to the kitchen to prepare some coffee for himself. The clamour woke up his wife, Shilpa, and as the milk boiled, she too entered the kitchen.

'Good morning, the coffee smells nice. Make a strong cup for me too.'

'Morning,' replied Dev without glancing at his wife as he busied himself with preparing their daily elixir.

Without noticing her husband's sombre tone, Shilpa continued, 'I'm planning to order pizzas for lunch today. A new pizzeria has opened up in our locality, and I've heard their hand-tossed, wood fired pizzas are scrumptious. It will be a real Italian treat.'

Dev was particular about the preparation of his morning coffee—the proportion of the full cream milk and the froth that it created had to be perfect. So while Shilpa was rattling on about their lunch plans, Dev was busy sprinkling coffee powder over the final preparation. After he finished, he quickly eyed the two cups and seemed satisfied with the final outcome and his attention to detail.

As he handed Shilpa a cup, he said, 'Yes, call for lunch at home. I won't be stepping out today.'

'You seem tense. Is anything the matter?' enquired Shilpa.

'Observing someone can reveal a lot about that person. We may be losing balance and control, and they need to be re-tilted in our favour,' replied Dev as he slowly sipped the hot coffee, the elixir sliding down his throat, warming him from inside.

Despite the caffeine triggering his brain cells, he was still perplexed about how to resolve his suspicions. He feared that the authorities above him would not pay heed to his suspicions, especially due to the lack of evidence. Yet, he knew he had to do something. He had a strong gut feeling about his observations.

While Dev was musing over his dilemma, his wife, who had not quite understood his comment, simply replied, 'After a few weeks, once you are done with your work, we could leave for Nainital and stay with your parents for a few days. It would be a nice break for us.'

Dev did not reply as his thoughts had wandered elsewhere.

Shekhar Banerjee, an ambitious, forty-eight-year-old man, was agile and robust for his age. He had a doctorate in economics from the prestigious St. Stephens College of Delhi University. He was a late child, and his parents had died of complications related to old age a few years after he had started working. His wife, Urmimala, was nine years younger than him. It had been a love marriage. Their union had borne them a set of twin girls. He was not of a patriarchal mindset and had been ecstatic at the birth of his daughters. He felt happy that they looked like him.

Shekhar had moved up the ranks of the Indian Administrative Service through hard work and smart choices. He had made the right contacts and had oiled the right parts of the government machinery to secure quick promotions. He could be a charmer when the situation demanded. After twenty years of rigorous work he had managed to become the nation's defence secretary. A position he had held for the past five years.

As the defence secretary, he was privy to all threats and security matters in and around the nation. He had been briefed about Vita, about the developments in Nepal and Professor Hamid Ansari's defection. R&AW had understandably only briefed the prime minister about their covert operation in Myanmar for fear of the information being leaked and their mission failing. It was standard protocol. The agency also had to maintain plausible deniability when operating on foreign soil, in case the operation went south. This would not be possible if the details of the mission were widely known; hence, a close-knit circuit of information was maintained.

Shekhar was particularly unhappy about Humayun Haq and the role he had played. After the agency had informed him that they had solid evidence that the high commissioner was a spy and had been involved in a conspiracy against India, he had detested the man even more.

32

A Time to Kill

The Rinchenling Gompa had accepted Mashal and her kids easily. A travel-worn mother with two children does not raise any eyebrows, even in this remote corner of the world. Looking at their condition, the monks gave them cups of hot tea made with thick yak milk and a broth with thick noodles. The food was rich in carbohydrates and fats as the body needs extra energy to survive at those high altitudes.

Not wanting to be a burden, Mashal gave five hundred dollars as a donation to the abbot and humbly explained, 'The monastery has upkeep expenditures, and it will ease our minds knowing that we contributed in a small way.'

From her gentle tone and voice, even the most perceptive sleuth wouldn't have guessed Mashal was a cold-blooded killer. The circumstances of one's life often force one to put up a front to maintain public impressions and preconceived notions. For Mashal this was such a moment.

The Ansari family settled in well at the monastery. They relaxed and joyously mingled with the locals and the monks. The following day, Aqsa and Ali readily participated in the chores of the monastery. For the monks, the Ansaris were like any other hikers and adventure tourists who occasionally came to the remote village to seek thrills and escape life.

Casually striking up a conversation with one of the monks, Mashal asked, 'Tell me about Limi Valley. What do the people do? What about basic facilities?'

With a smile on his peaceful countenance the monk replied, 'Most of the locals are simple pastoralists who graze their livestock in the pastures in the surrounding hills. Most households have at least one member who works at a construction site across the border, in China. They are often overworked and underpaid as compared to other Chinese workers, but they still earn a lot more in China than they would in Nepal.

'As for the facilities, electricity is scarce and phone and radio signals are weak in Limi Valley. So, heaters and other gadgets are not always functional,' the monk explained, seemingly unruffled by these deficiencies.

For Mashal this was a relief, as it meant the valley's inhabitants would be blissfully unaware that she was a wanted woman. Nonetheless, bad news travels fast, so Mashal decided that they would have to be back on the road in a few days.

In all the major towns and cities of Nepal, news broadcasts were being flashed about Mashal Ansari and her kids, Ali and Aqsa, murdering a man at the Kathmandu Guest House, setting a fire and running away. The investigating agencies felt that involving the media and broadcasting the culprits' photos on the news channels would put pressure on the fugitives and consequently push them to make an error.

But Vikram had another ace up his sleeve, and so with fresh resolve he called Secretary Wasim Khan.

'Sir, Mashal has escaped with Vita, but everyone knows that the device has a limited range and that is its limitation. Therefore, I believe that Vita will only be used as a distraction when Hamid Ansari is ready to execute his plan.'

'Even if your conjecture is right, we don't yet know Hamid's plan and we cannot wait till the last moment to find out what it is. By using Vita, they might cripple our ability to respond in time,' replied Wasim Khan, sounding downcast.

'Precisely, and that is why I suggest that you allow Ranbir and me to fly to Pakistan to capture or kill Hamid, while Naina can stay in Nepal. If the Ansari family doubles back and returns to Nepal, then Naina will be waiting for them,' explained Vikram.

'What happens if they don't return to Nepal and instead try to enter India? After all, it seems their target is Siachen.'

'Sir, even if that were to happen, Naina would be able to reach them faster than us and apprehend them if possible.'

'Okay. But first let my ground sources find out where in Pakistan Jahangir Niazi and Hamid Ansari are hiding. In the meantime, you and Ranbir are to take the first flight to Delhi.'

33

Deathly Silence

The following day, on Thursday morning, Naina took charge of the hunt for Mashal and began coordinating with the local authorities.

Meanwhile, Vikram and Ranbir took a flight to Delhi. They reached the R&AW office a little before noon and met Arvind and Parth to discuss their strategy.

Parth opened the discussions by stating, 'We now know that Humayun Haq was poisoned with arsenic. Logic dictates that the people who had Humayun murdered also ordered the hits on Shiv Narayanan and Yousef Lehri. Analysis of video footage from the hotel where Shiv was staying did not reveal anything. However, a camera installed at a shop across the street from the hotel caught two people climbing down the drainage pipe from the room where Shiv was staying. In all likelihood, these two men are our killers. Their faces were covered, but we have the number plate of the car in which they drove off.'

Then after glancing at everyone in the room, Parth continued, 'We still don't know the identity of the turncoat called Top Hat and are nowhere close to flushing him out.'

Arvind then opened his file and said, 'Another interesting development is that ISRO's chief, Satya Kulkarni, has taken an indefinite leave of absence from office. This happened after Shiv and Humayun's deaths. No one in his office knows where he has gone or when he will return. Although he has taken leave before, this time his behaviour has been erratic and suspicious. He rarely replies to his emails and keeps his phone switched off for days. He has no family left so tracking him is proving to be difficult.'

'What about Dev Burman?' asked Ranbir.

'He called me earlier today and sounded petrified. He said he wanted to discuss something in person. So, I'll be flying down to Mumbai this afternoon to meet him. I should be back by midnight,' said Arvind, adjusting his neckerchief.

'Why don't you save the taxpayers' money and your time and conduct a video conference with him?' suggested Ranbir.

'That's not a bad idea. Though I do think these ubiquitous technologies are not entirely safe and are prone to hacks, I'll give it a try,' replied Arvind with a smile.

After trying unsuccessfully for an hour to get in touch with Dev, R&AW decided to send two officers from their Mumbai branch to his residence to check on him.

At 2.30 p.m., two agents in plain clothes were standing outside the Coral Heights building in Chembur.

34

Dead Men Tell Tales

Twenty-four hours ago, on Wednesday afternoon, Dev Burman, who had taken the day off from work, was busy researching Professor Hamid Ansari. He had been uneasy since his return from his latest string of meetings. The news channels and online articles simply stated that certain anonymous sources had revealed that the esteemed scientist had been kidnapped because of his ground-breaking research on nuclear fusion. Yet, government officials maintained that there was no truth to the rumours and that the scientist was well and on an overseas expedition to further his research.

The ambiguity and the enigma surrounding the incident had prompted Dev to contact his associates, colleagues and confrères in the scientific and business communities to help him delve into the matter.

He spent most of the afternoon engaged in casual conversations with his contacts, which mostly started with, 'Hi, how are you?' then developed into a fruitful dialogue with, 'Don't you think the Indian economy needs a greater push?' and then shifted casually to current affairs with Dev slyly asking, 'Do you know what happened to Professor Hamid Ansari?'

Dev took notes on anything new that he learnt. A little before 5 p.m., he got a call from an unknown number.

'Hello?'

'Sir, we know you are the head of the R&D department of DRDO. We have developed a sensitive technology and would like to meet you to discuss its development. May we come to your office tomorrow morning?' a hoarse voice asked him.

'What is your company's name? Who are you?' enquired Dev.

'Sir, we would like to meet in person and explain everything in detail,' replied the man.

'I am in Delhi for the next couple of days. Contact me next week.'

'Sir, we can come to Delhi. Where are you staying?'

'The Ambassador Hotel,' said Dev and cut the call.

Dev had lied. He had realized that someone was onto him. As he continued with his phone calls, he paced around his house and kept peeking outside the windows to see if any suspicious vehicles were parked near his building.

Dev continued his calls and research well into the night. The following day, on Thursday, he made a few calls to his contacts in Pakistan. Immediately after that, at 10 a.m., he called Arvind Ghosh and requested a meeting. At the time, Arvind had told him that he would fly down to Mumbai and that they could meet in the evening. However, an hour later, Arvind had called back and requested they hold a video conference instead, at 12.30 p.m.

Just as Dev finished his conversation with Arvind, he noticed two hefty men tampering with the phone wires on the east side of his building. One of them took out a laptop from a huge blue bag and worked on it for about five minutes. As the man finished, Dev noticed that his mobile signal was down. He quickly checked his landline and found that to be dead too. Dev rushed to the window and saw the two men, now dressed as pizza delivery boys, enter the building.

Dev realized that his time had come. He told his wife to go to their friend's flat two storeys below and wait for him. As soon as his wife left, Dev locked the front door. He knew that if he wrote a note for Arvind, his killers might find and destroy it. Thinking fast, he first burnt all his notes as giving them to his wife would have endangered her. Then, he laid out a game of Monopoly on the dining table. By the time he was done, the killers were at his door, trying to break in. After setting up the game, Dev locked himself in his bedroom. But this effort only gained him fifteen minutes. The killers barged in and shot him in cold blood.

When at 2.30 p.m. the R&AW officers reached Dev's residence, Coral Heights, they found him dead and no sign of his killers.

When Arvind Ghosh was informed, he specifically asked the officers on site to ensure that nothing in the house was touched and that the apartment was sealed till he arrived. Dev's wife was located by the officers and while they took her statement, they denied the poor soul entry into her own home.

At 6.30 p.m., Arvind arrived at Coral Heights to inspect the crime scene. Normally, a senior officer like Arvind would never inspect a crime scene himself, but this was an exceptional circumstance. DRDO's R&D secretary had been found murdered a few hours after he had reached out to R&AW. Moreover, the spy agency was already in the midst of chaos thanks to Hamid Ansari and Vita. Given the timing of Dev's murder, everyone at R&AW concurred that his death was related to the ongoing chaos.

Arvind entered Dev's apartment and studied the scene meticulously. He asked the agency's photographer accompanying him to capture all relevant details of the crime scene. Arvind noticed the broken locks, the burnt papers and Dev's body sprawled on the ground near his bed. As Arvind came out of the bedroom, he noticed the game of Monopoly laid out on the dining table. Without giving it a second thought, Arvind went to speak to Dev's wife, Shilpa.

'I am sorry for your loss and am sorry for questioning you at a time like this, but your answers will help us locate his killers faster,' Arvind began gently as he offered her his handkerchief.

'Dev called me earlier today and requested a meeting. Did you notice anything strange in his behaviour lately?'

Shilpa, trying to control her tears and after blowing her nose into Arvind's handkerchief, said, 'He returned on Tuesday evening after attending a number of meetings across the country. He seemed paranoid after his return. He mentioned that he had not been able to reach his friend Satya Kulkarni for the past few days. Strangely, he also said that while observing someone he had deduced their character and intentions. I don't know what he meant by that.'

Ruminating over Shilpa's remarks, Arvind asked, 'Why had you gone to your neighbour's house?'

Her face red and puffy from crying, Shilpa replied, 'Dev had been very tense since yesterday. He had been making calls and taking notes. I don't know whom he called. He even lied and told someone that he was staying at the Ambassador Hotel in Delhi. After that call he kept peeking out of the windows.

Today, he made a few calls to Pakistan and then suddenly he told me to go down to our friend's house.'

Arvind pondered and paced in silence as he absorbed everything Shilpa had just said, lighting a cigarette to calm his nerves.

A few minutes later, Arvind enquired, 'Mrs Burman, were you by any chance playing Monopoly with your husband?'

With a dumbfounded expression, Shilpa simply shook her head indicating that she had no idea what Arvind was talking about.

With a sense of hope, Arvind rushed back to Dev's apartment. He observed the Monopoly board and found the 'Top Hat' token placed on Old Kent Road along with two coffee beans. All the other tokens were placed inside on the 'Go' marker. A few banknotes were placed under the 'Free Parking' marker. Removing the notes and flipping through them, Arvind noticed that on the back of one of them was scribbled the message, 'Go to the city in which the half lion–half man appeared.'

Taking the bank note and clicking a picture of the Monopoly board on his phone, Arvind exited the building. As he left, he silently prayed for Dev's soul and wondered about the clues he had left behind.

35

In It Together

On the following day, Friday, while Mashal and her kids were busy in Rinchenling Gompa, Naina was working tirelessly in Kathmandu to locate the trio. As Mashal had sprayed their hotel rooms with a cocktail of ground spices before escaping with the kids, the adept abilities of the sniffer dogs had been rendered utterly useless. The well-trained dogs kept sneezing and eventually had to be taken out of the room.

Naina, however, was determined. Other than seeking the help of the media, the young R&AW officer was questioning various roadside shop owners and taxi drivers who were operating in and around the Kathmandu Guest House that night. The NID was rounding up local suspects and goons in the hope of learning about Mashal's movements. Personnel working at the train and bus depots in and around Kathmandu were being extensively questioned about Mashal and her kids. Local travel agencies and travel companies were being contacted to check if the trio had hired a private vehicle or taxi. The airport did not seem like a plausible escape option, as the authorities had issued an all-points bulletin or APB almost immediately.

As Naina sifted through the heaps of clues and intimations about Mashal's movements on that night, phones kept ringing around her in the NID office, with almost all the callers providing some form of bogus or uncorroborated evidence. The locals were hungry for the prize money announced for Mashal and her kids. Often, the callers were just phoning in to enquire whether the prize had been claimed yet.

In New Delhi on that Friday, Vikram, Ranbir, Parth, Arvind and Wasim were all present in a conference room at R&AW headquarters. Arvind had shared whatever leads they had with everyone.

After playing around with some ideas, Vikram suggested, 'The Sphinx in Giza is said to be half lion–half human. Was Dev indicating Giza?'

Shaking his head, Parth replied, 'No. The Sphinx of Giza is half woman–half lion. The Sphinx never has the head of a man, even according to Greek mythology.'

'Moreover, the Sphinx was created. We need to search for a place where the half lion–half man *appeared*,' said Wasim Khan.

Typing on his laptop, his fingers working faster than a hamster in a wheel, Parth, his face glued to the screen, said, 'The search results for the phrase "half lion–half man" show Lord Narasimha. As per Hindu mythology, he was the fourth incarnation of Lord Vishnu. Most of the temples dedicated to Lord Narasimha are in Andhra Pradesh and others are in—'

'But temples are again a creation of man. Where did Lord Narasimha *appear*?' Wasim Khan cut Parth short.

Everyone started searching the internet.

A few minutes later, Ranbir said, 'There is a temple in Multan, Pakistan, called Prahladpuri. It is believed to have been built by Prahlada, son of Hiranyakashyap, the demon king of Multan, in honour of Lord Narasimha, who saved his life. The belief is that it was at this place that Lord Narasimha appeared out of a pillar to save Prahlada.'

There was a charged silence in the room.

Finally, Vikram said, 'It seems that Dev was pointing us towards Multan.'

Wasim Khan pondered for a moment then said, 'I agree with Vikram. Who or what is in Multan? We don't know. But we need to delve into this further. I will direct our local assets in Pakistan to keep an eye out for Hamid Ansari and Jahangir Niazi in Multan. If we get a confirmed sighting of either of them, then Vikram and Ranbir will have to visit our cantankerous neighbours again.'

'Now, let's move on to the second clue. On the Monopoly board, the Top Hat token along with two coffee beans were placed on the Old Kent Road marker. Clearly this seems to be an indication of Top Hat's possible location. Does anyone have any ideas?' asked Parth, looking around the room.

Vikram began by stating the obvious, 'Old Kent Road is in London. Could Top Hat be staying in London and operating from there?'

'Then what do the coffee beans signify?' enquired Ranbir.

'Maybe he is staying near a café on Old Kent Road,' replied Vikram, shrugging.

'It's a possibility. Based on the singular dimension of this clue, we can't rule out the obvious. So, I will ask our assets in London to check if any Indians are living on or near Old Kent Road. I will also inform Scotland Yard,' said Wasim Khan.

While the others were discussing the clues, Arvind had been fervently searching the internet and extensively using Google maps.

As Wasim Khan finished, Arvind looked up and said, 'There is only one property in India by the name Old Kent—the Old Kent Estate and Spa. The property is in Coorg in Karnataka, and is in the midst of a coffee plantation.'

Then looking at Wasim Khan, Arvind continued, 'Sir, I don't think Top Hat is in London. I think Dev Burman was pointing us towards Coorg and this specific property. I think I should go and investigate this resort.'

'Sir, I agree with Arvind and would like to go with him,' said Parth before the secretary could respond to Arvind's request.

'Very well. Take the first available flight to Coorg. Spend the weekend at the resort and find out everything you can about Top Hat. However, just to be doubly sure, I will speak to Scotland Yard.'

The meeting ended in under an hour. It was 11.30 a.m. As Arvind and Parth prepared to leave town, Vikram and Ranbir left for their respective homes. They needed to pack and be ready to leave at a moment's notice if the assets in Multan confirmed a sighting of their targets.

36

Time Zero

In Multan, a R&AW field agent casually walked around the shrine of Bahauddin Zakariya. The agent mingled with a crowd of tourists who had gathered around a local guide. The guide was talking about the saint and his squeaky voice could be heard in Delhi as he said, 'Bahauddin Zakariya, who lived from circa 1170 to 1262, was one of the most influential Sunni Muslim scholars and poets of his era and established the Sufi order of Suhrawardiyya in medieval southeast Asia, particularly around Multan, Pakistan. Via his tariqat or philosophical orientation, he preached that one must live a life with simple food and clothing yet rejected the Chisti assertion that spirituality lay upon a foundation of poverty. Zakariya spoke not only about the importance of fasting or keeping a roza, donating alms to the poor or performing zakat, but also fiercely advocated the need and relevance of gaining scholarship or attaining ilm. The scholar emphasized the importance of education for all humans, irrespective of their caste and class. This set him apart from the Hindu mystics of the time.

'In two days, on Monday, Multan will be celebrating the death anniversary or Urs of Bahauddin Zakariya. During the three days of remembrance, teachings of the saint will be recited and his beliefs and philosophies will be narrated at the shrine of this great scholar.'

Then throwing his hands in the air in a grand gesture the guide emphatically continued, 'People from around the world will pour into Multan to hear the recitals, pay their respects and donate to the poor of the city.'

Finally, the guide concluded, 'Even local politicians often attend the Urs to keep their image fresh in the minds of the people, whose votes they rely on to remain in power.'

The field agent had heard enough and decided to move away.

Based on the agent's report, in Delhi the spy agency concluded that this was a good time for their local agents to mingle in the bustling, overcrowded city and start looking for Hamid Ansari and Jahangir Niazi.

So, a second agent was designated to set up a fruit cart near the Kabootar Mandi on Haji Camp Road, where an array of pigeons of various shades and colours were caged and cooed continuously. Some sellers even kept parrots, parakeets, sparrows and goldfinches. The street smelt of bird droppings and feathers and the nauseating stench settled into the agent's nose. He could almost taste the filth on his tongue and he repeatedly spit on the roadside to rid himself of the sensation.

A third agent, whose plight was perhaps worse than his colleague's at the Kabootar Mandi, was to set up a paan shop on the north end of the road opposite the cattle hide and skin market known as the Chamra Mandi. Here animals were slaughtered, their hides sold to leather craftsmen and their meat to various butchers. The open sewer on the road carried a mix of blood and filth as the animals were routinely chopped up with the careless ease of one plucking a flower from a garden. The street smelt of death, and the whiff of the slaughtered meat and the anguished last cries of the animals made it difficult for the agent to breathe. To stop himself from retching, he lit a cigarette.

A fourth agent sat as a desolate beggar outside the fish market or the Machli Mandi on the corner of Eidgah Road. A variety of fish were being sold and cooked there. Some sellers were frying and serving the crisp fish sprinkled with red chillies, spices and ground herbs. Although the agent's mouth was watering, the role he was designated to play prevented him from going to a shop and eating to his heart's content.

Following this modus operandi, a fleet of twenty-one agents scattered themselves in and around Multan, especially around the shrine of Bahauddin Zakariya as it was located right next to the now disused Prahladpuri temple in the fort of Multan.

The spies were divided into seven teams of three, but no team knew about the presence of the others in the area. This was done to limit the damage-inflicting ability of anyone who got busted or decided to turn traitor. Each team was tasked with spotting Hamid Ansari or Jahangir Niazi. Photographs of the perpetrators, including the new alias of the scientist as Doctor Zulfiquar Ali, had been circulated to the seven teams. Instead of reporting to a local handler, who would have then relayed the information to New Delhi, each team was being monitored in real time by a dedicated team of analysts from R&AW headquarters itself. Minuscule cameras that had been discreetly placed either on the spies' bodies or in their vicinity, along with satellite imagery, allowed the analysts in Delhi to track what was happening on the streets of Multan.

Aside from watching the streets, R&AW was also monitoring the telephonic chatter in the city with key words being highlighted. Such flagged conversations were then handed over to a separate team of analysts who searched through the conversations to determine whether or not anything of relevance was said. By 3 p.m. on Friday afternoon, Multan had become an intense playing field for R&AW, and the analysts were crunching data faster than any financial bank.

37

Midnight Coffee Race

As the radio waves transmitted data from Multan to Delhi, Arvind and Parth landed at Mangalore airport. Their plan necessitated a discreet arrival in Coorg. They were not sure who in the government or R&AW was the mole, so they posed as tourists and hailed a cab to their destination. It would be a three-and-a-half-hour drive to Old Kent Estates and Spa, which was nestled amongst hills of lush coffee plantations.

As they neared the resort, Arvind, who was extremely fond of coffee and a self-proclaimed connoisseur of the beverage, lowered the window so he could take in the nutty and smoky aroma of the plantations around him.

Upon arrival at Old Kent Estates, the duo entered the main lodge, which was perched at a vantage point on the estate. This lodge housed the reception, behind which stood a short bald man wearing brown trousers and a crisp beige shirt. Looking at the guests and forcing as broad a smile as possible, the bald receptionist said in a north Indian accent, 'Welcome to Coorg and welcome to Old Kent Estate and Spa. I am Ayush, and I am the manager. I shall check you in and then escort you to your cottage.'

'How big is this property?' asked Parth as Ayush checked their credentials and booking in his system.

'Sir, the estate is set in a two-hundred-acre plantation. We have five cottages for guests, and in this lodge we have our dining room, home theatre, library and games area,' replied the manager as he handed the duo's driving licences back to them.

'Only five cottages? So not more than ten people can stay on the estate at one time,' replied Parth.

'We have a writer's bungalow also, hidden in one corner of the estate, but we usually only give it out to groups. The bungalow has three bedrooms along with a kitchen and a small library, so it is priced a little higher than the cottages. Often, artists or celebrities or people looking to spend some solitary time rent the whole bungalow for themselves and request not to be disturbed,' Ayush replied courteously as he escorted them to their cottage.

'How many staff do you employ to manage this property?' asked Parth.

'Other than the plantation workers, we are a team of ten people. We cook, clean and maintain the cottages and the writer's bungalow.'

The mist and the humidity prompted Arvind to light a cigarette and after taking a few quick drags, he asked, 'You have a north Indian accent. You're not a local?'

'No sir. I am from Delhi, but I have been the manager of this estate for more than a decade now.'

'Are there any other guests on the property at the moment?' asked Arvind as they neared their cottage.

'No sir. Presently, you are our only guests, and our next lot arrives two days after you leave.'

As Arvind stubbed out his cigarette, the spies entered their cottage.

After settling down and freshening up, Parth sat in the plush armchair and stretched his feet out on the foot stool in front of it, while Arvind sat on the sofa.

After a moment of silence Arvind said, 'We have two options, either we become friendly with the manager and slyly get him to reveal details about guests who have visited in the past month; or we break into his computer system at night and get the details of everyone on the roster.'

Parth considered the possibilities for a moment then said, 'We will have to hack into his computer. That's the only way to get accurate details of everyone who recently stayed at this property. Talking to Ayush is unlikely to yield a definitive result as he may not know which of the guests are government employees, much less if any is a turncoat spy.'

'Then tonight we observe the patterns and movements of the staff and find a window of opportunity for the following night,' replied Arvind.

Later that evening, after formulating their plan, the spies headed out to the main lodge to have their dinner.

Both relished non-vegetarian food and ordered the local Kodava cuisine. When the waiter arrived with their order of marinated pork curry, the air around the duo's table was filled with the intense aroma of spicy red chillies, fenugreek seeds, cumin and turmeric. The dish was served with steamed rice balls and soft flatbread, and as Arvind plunged his fork into the succulent chunks of pork, he could appreciate the time the chef must have spent in marinating the meat in local balsamic vinegar.

Through the meal Arvind was quiet, only stretching out a hand to take repeated helpings of steamed rice balls and flatbread. He was rarely so focused.

After their dinner the spies moved to the games room for a friendly match of billiards, wherein they were served locally brewed coffee that had been prepared from freshly roasted beans.

At around 11 p.m., as the spies headed back to their cottage, they noticed that Ayush had left for the night, and his post was being manned by one of his younger team members. The weary young man yawned and looked like he would drop off to sleep at any moment. To give him a nicotine hit and jolt him out of his stupor, Arvind offered him a cigarette which the young boy initially refused but after a slight nudge from Arvind quickly yet hesitantly took.

Lighting it and then another for himself, Arvind asked, 'Are you alone? Where is Ayush?'

'Yes sir. After you had dinner, the manager left and the kitchen staff cleaned up, closed the kitchen and left for the day. I shall be at the reception till 8 a.m.,' replied the young boy as he puffed on his cigarette.

'Do you need anything, sir?' asked the boy innocently.

Shaking his head, Arvind replied, 'No,' and the spies then silently walked back to their cottage.

As soon as they entered, Parth said, 'The young receptionist will soon be asleep. We can strike tonight.'

'What if he wakes up or doesn't doze off?' enquired Arvind, wanting to have a contingency plan.

'In that case we will have to outfox him by keeping him occupied.'

'When do we strike?' asked Arvind.

'At 3 a.m.,' declared Parth.

In the dead of night, at the designated hour, Parth and Arvind slowly crept up to the lodge. There they found the young receptionist slouching in his chair. He was asleep. The slight creak of the door when the spies entered had not woken him up. Without wasting any time, Arvind switched on the desktop and plugged in a pen drive. As the data was being copied, the spies kept a close eye on the receptionist. It took under seven minutes for the data to be transferred to the pen drive, but each second passed at a snail's pace for the duo. After the data was copied, Arvind silently pulled out the pen drive and switched off the computer before the duo crept back outside. The young receptionist remained fast asleep, unbothered by the mild disturbance.

No sooner had the spies stepped outside the lodge than Ayush came around the corner, holding an old-fashioned lantern with a thick candle burning inside.

Seeing him, Arvind's heart leapt into his mouth, and he stopped dead in his tracks.

As Ayush extended the lantern to illuminate whoever was in front of him, Parth said, 'What are you doing here at this time of night?'

'Sometimes I make random checks on the night staff to ensure they haven't dozed off. This receptionist is new, so I'm going to check up on him. I hope everything is well in your cottage? Do you need anything?'

'Ah...no, not at all, we just couldn't sleep, so we thought we would take a little stroll around the lodge,' replied Arvind quickly.

'Very well, sir,' replied Ayush, looking intently at Arvind before silently moving towards the lodge.

As Arvind and Parth entered their cottage, they could hear Ayush reprimanding the young receptionist for sleeping while on duty.

As Arvind plugged the pen drive into his computer, his jitters finally subsided. A few moments later, he confirmed that the data had been copied successfully. The spies then sent the data to headquarters for the analysts to work on, after which the duo slept peacefully.

38

Tread Lightly

The following morning, on Saturday, while Arvind and Parth were gorging on freshly steamed soft idlis and dosas, they were notified by headquarters that in the past thirty days, three men from the government sector had stayed at the resort at different times.

Reading the email from headquarters, Parth explained, 'The first name on the list is the secretary of overseas external affairs, Rahul Das. The second name is of our defence secretary, Shekhar Banerjee. And the last name is of the ISRO chief Satya Kulkarni. And interestingly enough, Dev Burman recently met all three of them.'

'When did each of them visit this resort?' enquired Arvind.

'Satya visited at the beginning of this month, much before this fiasco started. But he is now on sabbatical, and no one knows where he is. Rahul Das visited shortly after Satya and stayed here for four nights with his family. And finally,

Shekhar Banerjee stayed here recently for two nights but left the property a week before we got here,' replied Parth.

'We need to investigate and interrogate all three of them. We also need to track down Satya and trace his movements over the past couple of days. And we need to delve into the lives of the other two gentlemen,' said Arvind as he considered the best way to handle the investigation.

'The minister for external affairs won't be very happy about Rahul Das being interrogated. She is proud of her team, so we'll have to address the issue carefully with her first,' suggested Parth.

Nodding, Arvind added, 'Ideally, we would have asked the Intelligence Bureau to locate Satya, but we don't know who all are in cahoots with Top Hat, so I will put a few of our own agents on the job of locating him. Till then let's interrogate the other two.'

The spies then discussed their findings and intentions with Secretary Wasim Khan. It was decided that Parth would fly back to Delhi to interrogate Rahul Das. Arvind, on the other hand, would travel to the Machaan Wilderness Lodge near Nagarahole National Park, where they had discovered Shekhar Banerjee was currently staying. The defence secretary's office kept tabs on his movements and were cooperative with R&AW's request to reveal his location.

While the R&AW agents discussed their plans, the field agents in Multan were scouring the city in the hope of spotting either one of their targets. By 11 a.m. on Saturday morning it had been twenty hours since the agents had spread themselves in the field, but no result or relevant chatter had been retrieved so far. Some agents had acquaintances and friends in Multan and had started tapping them casually for information. Two of the agents, who had been living in

Multan for a while, had managed to get jobs as gardeners at the Bahauddin Zakariya University.

On the first day of the Urs, a Monday, a lecture on the teachings and philosophies of the saint had been arranged at the university. Many prominent personalities were to attend the lecture.

For R&AW this was going to be a patient hunt with a lot dependent upon sheer luck.

At the same time in Nepal, Naina was struggling to find hard evidence that would help her locate Mashal and her children. Inconclusive reports and local intelligence suggested that the family had fled westwards, but none of the information was definitive. Then, late in the afternoon, a little before 4.30 p.m., a call came in from Jumla, a district in Karnali Province in north-western Nepal. The caller was the owner of a small petrol pump, who had positively identified Mashal and her kids from the news flashes on the television. Electricity supply was sporadic in that part of Nepal, and it was the first time since the incident on Wednesday night at the Kathmandu Guest House that electricity had been available in the region.

With the only sliver of hope in her hand, Naina, along with two NID agents, departed for Jumla in the intelligence agency's only helicopter. It was a two-hour flight, and those one hundred and twenty minutes were going to be full of anxiety for Naina.

Elsewhere on that Saturday, Parth had left the Old Kent Estate for Mangalore airport. Arvind, on the other hand, had left for Nagarahole National Park. Both took a little over two hours to reach their destination. So when at 1.15 p.m. Parth was entering the airport, Arvind was at the gates of the Machaan Wilderness Resort.

Defence Secretary Shekhar Banerjee knew that R&AW's joint secretary for the Pakistan Desk was coming to meet him, but he had no clue about the purpose of the meeting.

Upon reaching the resort, Arvind was escorted by the receptionist to Shekhar's cottage. The receptionist rang the bell and upon hearing footsteps from inside, retreated to the reception.

Shekhar opened the door. He was taller than Arvind and had an air of confidence about him.

Extending his hand as he towered over Arvind, Shekhar said, 'Welcome. Come inside. Let's talk over tea.'

Although Shekhar was a suspect, a formal investigation had not been launched against him, so the interrogation had to be informal and casual.

Arvind stepped inside and Shekhar led him to the other side of the room, which opened onto the lawns and surrounding jungle, where spotted deer would sometimes visit.

As Shekhar boiled water in a kettle, Arvind casually asked, 'Your office told us that you often visit south India and prefer to stay in and around the various national parks.'

'My job demands that I liaison with the local leaders of the southern states as well as with those of our southern neighbour, Sri Lanka, to assess their political inclinations. It is critical to understand someone's thinking and intent if you want to maintain peace in the region. I prefer to stay and meet them around peaceful, tranquil areas. I like the melodious songs of the birds in these national parks, and the irregular cellular network gives me spells of peaceful time,' explained Shekhar while pouring hot water into two teacups before dropping a teabag in each.

After dipping the teabag a few times before removing it, Arvind slowly moved into an interrogative mode and asked,

'Whom did you meet at Old Kent Estate? You stayed there recently, but you also had a booking here. Why not call your guests here?'

'I went there to meet a Singaporean arms broker, Mark Teo. He supplies arms regularly to guerrilla forces in Sri Lanka, who at times also resell the arms to terrorists in India. I went to convince him to instead supply to our government and become a listed dealer.'

R&AW had the details of everyone who had stayed at Old Kent Estate. Mark was indeed an arms broker who had stayed there at the same time as the defence secretary.

Arvind made a mental note to cross-check Shekhar's story, but for now he decided to believe him and move on.

Draining his cup of tea, Arvind pressed further, 'Dev Burman recently attended a meeting with you. He was found murdered in his apartment. Do you know anything about that?'

'He was an acquaintance. I did not know him well. But in the last meeting, he seemed jittery and anxious, especially when our army chief offered condolences for High Commissioner Haq,' replied Shekhar.

'Are you suggesting Dev was involved in some surreptitious activities with the late high commissioner or that he was a spy?'

With a slight smirk, Shekhar said, 'I am not suggesting anything. I am just telling you what I observed.'

'Did you know Humayun Haq? Were you close to him?' enquired Arvind, now desperately fishing for information. He thought that if he kept pushing Shekhar, the latter may slip up and say something.

'By virtue of my post, I have had many interactions with the consulates of various countries. And since we have a sweet and sour relationship with Pakistan, their high commissioner cannot be avoided. So, yes, I met the high commissioner several times, and if you like, I can ask my office to share the minutes of those meetings with you.'

After a slight pause Shekhar looked straight into Arvind's eyes and asked, his voice steady, 'Why is R&AW interested in Dev Burman's death? Shouldn't it be a local police case? And why am I a suspect?'

Arvind knew he couldn't give a straight answer, yet he could not lie, so without giving up much, he explained, 'Sir, you are not a suspect but were one of the last few people to have met Dev. Therefore, your testimony is important. Dev was involved in a secret project that entailed building a novel overriding device. That device was stolen. We think Dev was murdered because of that device, which is why we haven't transferred the case to the local police or to the Intelligence Bureau.'

'I see,' said Shekhar, nodding.

Then he pointed to a little trail going into the surrounding jungle and said, 'Since I am not a prime suspect in your investigation, come, let's go for a little stroll in the woods and continue our chat while we walk.'

Arvind got up and followed the defence secretary into the jungle. It was 3.45 p.m.

39

Big Little Lies

At that time, Parth, who had flown to Delhi in R&AW's small charter plane, had landed and was heading towards the South Block of the Secretariat buildings located on Raisina Hill. As the additional secretary of R&AW he had priority clearance at the airport, which allowed him to depart the facility faster than anyone else.

It took Parth about fifteen minutes to reach his destination. The South Block houses the PMO, the Ministry of Defence and the Ministry of External Affairs. Parth headed straight for the office of the minister of external affairs. The minister, a stout lady, was perceptive, intelligent and worldly.

The minister's secretary showed Parth in, who, upon entering, gave a quick salute to the minister and took the seat opposite her at her desk.

'Ma'am, good afternoon. I am here to seek your support as I am about to interrogate a senior member of your team.'

'You wish to interrogate the secretary of overseas external affairs, Rahul Das.'

At Parth's bewildered look, the minister explained, 'Secretary Wasim Khan called me and briefed me on the situation.'

'Yes ma'am. The R&D chief of DRDO, Dev Burman, was recently murdered in his house. The secretary was one of the last persons to have met Dev. Moreover, one of the clues left behind by Dev hints at the secretary's possible involvement in the matter,' explained Parth without giving too much away.

The minister gave Parth an appraising look before ordering coffee for herself.

She then said, 'I am guessing the matter is much more convoluted than it appears, and you are not yet ready to share all the details with me.'

Parth shifted in his chair, but before he could reply, the minister raised her hand to silence him and continued, 'I shall not stall your investigation. Please feel free to question the secretary.'

With a sigh of relief, Parth got up, saluted the minister and left for the secretary's office.

R&AW did not have an arrest warrant for Rahul Das nor did they want to approach the courts and act as per procedure. The judiciary would have required probable cause to be established, which would have taken time and blown any chance of secrecy. Under these circumstances, had the minister of external affairs not given her support, R&AW's investigation would have stalled. Moreover, R&AW is not supposed to actively work in India. It was set up to operate outside the country. The government had set up the Intelligence Bureau and NIA to deal with domestic matters of security. But given the intelligence gathered recently, the officers were not sure whom they could trust and which agencies had been infiltrated.

At 4.10 p.m., Parth entered the secretary's office. Rahul Das had been informed a few minutes earlier that the additional secretary of R&AW was coming to meet him, but he had no idea what the meeting was about and was nervous about interacting with the spy.

Gesturing Parth towards a chair opposite him, the secretary said, 'To what do I owe the pleasure? How can I help you?'

Parth hated beating around the bush and making unnecessary small talk, so he got straight to the point. 'Sir, you recently met Dev Burman. Two days ago, someone killed him in his apartment. Could you tell me about your last meeting with Dev? What was his behaviour like? Was he nervous or frightened?'

'I am sorry to hear about Dev. May his soul be liberated from the arduous cycle of rebirth,' said Rahul before he continued, 'The last time I met Dev was at a joint meeting of the Ministry of External Affairs, DRDO, ISRO and a delegation from Israel. Our country, under the guidance of DRDO, recently carried out an anti-missile satellite test. The success of the test established our capability to interdict and intercept satellites in outer space. The technology that we used was indigenous, but Israel supplied a few of the key components required for the development of the missile and satellite detection programme. The Ministry of External Affairs was liaising between DRDO and Israel. I was in charge of the liaising team for this programme. At the meeting, the Israelis wanted to increase the price of the components. However, we were able to counter their greed by placing a larger order.

'Dev, however, was not impressed by their behaviour, and after the Israelis left, he said that we should develop the components ourselves. But we don't have any local manufacturers for those particular components and Satya, ISRO's chief, was doubtful if local manufacturers could match the quality of the Israeli products. Dev argued with us and finally left in a fury.'

'Was the matter about the purchase of components concluded?' enquired Parth.

'No. Our bulk order will provide components for only about a quarter of the anti-missile satellites that we wish to produce. But now, after Dev's death, whoever is put in charge of the project shall have to decide on the future course of action,' explained Rahul.

As Parth absorbed the information, the secretary asked, 'Why is R&AW investigating this matter? Shouldn't this be a case for the Intelligence Bureau or the local police?'

Parth did not appreciate the secretary asking such probing questions. He knew Rahul was a grey character and was making money from the deal with the Israelis and so had benefited from Dev's death.

His displeasure clear in his voice, Parth replied, 'I am not at liberty to discuss that with you.'

Then, pressing the secretary further, Parth enquired, 'Why did you visit Old Kent Estate in Coorg?'

The secretary had not expected R&AW to have delved into his travel history, and his eyes widened in surprise.

He explained, 'I went there with my family for a short holiday. I love the coffee plantations and the serene trails around the estate. It's a beautiful property.'

'Mr Secretary, we know you met one of your Israeli suppliers at Old Kent Estate. The holiday was just an excuse,' replied Parth, his expression grim.

The secretary went red in the face. He was of a fair complexion and the colour suffused his cheeks and ears so fast, it was as if someone had painted him red. Overcome with feelings of fear, shame and guilt, the secretary looked down and fell silent.

'I hope you have not been as dubious in answering my questions as you are in your dealings, Mr Secretary. Please do not try to run or leave town. We will be watching. I may ask for your presence in the future, and I hope you shall make yourself available.'

'I shall be readily available whenever you call me, sir, and shall not leave town. I am sorry for the bribes that I took.'

'No, you're not sorry, you're scared. But I hope you have the sense to become a better man in the future. You chose the job, this job did not choose you,' said Parth sternly and walked away.

It was 4.30 p.m.

As Parth was leaving Secretary Rahul Das's office, he heard a message ping on the secretary's phone.

In Karnataka, Arvind and Shekhar Banerjee had returned from their short hike. Arvind was preparing to leave, and as the defence secretary entered his cottage, his phone beeped, indicating that he had received a message.

40

Bitter and Sweet

Nepal is fifteen minutes ahead of India, so at 4.30 p.m. in India, which is 4.45 p.m. in Nepal, Naina, along with two agents from NID, was preparing to board the chopper that would take them to Jumla district.

During the anxious ride of a little over two hours, where time had sadistically decided to slow down, Naina bit off almost all her fingernails. When she wasn't biting her nails, she drummed her fingers on the window beside her seat. Towards the end of the journey, anxiety had caused such an adrenaline release that her leg muscles twitched and Naina started tapping her foot to calm herself down. The young R&AW agent knew that the alleged sighting by the petrol pump owner was the only lead they had, and the pressure to extract the required information from him weighed heavily upon her.

The Nepali officers accompanying Naina were Imay Lama and Sejun Pokharel. Both were fit and had been serving in the NID for over five years. Sejun was the younger of the two and traced his ancestry to the early Brahmins of Nepal, while Imay belonged to the Tamang tribe, who were said to be descendants of the horse-riding warrior tribes of Tibet.

Just before take-off, Sejun had surreptitiously sent a text message to someone and had almost instantly received a reply.

The officers were professional, and no one made any unnecessary small talk during the two-hour journey.

At 7 p.m. in Nepal, the helicopter landed near the dilapidated structures that surrounded the Jumla petrol pump.

For generations life had been slow and defined by routine for these simple mountain-dwelling people. The arrival of the helicopter and the owner of the petrol pump claiming to have spotted a wanted terrorist had filled the local people with excitement and inquisitiveness. Anticipating drama and to quench their curiosity, a group of them had assembled at the petrol pump and while listening to the owner's narration of events had decided to declare him their local hero.

Witnessing the crowd as they landed, Naina and the two NID agents cursed under their breaths. The presence of a crowd complicated the situation and would make the interrogation tougher.

The trio, all equally tense, flashed their credentials as they pushed their way through the crowd to reach the pump. The owner was an old frail man with a deeply lined and creased face. With a smile stretching as far as it could between his sunken cheeks, the man stood surrounded by a group of people, who seemed more than eager to bask in his glory and partake in his fame.

As Imay and Naina made their way to the old owner, Sejun started clearing the crowd, moving the people back and forming an imaginary periphery. In spite of his efforts, however, the curiosity of these simple people demanded that they stay put and hear the story straight from the horse's mouth, while in the presence of the authorities. Many felt involved in the incident through the pump owner's experience.

Naina flashed her credentials and said to the owner, 'What is your name and what did you see?'

Before the man could reply, his new-found friend spoke for him, 'Will you be recommending him for the Nepal Ratna, our country's highest civilian award?'

'And will the government now provide this area with electricity and water?' asked another, tired of the lack of basic necessities in his life.

Irritated by the interruptions, Naina sternly warned the owner, 'If you do not reply to my questions, I shall drag you to jail. Time is a luxury I don't have.'

The old man squinted as he said, 'I have lived all my life amongst these mountains in poverty, while scrambling for basic needs. I am at the far end of my life, your threats don't scare me. I have nothing to lose. Why shouldn't I enjoy this fame?'

Naina looked helplessly at Imay.

The NID officer gently replied to the old man, 'If you answer this lady's questions, I will get you an exclusive interview with a news channel based out of Kathmandu. You shall be famous all over Nepal.'

The old man smiled and said, 'I am at the fag end of my life and your worldly gifts don't excite me. Still, I shall help you as I do not want to die with any regrets or with a heavy heart.'

The man then looked around the crowd for affirmation and found many nodding in agreement.

Observing the scene, Naina silently wondered at how easy it was for humans to influence their fellow beings. The scene was a textbook example of how to become a popular leader, as written by an amateur who had found early and easy success in his venture, that too by a stroke of luck.

The owner calmly waited for the murmurs to die down then confidently said, 'My name is Baburam Khappanggi. I run this petrol pump which my father set up when he was young. The lady and two kids you are looking for were travelling with some monks in a rickety Matador van. They stopped here for refuelling. They were headed towards—'

Before Baburam could complete his sentence, a loud bang reverberated through the pump and a few seconds later the reports of two more gunshots were heard. Of the three, two shots hit Baburam in his chest, while the third missed and hit one of the bystanders in the leg. The two bullets punched clean through his chest, making large exit wounds as they escaped from the other side of the frail man's body. A few of the bystanders caught Baburam before he hit the ground, but the damage had been done. Blood oozed out of his body.

Without caring for the shooter or for her own life, Naina put her ear near Baburam's mouth in the earnest hope that he would point her in the right direction before breathing his last.

As Naina was bent over Baburam, two more shots were fired. While one hit the ground, another hit Baburam in his leg. It all happened in under fifteen seconds. This time Naina turned around with her gun pointing towards the crowd; everyone was chaotically running around, not wanting to get caught in the crossfire. Looking towards a deep ditch at the end of the road, Naina noticed that Sejun was running towards the woods with Imay chasing after him.

She quickly took out her mobile, called Secretary Wasim Khan and while looking at the lifeless body of Baburam said,

'Sir, a petrol pump owner in Jumla District has identified Mashal and her kids. They were travelling with a group of monks. While I was interrogating the man, one of the NID agents betrayed us and shot the informant.'

Wasim Khan was a seasoned spy and realized that this was not the time to get upset so he calmly asked, 'Was the informant able to provide us with a definite direction before he died?'

'Yes sir. They went to Rinchenling Gompa, a Buddhist monastery in Limi Valley,' replied Naina.

'Very good. Take a team to the monastery to tail Mashal and her kids.'

'Sir, I feel we should also pursue Sejun, as he may be working with the mole in our system. By catching Sejun, we may catch Top Hat.'

'A bird in hand is better than two in the bush, Naina. I will ask one of our local assets to coordinate with the NID and pursue Sejun. But you need to head to the monastery without further delay.'

'Understood, sir,' said Naina and cut the call.

By the end of the day, Naina was heading to Limi Valley, Parth had returned to his house and Arvind, who had landed in Delhi, was also heading home for the night.

41

Dying to Meet You

The following day passed without much activity. For the various teams of R&AW agents in Multan, time had slowed, and their eyes were sore from continuously concentrating on their surroundings. They had to remain alert and could not afford to daydream if they were to identify their targets.

In Delhi, Parth and Arvind exchanged notes about their respective interviews and concluded that neither of the suspects could be ruled out at the moment.

For Vikram and Ranbir, it was a game of waiting. The duo were spending time with their respective families and trying to be a part of the everyday lives of their partners.

The helicopter in which Naina had flown to Jumla had malfunctioned after the shootout at the petrol pump. The archaic bird had stalled when the pilot tried to fire the engine. After it had stuttered for the fifth time, Naina had decided to reach her destination via car. A rickety old white SUV, which smelt of rotten salami, was borrowed from the district's Transport Management Office. The rusty vehicle came with an equally old and feeble driver, who looked like he could die if he sneezed too violently.

After filling the petrol tank and a few extra canisters with the liquid gold, Naina had begun her arduous journey to the monastery. The smell of petrol from the canisters did nothing to mask the odour of salami in the car, but now was not the time to complain.

The old man, much to Naina's surprise and horror, drove in a frenzy. It was almost as though he had made peace with the fact that he would soon meet his maker. He occasionally drove the car right along the edge of the narrow road winding up the mountains, with Naina frantically praying to God. After about three hours, Naina had finally felt confident about the old man's driving abilities and had let her fears go. A while later she dozed off.

On Monday at around 7 a.m., Naina reached the monastery. Without wasting a second, she went to look for the abbot. The abbot, wearing the traditional red kasaya, was meditating, and Naina wondered if in the name of national security, she should disturb the pious man. As she stood conflicted, a young monk passed by.

Naina gently tapped him on his shoulder and asked, 'I am sorry to bother you, but I am looking for a lady and her two kids. Are they staying here?'

Before the young monk could reply, the abbot, who had also heard Naina's words, opened his eyes and asked, 'Why are you looking for them?'

'Father, they are wanted criminals. They murdered a man and fled with an important technological device. The lady's husband is a nuclear scientist who has defected to Pakistan. We need to find them before they unleash chaos.'

The abbot smiled and said, 'I suggest you and your driver eat, regain your energies and fill up your petrol tanks. The lady and her children left three hours ago. I cannot say where they were headed, but they purchased our jeep, and that vehicle is now very old. You should be able to catch up with them.'

'Should we not leave instantly?' Naina wondered out loud.

The abbot smiled and quipped, 'Is it not better to sharpen your axe before you deliver the blow?'

Naina understood the wise abbot's point and nodded in agreement.

At 7.30 a.m., Naina resumed her pursuit. She and her driver had eaten some bread with butter and drunk a well-brewed black tea. They could not fill their bellies lest it made them drowsy. Once they descended from the monastery, Naina would occasionally stop the car and ask the small roadside tea shop vendors if they had seen the monastery's jeep come down the road. Traffic in that remote corner of the world was sparse, and the shops opened quite early in the morning. As Naina and her driver wound their way downward, she found help from many of the locals who had spotted the jeep driving down into the valley.

Once they hit the valley floor, however, few locals had seen the jeep, but Naina told the driver to keep heading west, towards Himachal Pradesh, in India. Naina's gut told her that as Mashal was wanted in Nepal, she would not risk doubling back into the country.

A while later, they crossed a young shepherd girl walking with her flock of sheep and herd of goats. The sheep had numbers painted on their heads while the goats had small bells tied around their necks, which tinkled as they moved. The young girl, clad in a traditional knee-length grey robe of yak wool, was walking behind the herd with a long staff in her hand.

Naina noticed her black boots had mud and grass stuck to them, indicating that she had just descended from the mountains.

Relying on her gut instinct, Naina stopped the car, rolled down the window and gently asked her, 'Hey, young lady, while you were up in the hills, did you see a jeep speeding down this road?'

'Do you think I care about cars speeding on the road?' replied the young girl. 'Besides, what makes you think I could spot a specific car from the hills?'

'The hills give you a nice vantage point. You have sheep, which tend to graze on the grass and weeds found on flatter ground, so you wouldn't have gone too high up into the mountains. Hence you may have had a view of the road below.'

The girl looked impressed by Naina's reasoning but decided to test her further. 'I also have goats.'

'Goats prefer to eat small bushes and young saplings which can be found easily on the lower elevations of these hills,' replied Naina, accepting the challenge.

'Who are you?' asked the young girl, impressed by Naina.

'I am a spy and am chasing some very nasty people. Will you help me now?'

'Nothing in this life is free, not even for the virtuous who are doing their duty,' said the girl excitedly, ready to milk the opportunity in front of her.

Naina quickly took out a few hundred-rupee notes and handed them to the girl, wondering at how quickly the ways of the world corrupted even young and innocent children.

The girl pocketed the notes and said, 'A while ago, a jeep driven by a lady zipped passed me. At the time I was about to take my sheep and goats up into the hills for grazing. I also noticed that a young boy and girl were sleeping in the back seat. They were headed west.'

'Thank you,' said Naina and waved her hand forward, indicating to the driver to continue the pursuit.

It was 9 a.m. in Nepal, and Naina was hot on Mashal's heels.

42

The Scars Remaining

Early on Monday morning in Multan, crowds had started pouring into the city to attend the Urs of Hazrat Bahauddin Zakariya. In fact, many pilgrims had arrived the previous day, late at night or in the early hours of the morning, before the crack of dawn. Most had come via bus or train. People had come not only from the neighbouring towns and cities but also from India, Bangladesh and Afghanistan. The majority of the pilgrims were Sunni Muslims who had come to pay homage to their saint and pray for a prosperous life.

The mayor of Multan, Mamnoon Hussein Qureshi, who claimed descent from Saint Zakariya himself, had organized tents, portable toilets and stalls of food and water for the pilgrims. The mayor was also the finance minister of the country, and providing facilities for the pilgrims was more of a political move than a genuine gesture. Humanity seemed to have come to a point where providing basic amenities to religious pilgrims also served a greater purpose.

Several police teams had been assigned around the shrine and had put up check posts and barricades. Every pilgrim would be frisked before being allowed to enter the shrine.

By 7.30 a.m., media vans had started rolling up and their teams dispersed in and around the shrine to cover the prestigious event.

When at 9 a.m. Mamnoon Hussein Qureshi stopped at the gates of the shrine, certain street vendors across the street selling tea and fritters were also transmitting data back to New Delhi to R&AW headquarters.

So as Mamnoon stepped out of his white Mercedes, his red suede shoes were clearly visible on the monitor in Delhi.

Mamnoon and his family were seen entering the shrine. A few minutes later one of the R&AW agents also entered the shrine. He was frisked, but the police did not find his video camera nor the pen that he was carrying to be odd.

Wasim Khan, Parth Sinha and Arvind Ghosh were all on the operations floor witnessing Mamnoon and his associates bathe the revered saint's grave and then cover it with ornate and intricately embroidered blankets as a mark of respect to the great saint.

The agent was the sole eyes of R&AW inside the shrine. The spies did not want to risk exposure by putting too many variables in the equation. Each asset on ground was vulnerable to getting caught and could potentially disrupt the operation, and hence were referred to as a 'variable'.

After paying their respects, Mamnoon and a few other scholars discussed the teachings of Hazrat Bahauddin Zakariya, particularly his emphasis on the importance of education for all. After the evening prayers, Sufi songs and qawwali were sung, and some of the pilgrims even danced in a trance-like state while remembering the saint and his teachings.

By 9 p.m., the celebration came to a close, and there had been no sign of Jahangir Niazi or Professor Hamid Ansari. The tired and dejected teams of R&AW agents returned to their respective safe houses and quarters.

The set-up for the following day would be similar, except a different agent would go inside the shrine with a camera and the transmitter concealed inside the pen.

For Mamnoon the night was still young as after the celebrations ended at the shrine, the prominent finance minister hosted important dignitaries at his residence. All were from the country's ruling party, yet none of them were aligned with the affluent factions of the Punjab region that controlled the party and by extension the country. In the coterie were the country's minister of industries, Ghulam Khan, the education minister, Tariq Haque, the minister for national food security and research, Imam Ali Zaidi, the railways minister, Ahmed Shafat, the minister for religious affairs, Noor Ali Khan, and the minister for national water resources, Sahabzada Arbazz Sultan. These ministers all held weak portfolios and were disgruntled about their career growth and prospects. Their departments neither received the cream of the bribes nor were they given the opportunity to craft schemes for the welfare of the nation and by extension of themselves. Since Mamnoon was the finance minister, they all looked up to him, and it had been easy for him to sway the disgruntled lot in his favour.

Aside from these cabinet ministers, various junior members of the National Assembly or the Lower Legislative House were also present.

As the guests circulated and mingled in the ornate drawing room making small talk, their host eyed them carefully while standing tall in a corner of the room by a large window that overlooked the sprawling, lush lawns of the lavish estate.

Mamnoon realized that he was playing a dangerous game. He had old money and had grown up seeing power. His father and grandfather, like him, had been the country's finance ministers and had amassed great wealth and power over the decades. But the feel of the silky Kashmiri carpets under his feet or of the expensive white mulberry silk shirt that he was wearing meant little to him. He was not ambitious but felt frustrated about the despicable state of the nation and the lack of vision of the leaders who exerted real power. Corruption was not the issue, for he realized that to remain in power, a steady flow of funds was required. But the lack of will of the country's leadership to tackle issues like inflation, the growing national debt, the insurgency from Afghanistan that brought rampant arms and drug trade, droughts and the lack of facilities and support for the farmers, and the never-ending debacle that was Kashmir was causing distress amongst the masses.

Mamnoon realized that being a prominent minister of a failed State had no meaning. However, if he were able to turn things even slightly around, he would be hailed as a hero, and his legacy would be sealed in the history of Pakistan. Thinking as much, he sipped his scotch while looking out the window at the apiary in his garden below. The honeybees were resting for the night, and it was time for him to rest too. The following day was going to be essential for his journey to becoming the next prime minister of Pakistan.

Despite the hubbub in the room, Mamnoon's keen ears could hear the seconds ticking away on the Mont Blanc clock hung on the wall next to him, and the feeling that it was not time but rather life that was ticking away was reinforced in him.

Mamnoon was disgruntled, and a disgruntled man is capable of doing anything.

43

Queer Lodgings

By nightfall of that same Monday, under the bright twinkling stars that were clearly visible in the pollution-free sky over Uttarakhand, Mashal and her kids reached Lansdowne. They had entered India via the border town of Dharchula, and it had taken them over thirteen hours to reach their destination. Naina was right behind them. She could have intercepted them, but since the R&AW agents in Multan hadn't picked up any sign of Professor Hamid through the day, Wasim Khan wanted Naina to tail the targets and observe Mashal from afar. An arrest and interrogation would have yielded results but could have prompted Hamid Ansari to slip away if he was back in India. This was a chance that R&AW was not willing to take yet, so Naina had been instructed to play it safe.

However, Lansdowne wasn't Mashal's final destination. After a two-hour drive she reached the northern tip of Jim Corbett National Park. There on the banks of the Palain

River was a three-cottage property called Ramisera Wilds. It was a unique property, for these cottages were a homage to the British-era forest rest houses except for the fact that they had been constructed with pre-fabricated, sustainable materials. These 'A' shaped cottages could be unbolted and dismantled at any time, allowing nature to reclaim the land.

An all-out APB had not yet been issued for Mashal and her kids in India, and therefore the property manager had no clue about Mashal's true identity or the fact that she was wanted. Mashal had cleverly booked all three cottages. These were right in the middle of the jungle, and Naina, who had been observing them via her military-grade binoculars, found herself to be in a fix. The only way for her to keep Mashal under observation was by staying put and potentially spending the night in the rusty, putrid vehicle. Cursing the situation and muttering under her breath she stepped out of the vehicle to stretch her legs. She then sent the old driver to the town to get food, a tent and mosquito repellent, while she canvassed the area. Since there were no other structures around, Naina couldn't risk flying a drone lest it was spotted by Mashal. This was going to be a manual operation, and it was going to be a long night for Naina.

A little after midnight the lights in all three cottages were switched off, indicating that Mashal and her kids had finally gone to sleep.

A chorus of trills and the croaking of frogs and toads along with the calm burbling of the river could be heard in the silent night. Not wanting to disrupt nature's rhythmic and cathartic music, Naina put the jeep in neutral gear and then, without turning on the ignition, pushed the car behind some bushes. Next, she instructed her driver to sleep in the car. After ensuring that the driver was settled, Naina hiked up the hill behind the cottages. After a steady climb of about twenty minutes, she found a relatively flat piece of ground where she could set up camp. It took her about ten minutes to set up the tent, a skill she had learnt during her training days at the National Cadet Corps or the NCC.

After setting up the tent, Naina camouflaged the area and her tent with leaves, twigs and branches. She even found two empty nests in a nearby tree and placed them on the bushes around the tent to better blend in with the surroundings. Lastly, she set up a thin trip wire three inches above the forest floor, forming a fifteen-metre perimeter around her tent. She did this so she would be able to hear any wild animal or human that came in the vicinity of the tent. And a distance of fifty feet was more than sufficient for her to decide whether to confront or run from the danger.

Finally, at 2 a.m., Naina lay flat on her belly inside her carefully set up tent, from where she had a clear view of all three cottages below. Satisfied with her observation post, Naina fell asleep after an hour of no activity.

44

Hello Again

The following day, in Multan, the scene was similar to the previous day. Most of the R&AW agents retained their acts and guises. A few moved their carts and stalls. Another agent was chosen to go in with the camera and radio transmitter. The transmitter was embedded in the video camera itself and hence the agent was not required to carry a pen. The transmitter, using the radio waves of satellites, would allow the camera to transmit a live feed to R&AW headquarters in Delhi.

The day was overcast with stratus clouds spread across the Multan sky.

As the Urs began, a tall, bearded man in a white Pathani suit walked up to one of the carts that was stationed across the shrine. The cart vendor was roasting corn on charcoal, one hand holding and turning an ear of corn and the other fanning the coals. Glimpsing the man, the feeble cart vendor, who was wearing a vest with holes and had a striped piece of cloth wrapped around his waist, quickly prepared some corn on the cob, sprinkling it with salt and red chilli powder, squeezing a lemon over it and wrapping the hot corn in its own husk before presenting it to his salivating customer.

As the bearded man took the corn, he casually remarked, 'The weather demands such flavoursome street food.'

'Yes sir,' remarked the vendor.

Hungrily chewing on the corn, the man turned and was about to leave when the vendor remarked, 'Sir, that will be thirty rupees, please.'

The man grunted, placed the corn on the cart, took out his badge and flashed the Markhor sign in front of the vendor.

The vendor backed off. The man then took his corn and walked back towards the shrine.

Once the bearded man was back at his station, the bony vendor said softly to his assistant, 'Relay the news to Delhi, our local brothers are in play today. Everyone needs to be extremely vigilant.'

Fifteen minutes later, Wasim Khan along with Parth Sinha and Arvind Ghosh received the update. R&AW then circulated the information to the other teams operating in Multan. As the news circulated, the teams started scanning the crowd for ISI agents. Behavioural cues and body language were keenly observed and whenever an agent was spotted, the team would relay the information to Delhi, and R&AW headquarters would in turn circulate the identity of the said agent to all other teams. This exercise was necessary to ensure the safety of all Indian agents in play. If there was any slip-up leading to the capture of anyone, the entire mission would be in jeopardy and would most likely culminate in the death of the captured agent.

A while later Mamnoon's family started arriving at the shrine. Mamnoon's own entourage followed shortly after.

Similar to the previous day, the holy rituals were carried out, followed by lectures on the teachings of the great Sufi saint.

For the R&AW agents in play, the day had not brought any major changes so far. The agent that had gone inside the shrine mingled with the crowd and other journalists and recorded the event. The live footage was transmitted to Delhi.

As dusk fell over the city, the lectures and the sermons drew to a close. The scene for jubilant celebrations was being set again. The wealthy members of the city including Mamnoon's family members started departing. The agent recording the event was about to switch off his camera when he noticed that Mamnoon was heading towards the rear gate of the shrine. Previously, Mamnoon had always entered and exited via the front entrance. Noting the obvious variance in behaviour, the agent immediately alerted his team, which in turn alerted Delhi.

Another team, which had been selling corn on the cob across the shrine, noticed Mamnoon's car zip into the shrine through the rear exit. They too relayed the development to Delhi and added that there may have been a passenger sitting behind the chauffeur. The car had zipped past so quickly that the agents had barely got a glimpse of its occupants.

At this point, Parth, seated in the conference room of R&AW's headquarters, declared, 'We need to identify the passenger in Mamnoon's vehicle now—we won't be able to conduct a surveillance operation inside Mamnoon's bungalow as it is highly guarded.'

The decision was conveyed to all teams in Multan. While one team made its way to the rear exit of the shrine, another positioned itself on the roadside to get a glimpse of the said passenger.

The agent with the camera moved through the crowd and ran after Mamnoon. As he cut through the crowd and got to the area behind the stage, a set of police officers stopped him and authoritatively enquired, 'Where do you think you're going? Who are you?'

'I'm a freelance reporter and was hoping to interview the esteemed minister,' came the crisp and rehearsed response from the agent.

Then quickly taking out his identity card and papers, he handed them over to the officers.

After glancing through his papers, one of the policemen handed them back to the agent but did not allow him to pass through.

The officer in charge simply stated, 'The minister is a busy man and will not talk to unestablished reporters like you. Go away.'

The dejected agent walked back into the crowd. He had lost his chance.

By this time Mamnoon was comfortably seated in his car. The chauffeur reversed the vehicle and the entourage left.

The R&AW team that had managed to reach the rear exit of the shrine also did not get a glimpse of the passenger as they were too far away to discern anything clearly.

Mamnoon's entourage then zipped past the shrine's front entrance but came to a screeching halt a few feet ahead of the corn cart. The vehicles reversed, and Mamnoon's car stopped right in front of the cart. Mamnoon rolled down his window and instructed the lanky corn seller on how to prepare his corn on the cob. Mamnoon was extremely fond of this street food but was equally particular about its preparation. Then Mamnoon asked his guest if he would like one. The guest leaned forward to peer at the corn seller and ordered an extra tangy and spicy corn on the cob. As he peered out the window, the tiny cameras on the cart and on the shirt buttons of the corn seller's young assistant captured a photo of Professor Hamid Ansari, aka Doctor Zulfiqar Ali.

The lanky fellow prepared the corn cobs as instructed, rapidly fanning the charcoal to evenly roast the corn.

As the vendor handed the two corn cobs to Mamnoon, the finance minister, while giving him a crisp five-hundred-rupee note remarked, 'The weather demands such scrumptious food.'

As he took the first bite, he nodded approvingly. 'Keep the change,' then with a grunt indicated to his chauffeur that it was time to move on.

Five minutes later, the photographs were being analysed by R&AW in Delhi.

At 7 p.m. on Tuesday evening, out of the seven teams that were operating in Multan, five had been asked to withdraw. Of the two remaining teams, one was tasked with setting up a staging area and an observational platform near Mamnoon's house. Their task was to tail Professor Hamid the moment he set foot outside Mamnoon's mansion.

The other team was kept in reserve.

At this point, Vikram and Ranbir both got a message. 'Intel on HVT confirmed. Wheels up at 22.00 hours.'

The two knew that the high value target being referred to was Hamid Ansari. Their bags were packed and ready; both had been mentally prepared to leave for Multan since the mission had begun.

Ranbir had spent much of the day with his daughters and had even helped his wife Mousumi cook a scrumptious pomfret for lunch.

Vikram too had spent time with his family. They had all played cards in the afternoon, followed by a lengthy game of carrom.

When the message came, Vikram and his wife Sanyukta were alone in their room. Watching Vikram as he read the message, Sanyukta understood that the call of duty had come. There was an air of tension in the room.

Vikram and Sanyukta were planning on starting a family, so after Vikram gave her a tight hug and was preparing to leave, she said, 'Vikram, we need to have a stable life with a stable income to be able to start a family.'

Vikram nodded in agreement, smiled and said, 'I understand. Once I am back, we shall work towards it.'

45

An Unexpected Party

At 10 p.m., while a team of R&AW agents keenly observed Mamnoon and Hamid from the rooftop of an adjacent bungalow, Vikram and Ranbir were boarding their flight to Multan. The information from Dev Burman's contacts in Pakistan had paid off, but his enquiries into the clandestine matter had raised the alarm, which had led to his murder.

The R&AW agents had discreetly clambered onto the back wall of the adjacent bungalow, and using the rear staff staircase, had tiptoed their way to the terrace. There was one guard at the other end of the bungalow's driveway, and he was asleep. The owners of the house were also asleep, and all the lights were out.

From the terrace the agents had a clear view into Mamnoon's plush Victorian drawing room. They could see Mamnoon lounging in an armchair, one ankle resting on the knee of the other leg, his posture reflecting his power and arrogance.

Hamid, on the other hand, was sitting on one end of a long sofa, his right leg neatly crossed over his left one, his clasped hands carefully placed on his thighs indicating his submissiveness and the slight tension that he was under.

In the world of espionage, every move and gesture is recorded. Every action has a meaning and is analysed. The agents clicked photographs and sent the files to Delhi where analysts scanned them and sent their initial observations to their seniors for review.

It was not yet clear to R&AW in what capacity Hamid was involved with Mamnoon Qureshi. There was no known history or family ties between them, so his presence in the prominent minister's house had come as a rude shock to the agency.

When R&AW had established Hamid's presence in Multan, they had expected to catch him meeting some mid-level official from the central ministry or the ISI. No one in their wildest dreams had imagined Hamid sipping hot tea in a Noritake cup with Pakistan's finance minister Mamnoon Qureshi.

Parth was particularly anxious about the conversation that was taking place between the two and hence suggested, 'Should we send someone to the house? If we are able to plant a bug, we may be able to hear what they are talking about.'

'We cannot risk exposing ourselves yet. A whiff of suspicion and their whole network will go underground,' replied Arvind.

He had been head of the Pakistan Desk for over five years now. He had significant experience and insight into their behaviour and antics.

By 11 p.m., this information was relayed to the prime minister's secretary so he could incorporate the same in his daily morning briefing to the PM. The development was important but not yet critical enough for R&AW to wake the prime minister up.

46

Three Blind Mice

In the Garhwal region, Naina had spent the night in her tent surrounded by the continuous chorus of crickets, the soft chapping of geckos and the haunting calls of the nightjar, which sounded more like an old spoilt fax machine than a nocturnal bird.

The first hue of the red dawn, of the same Tuesday morning, brought with it the musical notes of blackbirds, magpie-robins and cuckoos, to which she awoke. As the sun's warmth bathed her tent, Naina silently crept out and observed the Ansari family down below. They were all still asleep. Naina then trekked up about three hundred feet, till she found a spot where she could freshen up. She washed her face and arms and used some dry shampoo to feel clean again. Then she trekked back down and prepared some breakfast for herself and ate in silence.

The camping and monitoring of the Ansaris were proving to be exhausting for Naina. Sitting in her tent, Naina muttered to herself, 'If the Ansari family does not get back on the road sometime today, then I'm going to call for some backup. At least that way I will have some company.'

She had instructed her driver to park the SUV five kilometres down the road and sleep in it. The old man had led an unadventurous and melancholy life. The hunt and the chase, as well as being associated with a R&AW agent, was an exhilarating experience for him, so he had not complained.

As the hours passed by, Naina observed the family in silence.

Late that afternoon, at around 3 p.m., she called up Parth Sinha.

'Sir, as you know, I have been tailing Mashal Ansari and her kids. I have been observing them from the vantage of a hill. I don't know how many more days they intend to stay here. I need a backup team and proper surveillance equipment. We need to be ahead of them this time.'

Parth, who was focused on the events unfolding in Multan, hurriedly responded, 'I'll scramble a backup team of four and the required equipment. They should be at your location in the next three hours. Till then sit tight. In case the family moves, tail them and inform me of your then current location. Lastly, if and when you identify Vita, send us a signal.'

Parth did not wait for a response and disconnected the line.

As dusk fell, Naina observed the family through her binoculars playing a game of snakes and ladders.

At around 7 p.m., just as Mamnoon and Hamid Ansari bought their corn cobs in Multan, Naina's backup team, comprising two females and two male agents, reached her location. The agents had flown from Dehradun to the nearby town of Silwar, and from there they had driven to the vicinity of the property. They had left their car five kilometres before the cottages and had hiked their way to Naina. Once they arrived, they too set up their tents and then began meticulously setting up their equipment.

By 10 p.m., as Vikram and Ranbir were boarding their flight to Multan, Naina's team was fully geared up with spy cameras and voice recorders and had devised a plan to infiltrate the cottages at night to bug the belongings of Aqsa Ansari. The team had chosen the young girl as their target as they thought that even if she woke up, it would be relatively easy to subdue her.

At 2 a.m., as the family slept, the two female officers along with Naina crept up to the cottages. They quietly picked the lock of Aqsa's cottage, using a combination of a hook pick and some bump keys.

The sitting area below was strewn with Aqsa's belongings, while she herself was in deep sleep on the floor above. While the team quickly bugged her shoes, her handbag and stitched a microphone into the lining of her jacket, Naina crept up the ladder to ensure that their target had not woken up. When the team gave her a thumbs up, Naina softly climbed down.

Just as they were about to leave, they saw the lights in Ali's cottage come on. The team stopped dead in their tracks. Everyone was nervous. If their presence was detected, they would have no option but to arrest the Ansaris.

Ali came out of his cottage and casually strolled towards the river. A few seconds later he unzipped his pants and peed into the flowing water. Then after wandering about for a few more minutes, he went back inside and shut the lights. The agents waited with bated breath for the next fifteen minutes. When no other sound was heard, they swiftly and silently exited Aqsa's cottage and hiked back to their tents.

Ali was still awake and lying in his bed trying to get some sleep, but he had no idea what had just happened.

47

Sea of Greed

The sky over Delhi was hazy on Wednesday morning. It had been twenty days since Captain Akbar Moeen, Arvind Ghosh's spy in the Pakistani army, had warned Arvind about the fiasco that would unfold in the next thirty days. Also, twenty-one days had passed since the notorious scientist had orchestrated his own kidnapping.

The situation was frustrating Arvind and Parth, who were sitting in the conference room at R&AW headquarters.

Arvind was the more meticulous of the two, and looking at his notes, he said, his expression glum, 'Six days have passed since we found Dev Burman murdered in his apartment. And we have three suspects following our initial investigation—ISRO's chief Satya Kulkarni, Secretary of Overseas External Affairs Rahul Das and Defence Secretary Shekhar Banerjee. Satya has been underground for quite some time, and we haven't been able to locate him. Our extensive hunt for him only led us to his flight records, which showed that he had taken a flight from Mumbai to Karnataka. After that, his trail has gone cold. Our team is still actively looking for him in the southern states, but we haven't had a sliver of a clue so far.'

'What about Rahul Das?' enquired Parth, going through his own set of scribbled notes.

'One of our field teams is observing him. We have flagged his passport, lest he tries to run. After you met him, he was quite shaken up. He has been drinking every night since you questioned him and has also fought with his wife a couple of times. Maybe he is scared or angry or both. Moreover, other than the bribe he took from the Israelis, he has been trying to broker deals with Pakistan under the garb of improving Indo-Pak relations. He is specifically trying to get permission for India to sell satellite technology to Pakistan. He seems our top contender as the turncoat. Yet, we haven't been able to bug his house or trace his calls. Unfortunately, thanks to the turncoat Top Hat, we can't send a request to the State Home Ministry for tapping his phones.'

Flipping through his notes, Arvind continued, 'Shekhar Banerjee is still touring around south India. We have him under surveillance too. But he leads a routine life, holding meetings pertaining to his work, and he is efficient and prompt in his responses to the defence minister. Nothing about him is surreptitious. Although he is in a prominent position, he has a clean track record. But I feel that the most straightforward people can also go astray, especially under the garb of their pedantic nature.'

Then looking at a report from Nepal, Arvind added, 'Nepal's NID is still trying to trace Sejun, the officer who shot the informant and owner of the petrol pump in Jumla. Although the NID is mortified by the treacherous act of their officer and is cooperating fully, I have assigned two junior officers from Naina's team to participate in the hunt.

'Lastly, although we identified the number plate of the car Shiv's killers used that night, we haven't been able to trace the killers yet. We found the vehicle burnt near an abandoned farmhouse on the outskirts of Delhi. Our team is on the lookout, and I hope we get some results soon.'

Parth pondered over all the information Arvind had just given him.

As he thought through the entire timeline and the events chronologically, a realization dawned on him. Parth suddenly sat up in his chair.

Looking at him, Arvind asked, 'What's wrong?'

'I gave the papers to Shiv Narayanan to present to Humayun Haq. That means Shiv laced those papers with arsenic. It looks like someone promised him a secure future and enticed him to betray us, then later shot him to cut loose ends. This looks like the work of our turncoat Top Hat,' said Parth.

Continuing his train of thought, Parth said, 'We delved into Shiv's call logs, and they were clean. This means someone brainwashed him in the high commission, right before he met Humayun Haq.'

At that moment Wasim Khan entered the room and said, 'Vikram and Ranbir have reached Multan safely. They landed at 4 a.m. this morning. While they were refreshing themselves at our safe house, the team keeping watch on Mamnoon's house informed us that Hamid was still at the finance minister's residence. He spent the night there and has just had his morning tea. He may leave soon.'

It was 9.30 a.m. in Delhi, and the top brass of R&AW were collecting their notes and preparing to go down to the operations floor to monitor the situation in Multan.

While Arvind and Parth were discussing the investigation, Satya was having his morning tea in a remote tea plantation in south India. He was not yet prepared to face the outside world. Even in this remote place he often carefully searched his surroundings for signs of any unwanted elements or surprises. Even to the local staff he appeared paranoid.

A few hours prior, at about 2 a.m., in Multan, Mamnoon and Hamid were having a serious conversation.

While sipping on his scotch, Mamnoon explained, 'It took me years to chart out this plan. Slowly and steadily, I developed my team. Two years ago, at a joint Indo-Pak meet, I met a young energetic bureaucrat from India. After our meeting, I kept in touch with him. Slowly but steadily, I turned him. I gave him the code name "Top Hat" and became his handler. With his connections he found out that a captain in our army called Akbar Moeen had been spying for India. He was also instrumental in orchestrating your kidnapping and laying out the intricacies of my plan. When Humayun was sloppy, he reprimanded him, and when his cover was blown, he used the scared Shiv to kill Humayun.'

He paused to take a sip of his scotch before continuing with a smirk, 'Afterwards, he even bumped off the unassuming Shiv. If all goes according to plan, I shall call him here to Pakistan. He can be my aide and right hand.'

'So is your goal just to become the prime minister of Pakistan?' asked Hamid as he sipped on his tea.

'I am a finance minister with almost no powers or say. I want to replace the Punjabi Pakistanis and create a more inclusive government. After you carry out your attack, the farmers will have no water, and famines and drought will strike. Pakistan will become a failed State, and as an added advantage of your attack, a war will break out with India; consequently,

I will be able to overthrow the existing government and establish myself as the face of change. Through my schemes and relations with China, I will pull Pakistan out of misery and my legacy shall live on forever.'

Setting down his cup of tea, Hamid casually replied, 'Well, I don't have such deep ambitions, but the money you and the Chinese government offered me was more than I could have made in seven lifetimes. So, here I am executing your plan. I will, however, retire to Europe, away from the chaos that I unfold.'

Smiling, Mamnoon slurred a little as he said, 'Well, then, I shall celebrate a white Christmas soon.'

'Amen to that,' replied Hamid soberly and cheerfully.

48

Red Herrings

On the Wednesday morning, while the R&AW team was assembling on the operations floor and the morning shift of analysts had all had their teas and coffees and were firing up their computer systems, Naina and her team were camouflaged in the thickets above the Ramisera Wild cottages.

Mashal and her kids had woken up and were exercising near the river when Mashal's phone pinged.

She walked over to it and looking at it, said, 'It's a message from your father. He asks us to prepare for the strike.'

Thanks to the bugs the team had planted in Aqsa's belongings, Naina was able to clearly hear the conversation.

Naina said to her fellow agents, 'Vita will be activated near a big city or a large town. Start packing up all non-essential items. For us to tail Mashal, we must be able to leave at a moment's notice.'

At 11 a.m. in Multan, Hamid Ansari was spotted by the spies who had been observing him stepping out onto the front porch of Mamnoon's bungalow. He was accompanied by Mamnoon. A black Mercedes drove up and stopped before them. As the scientist was exchanging last minute pleasantries with Mamnoon, the chauffeur quickly came around and opened the door for Hamid. This was the cue for the spies, who quickly assembled their equipment and quietly rappelled down from the terrace of the adjoining bungalow into the vacant plot on its other side.

Although the occupants of the house they were spying from had awoken, no one had bothered to climb up to the terrace. It was sheer dumb luck for the spies. They had armed themselves with hallucination darts and were prepared to strike had someone come up to their hiding nest.

As the Mercedes exited Mamnoon's bungalow, the spies got into their Toyota Prius, which was parked nearby. The hunt was on. The spies were relaying the developments in real time to Delhi. Vikram and Ranbir had been instructed to stay put at the safe house till Hamid's destination was ascertained.

The Mercedes smoothly rolled onto Canal Road, which was behind the cantonment area. Thereon, it cruised at a speed of 40 kilometres per hour. The spies kept at a considerable distance from the Mercedes, and the traffic on the road allowed them to occasionally hide behind other vehicles.

After about thirty minutes, the Mercedes took a right turn onto a narrow dirt road, which was flanked by thickets of trees. The spies followed at a safe distance, and as they slowly drove past the thickets, they could make out that a villa with high walls was located behind the trees. Just a few meters ahead on the dirt track was Afzal Fruit Farm. They stopped in front of it. Two of the spies got out and went inside to purchase some fruit, while the third waited in the car with his eyes glued to the rear-view mirror.

The two spies who had gone in decided not to ask any questions about the villa that Hamid had just entered, lest their covers were blown. They opted to act as travellers and make their purchase and leave.

While the two spies made their purchase, the third spy observed the black Mercedes emerging from the trees and driving back down the dirt track. The spy was able to make out that there was no passenger in the car.

It was 12.30 p.m. and Hamid Ansari's location had been confirmed.

The spies were instructed to wait down the road and keep a watch on the area till Vikram and Ranbir joined them. Half an hour later, Vikram and Ranbir arrived. The villa where Hamid had been dropped off was the only property on that side of Canal Road. For a kilometre on either side of the villa were just trees, shrubs and a few plots of barren farmland.

The spies parked their vehicle further up the road and decided to canvas the area to determine the presence of bodyguards in and around the villa. Slowly and steadily they closed in on the villa from three sides. Then they climbed up into the nearby trees to get photos of the villa and to count the number of guards that were visible. After observing for an hour, the spies counted about thirty-four guards in and around the villa. All of them carried at least a handgun if not more.

Ranbir and Vikram were in a fix as they had no secure vantage point from where they could observe the villa, and they clearly could not breach it and get into a fight with the guards. Observing from the trees for a long period of time was not an option as the risk of being noticed either by the guards or by the vehicles going in and out of the villa was far too great. If their cover was blown the entire mission would be in jeopardy.

Ranbir relayed their tough situation to Wasim Khan. The veteran spy asked them to stay put while a solution was thought of.

For over an hour, Parth, Arvind and Wasim Khan minutely analysed satellite images of the area surrounding the villa and Afzal's Fruit Farm.

Finally, with a heavy heart, Wasim Khan called Ranbir and said, 'We have carefully analysed every possible nook and corner of the area, but it seems that this villa was very carefully chosen for Hamid. There is absolutely no vantage point. You and Vikram will have to observe the villa from your vehicle. The team with you now will help you change vehicles every three hours.'

'But sir, we need to see what is going on inside the villa. Otherwise, we won't know what we're up against,' countered Ranbir.

'We cannot storm the villa. That would be a suicide mission and will invoke the wrath of the ISI. You will have to stay put, and when Hamid exits and the security around the villa reduces, you and Vikram can infiltrate the compound to gather whatever clues you can.'

'Understood, sir,' replied Ranbir, feeling helpless.

'Don't be disheartened, Ranbir,' said Wasim, sensing the heaviness in his voice. 'We will get our chance to strike at them.'

'I hope so, sir,' said Ranbir and then Wasim cut the call.

While the spies had been canvassing the villa and refining their strategy, Professor Hamid Ansari along with Jahangir Niazi had been busy in the basement. The professor was fine-tuning his creation, and by the time Wasim Khan cut the call, he was ready to arm the device.

Marvelling at his creation and slyly smiling at the thought of all the money he was going to make, he messaged Mamnoon: 'The suitcase is ready.'

He next sent a message to his wife Mashal: 'It is time. Reach the capital.'

When Mamnoon got the message, he forwarded the same to a man in Beijing. The man, who was dressed in a traditional black Manchu robe or changpao, immediately sprang into action, running across the serene garden of Zhongnanhai, the seat of the Chinese Premiere. Upon reaching the main compound, he slowed to a brisk walk. He entered the central building and headed straight for the top floor. There, he told the receptionist he had urgent business with the Premiere. She got up and softly tapped on the door of the leader's office and after being allowed in, disappeared inside. A few seconds later, she came out and beckoned for him to go in.

The man walked in and whispered something in the ear of the Chinese Premiere. Since the fiasco in India had begun unfolding, this was the first time the Chinese Premiere Jiang Zemin was pleased with his master plan and sighed with relief.

At 3.30 p.m., while the Chinese Premiere was musing over his yet to be achieved success, Mashal had started on her arduous, seven-hour journey towards New Delhi.

49

Well, That Didn't Work

At 4 p.m., Hamid Ansari, Jahangir Niazi and a small company of bodyguards left for the Multan airport. Vikram and Ranbir decided to follow the motorcade, while the three other spies were asked to canvas the now empty villa and look for any possible clues.

Fifteen minutes later the spies called Vikram and informed him that Hamid and his people had taken all their documents, laptops and papers with them. They had burnt all unnecessary papers and equipment including some burner phones and SIM cards. Except for some wires, nuts and bolts and other such inconsequential material, nothing had been left behind by Hamid's team.

The next fifteen minutes passed by quickly, and then Vikram got a rude shock as he saw Hamid's motorcade moving towards the cargo hangar of the Multan airport. Vikram and Ranbir did not have the required documents to infiltrate the facility, so they parked their car outside and raced to the rooftop of the nearest building. Vikram had a pair of small military grade binoculars with him. Peering through them, he saw Hamid, Jahangir and two bodyguards getting into an Eclipse 500, a small light jet that could fly up to six people including the pilot.

Ranbir and Vikram could not determine Professor Hamid's destination, so feeling helpless and fearful, Ranbir called Secretary Wasim Khan.

'Sir, I thought we had more time, but it seems that Hamid is on his way to execute his plan.'

'Do you know where they are headed?' asked the Secretary, the fear clear in his voice.

'No sir, they cleared out their safe house. We had it searched. They left no clues whatsoever.'

Vikram interjected and said, 'General Soe Min had claimed that India would lose Siachen. We have to assume they are bound for Siachen.'

Ranbir shook his head and said, 'The moment that jet enters Indian airspace, especially the skies over Kashmir, our air force will shoot it down. Besides, other than the delusional general's word, we have no other proof that Siachen is the target.'

Vikram countered, 'The jet they are using can easily fly under the radar. And in all probability, they will enter Siachen via the Gilgit-Baltistan route and not fly over Kashmir. It will take them longer but will help them avoid detection. If I were in Hamid's position, I would have done the same.'

He paused before continuing, 'Sir, I think we should get on the next flight to India. We will need you to get it diverted to Kashmir. From Srinagar the army can take us to the base of the glacier. In the meantime, the army needs to point all its radars towards Siachen to detect the aircraft if possible.'

'Okay. I will issue a red alert and notify the army. Both of you get to Multan airport and let me know which flight you are on. I'll get the same diverted.'

It was 4.45 p.m., and Vikram had managed to secure two seats on an Indian airline flight going to New Delhi. The flight was due to depart at 6 p.m.

Once the flight had crossed Pakistani airspace, the air traffic controller from Delhi contacted the aircraft and patched in Secretary Wasim Khan. The R&AW chief instructed the aircraft to first land in Srinagar, deboard the two required passengers and then continue onwards to Delhi.

Had Hamid taken the route over Kashmir, he would have reached Siachen in about four hours, but flying to Gilgit-Baltistan first and then proceeding east towards Siachen would add another five hours to his journey. He would now reach the icy heights of the glacier at about 1 a.m. on the following morning.

At 9 p.m., Vikram and Ranbir landed in Srinagar. An army escort was waiting to take them to Siachen Glacier. The officer in charge of the operation was Colonel Nikhil Rai. He was a decorated officer and part of the equally decorated regiment, the Gorkha Rifles.

After receiving the spies on the tarmac and while leading them to the helicopter nearby, Colonel Nikhil said, 'R&AW has informed the PMO. Since you left Multan we have worked out possible landing sites for the small jet, and we believe that the most plausible option for them is the Vigne Glacier. Siachen is just fifty-two kilometres from there. But even the most experienced pilot would find it daunting to land the jet at night on the icy glacier.'

Shaking his head, Vikram replied, 'These perpetrators have been planning this mission for quite some time now. I am sure they would have installed anti-skid tyres and a CAT III system to allow them to land in zero visibility on a snowy platform.'

'Well, if they are that well equipped then they could land the aircraft anywhere,' replied the colonel, sounding tense. He then handed Vikram a map of the region with possible landing sites marked in red.

'But the Vigne Glacier will offer them the longest straight line path and even the best technology will require the assistance of a straight path to reduce traction and ensure a safe landing,' said Vikram as he looked at the map and calculated the possible options.

It was 9.30 p.m., while Vikram and Ranbir were en route to the Vigne Glacier, Mashal and her kids were an hour away from New Delhi. Naina and her team had been following them from a safe distance, and halfway through the journey they realized that Mashal was in all probability heading towards the capital.

Naina immediately informed Parth Sinha, who said, 'Mashal may strike around the same time as Hamid. Their plan is probably to curb our ability to respond. Keep a close eye on them. If you feel she is about to use Vita in Delhi, arrest her. If she or her kids resist, shoot them all.'

'Understood, sir,' replied Naina and cut the call.

At 11 p.m., Mashal reached R&AW headquarters and parked her car under a tree opposite the building. Naina asked her fellow agent to drive past Mashal's car and stop at a point ahead of it. That way Mashal would not get suspicious. Naina then told another one of her fellow agents to head across the pavement to a paan shop and surreptitiously observe Mashal's car from afar. A while later Naina rotated the agent.

By midnight the agents observing Mashal had the same thing to report—she kept looking at her watch, while her kids slept in the back seat.

By this time Vikram, Ranbir and a company of soldiers comprising 120 men were nestled in the mountains surrounding

Vigne Glacier. All of them were dressed in white camouflage uniforms.

At a quarter past midnight, much before the expected arrival time, Ranbir noticed a solitary man moving along the icy glacier. A while later he took out a small gun and fired seven shots of illumination flares. They temporarily lit up the night sky with an amber hue, but the light was enough to guide the incoming jet to the centre of the glacier.

At 12.20 a.m., the jet descended and despite the traction control system, the anti-skid tyres and the CAT III technology, it did skid a bit before coming to a halt. A few minutes later, the pilot along with Hamid Ansari, Jahangir Niazi and two men dressed in Pakistani Army uniforms climbed down onto the glacier.

The man who had fired the flares received them. He had a jeep equipped for icy terrain with him. As soon as all the men had assembled, the man in a flash took out his gun and shot the two men who were in Pakistani Army uniform.

Vikram and Ranbir were confused about what was going on, and as they clambered up from their hiding place to move down to Hamid and his accomplices, they saw the man with the jeep loading the dead bodies into the back of his vehicle. The eccentric scientist was standing beside Jahangir Niazi and the two seemed to be having a conversation.

Looking at the bodies without remorse, Jahangir said, 'You will be fondly remembered by the people of Pakistan. Your endeavour will change the fate of southeast Asia. Once we have successfully carried out this blast, I will help you sell this technology to the Iranians and the Syrians. The Arab nations are unstable and while they tear each other apart, we can make billions of dollars.'

Nodding and smiling, Hamid started fiddling with his gun and then suddenly squeezed the trigger and shot Jahangir Niazi in the leg.

Jahangir was not prepared for this. Although he knew that the two men dressed as soldiers were going to be used as patsies and were to be martyred, he was completely unprepared for that shot in the leg. His adrenaline was down, and the bullet wound stung badly.

Looking up with a perplexed expression he screamed, 'What the hell are you doing? Why did you shoot me?'

Hamid calmly explained, 'Change of plans, Jahangir, I am not going to bomb Siachen. Instead...'

At that point a sniper from the Indian army shot the man who had aided the landing of Hamid's plane. Hamid and Jahangir were taken aback, but before their shock could wear off, the soldiers along with Vikram and Ranbir surrounded Professor Hamid Ansari.

As Jahangir was bleeding profusely, an army medic performed first aid.

Hamid had still not lowered his weapon, and now pointing it at Ranbir, he exclaimed, 'I am not a traitor. I was recruited by the NIA. My family and I have been working directly for the director-general, Vishal Chauhan. You need to let me go.'

'What is your plan? Do you intend to bomb Siachen and start a war?'

'A war will happen, but not between India and Pakistan, rather between Pakistan and China. My mission is to bomb Aksai Chin, and I will leave the bodies of Jahangir Niazi and the two Pakistani soldiers near the blast site. The Chinese will retaliate, and we shall gain while they fight.'

Vikram was flabbergasted by the professor's explanation. He was at a complete loss for words. He stuttered and when he could finally speak, he said, 'You mean, the director of NIA recruited you and devised this elaborate plan?'

'The NIA conducted a raid on a local terrorist faction in Delhi. They interrogated the men they managed to capture alive. One of them had been in touch with Jahangir Niazi and said that the ISI is planning to kidnap a nuclear scientist from India. That was when Mr Vishal came to me and told me to offer myself up as bait. So, I contacted the ISI and orchestrated my kidnapping.'

'But what you are doing will start a needless war,' objected Ranbir.

'No! We are ensuring that India remains the most dominant force in southeast Asia, and I am helping end the alliance between Pakistan and China. The Pakistani finance minister Mamnoon Qureshi wanted to topple his government and establish himself as the prime minister. The Chinese supported him, for they believed that it would be easier to control the Pakistani government if the leadership was made up of Pashtuns, Sindhis and other local factions. The current leadership of Punjabi Pakistanis, who have amassed too much wealth and power, are making it difficult for the Chinese to establish trade routes, ports and an economic presence in Pakistan. In this evil game, neither of them realized that their ace of spades is actually an Indian spy.'

'So, do you know the identity of Top Hat? Is he also a part of your master plan? And did you know that your wife murdered Bhim Singh and stole Vita?' asked Vikram, still unsure about Hamid's innocence.

'Vikram, why don't you try and see things from a different perspective? Life isn't a linear equation. Neither me nor DGP Vishal know the identity of Top Hat. I spoke to the turncoat once over the phone, when I was in Pakistan, and he handed Vita and Bhim Singh to us on a platter. He wanted us to murder Bhim Singh and steal Vita from him. I discussed the same with DGP Vishal, and he asked me to execute Top Hat's plan, but instead of stealing the device and coming to Pakistan, Mashal hid in India and is now going to surrender herself at R&AW headquarters. She could have gone to NIA, but I was no longer sure if Vishal Chauhan could be trusted. And we felt that Vita would be safer with us, and Mashal had to hide and be on the move in case Top Hat's stooges were following her.'

Still doubtful, Ranbir slowly said, 'Does the prime minister know about your plan? Has he sanctioned the actions of the director-general?'

'No! Nobody in the administration knows about our plan. DGP Vishal Chauhan wanted the prime minister to have plausible deniability.'

When Hamid's plane had landed at 12.20 a.m., Mashal had exited her vehicle and along with her kids approached R&AW headquarters. At the entrance, a trio of guards stopped her. But just as she declared that she was a wanted woman and had come to surrender, the guards pressed a buzzer, alerted the authorities inside and surrounded her. As the hooter sounded inside the R&AW complex, Naina and her team reached the main gate. Naina quickly took charge of the situation and escorted the Ansari family inside. Upon reaching the main lobby, the trio was frisked. Their belongings, along with Vita, were confiscated. None of them objected.

A few minutes later Mashal and her kids were separated, and each was taken to an interrogation room.

While Hamid had been explaining his intentions to Vikram and Ranbir, Secretary Wasim Khan and Joint Secretary Arvind Ghosh came to interrogate Mashal. Parth remained on the operations floor to coordinate the situation at Siachen.

Mashal gave an explanation similar to Hamid's to her interrogators.

50

Walk through Fire

Upon learning of the developments in Siachen and relaying news of the surrender of Mashal to Vikram and Ranbir, Arvind decided to first brief the PMO.

The prime minister was furious about the unilateral actions of Vishal Chauhan and exclaimed, 'There is a fine line between being a patriot and a fanatic. We cannot allow political fervour to be an excuse for fascism. Apprehend him immediately.'

Within the hour a team of agents was sent to DGP Vishal Chauhan's residence to arrest him.

A major catastrophe had been avoided, and the perpetrators were now in custody. Hamid had been forced to surrender. The old Russian suitcase nuke that he had modified with his novel fusion technology had been deactivated. The timer had been removed and the wires of the detonator had been cut. Jahangir Niazi had passed away due to excessive bleeding while he was being flown back to Srinagar's army hospital.

Hamid was being transported to R&AW headquarters in Delhi by Vikram and Ranbir for further questioning.

By the time Vikram and Ranbir entered the headquarters it was 5 a.m.

As soon as Arvind saw Vikram, he gave him the latest field update. 'Our agents found DGP Vishal Chauhan at his house. We brought him here for further questioning. You can watch through the two-way mirror as Secretary Khan interrogates him.'

During his interrogation Vishal carefully explained, 'About twenty-five days ago I received an anonymous tip about the location of the terror financier Mirza Ghulam Khan. Following the tip-off, my team captured Mirza Khan in Vrindavan, but in the fight that ensued he was perilously injured. Before dying Ghulam told me about Pakistan's finance minister Mamnoon Qureshi's nefarious plan to uproot the existing government and establish himself as the nation's prime minister. The Chinese wanted to support him as they believed it would be easier to establish trade routes, develop and indirectly control the seaports of Karachi and enhance their economic and military presence in Pakistan under his rule. I formulated and put a plan in motion that would not only end the relationship between Pakistan and China but also secure our nation. Detonating a nuclear bomb in Aksai Chin would destroy this major freshwater source. This would not only hamper China's agriculture but also disrupt their industries that depend upon this freshwater resource, in particular the factories manufacturing microchips and defence technologies. This was a unique opportunity for us as we would not only stop a terrorist attack but also ensure that we emerged as the most dominant force in southeast Asia. Professor Hamid Ansari is a patriot, and I request the authorities not to arrest and prosecute him.

'Lastly, I know through my local intelligence sources that R&AW is looking for a turncoat called Top Hat who is deeply embedded within our system. I would like to clarify that I am not that turncoat nor do I know his identity. Although he contacted Professor Hamid while he was in Pakistan and gave him Vita on a platter.

'Our actions are like an arrow shot from a bow, once the wheels of destiny have been set in motion there can be no going back. But my action was aimed at improving our great nation. I am a patriot, yet I know I will be branded as a traitor and prosecuted as such. I am prepared to face the consequences of my actions and have no regrets whatsoever.'

Taking a sip of his coffee to keep his brain cells active, Parth remarked, 'Either he is Top Hat and is lying about it or he genuinely doesn't know who the turncoat is. I don't know if we will ever be able to uncover his identity. This turncoat is a deeply embedded mole in our system.'

Naina, who was standing close by, silently listening to the conversation, knew that she had an ace up her sleeve. But she did not say anything just yet.

While R&AW had been busy arresting and interrogating the culprits, Mamnoon Qureshi and the Chinese Premiere Jiang Zemin were having a sleepless night as they anxiously waited for Hamid Ansari's phone call confirming the success of the mission.

The following morning the PMO was briefed on the situation and how events had transpired. R&AW submitted a detailed confidential report highlighting the intentions of the Chinese to support the weaker and the frustrated factions in the Pakistani government to fulfil their own agenda. Arvind and Wasim had included their opinion that Mamnoon Qureshi was a man with a dangerous mind and plentiful resources and hence should be eliminated. Parth, however, was of the opinion that the ISI and the top brass of the Pakistani government should be informed and left to deal with their own demons and that India need not interfere just yet.

A week after the chaos had unfolded, the prime minister called Secretary Wasim Khan to his office and said, 'I have gone over your report in detail and have given it serious thought. After much deliberation I have decided that we shall inform the ISI and Pakistan's prime minister about Mamnoon and his devious plans. We will not interfere at the moment. However, this does not mean that Mamnoon cannot have an unfortunate accident in the near future.'

The secretary was a seasoned spy and understood the prime minister's insinuation. By telling the ISI and his Pakistani counterpart, he would not only be extending a hand of friendship but also ensuring that following Mamnoon's death, the fallout would most likely impact the ISI and the Pakistani government.

Wasim Khan smiled and replied, 'Understood, sir.'

Then the prime minister got up, and looking at him, the secretary also began rising from his chair, but the prime minister gestured at him to remain seated.

Walking up to the French windows in his office and looking out at the gardens, the commander-in-chief said, 'After much thought I have decided to let Hamid Ansari and his family go free. I do not want to condemn him to death, and I also don't want his intelligent and impressionable mind to be exposed to criminals in jail. Put the family under house arrest. Let the professor continue his research from there but monitor the family's movements and activities.

'Similarly, we shall have to ask Vishal Chauhan to resign and put his family and him under house arrest. Extremism of any kind is harmful and must never be rewarded. A mind driven by zeal can bring out our most devilish faces. We cannot let power ruin us.'

'Very well sir,' replied Wasim Khan and then excused himself, leaving the prime minister to ponder on his thoughts.

When the blasts had not gone off, Mamnoon had understood that Hamid and Jahangir had either been captured or killed. Through the course of the night, he spoke to the Chinese Premiere multiple times and assured him that his financial investment and master plan would not go down the drain. Anxiety and nervousness did not allow either of them to sleep.

Mamnoon had been drinking heavily to curb his jitters, for his future depended on the success of the plan.

Despite being intoxicated and slurring while mumbling to himself, Mamnoon was looking at a list of other nuclear scientists from India. As he was lost in this task, a team of ISI agents swarmed into his house. Mamnoon was taken into custody and over the next week he was thoroughly grilled by the ISI. The ISI leaked news of his arrest to the media to defame him and curb his power. Numerous rumours were leaked about Mamnoon, some reports stating that he had stolen the State's finances, others saying he was hand in glove with the local mafia and the Afghani opium and weapons dealers. These incidents and rumours were also picked up by the international media. After a few weeks, it was reported that Mamnoon had been allowed to return home. There were unconfirmed reports that he had paid a hefty bribe to the ISI and the Pakistani prime minister and had promised to stay in line.

Epilogue

After the chaos had settled, Vikram and Ranbir had both handed in their notices to Secretary Wasim Khan. The secretary was unhappy about their decision to retire from R&AW but understood that the job was very challenging and frequently led to burnouts amongst agents, especially those who were regularly assigned field jobs. The constant fear of being caught in a foreign land along with the pressures of foiling the nefarious intentions of terrorists could be extremely taxing.

The secretary was a seasoned officer and understood the predicaments of young minds, so without any anger or malice he asked the duo, 'Have you both thought of what you will do next?'

Ranbir was the less calculative of the two and had an easy attitude towards life, so he said, 'I haven't thought of that yet, but I need a break. I don't know what the future has in store for me.'

'I am working on a few options, but I too haven't decided yet,' replied Vikram, as the secretary's gaze fell on him.

'Well, I wish you both the best of luck in your new endeavours. But be careful about your appetite for risk, Vikram.

Had we apprehended Hamid early on when we had the chance, we could have avoided this chaos altogether. Remember, life is not a gamble and cannot be lived on chance. I hope you do enjoy your new life.'

Then turning to Ranbir he continued, 'I am fond of both of you, so whenever you can, drop in at my home, and we can have a drink for old time's sake.'

Thanking the secretary, the duo walked out of his office and went to their respective homes.

That night dinner was at Vikram's house. Sanyukta and Vikram had prepared the Indian version of Chinese food. While not overly fond of cooking, Vikram was a decent cook and helped out to show his love for his wife.

Over dinner, Vikram's father asked him, 'So what will you do now?'

'Ranbir and I shall open a private detective agency. We have good connections with the cops and the intelligence agencies, which we can use to our advantage while solving local crimes. The pay will be better, and we won't have to travel much, unless we are approached by an outstation client,' replied Vikram immediately.

'Although I love the idea, it looks like you had already thought of a plan and knew what we were going to do, so why didn't you say so in Secretary Khan's office?' enquired Ranbir, a bit taken aback by Vikram's clear forethought.

'I didn't want the secretary to think that I already had a plan as he may have felt betrayed. He understands that we have grown tired of the job and want to quit and try something different, but he hopes that we will go back. If I gave him a straight answer, he would have lost that hope and felt let down. I respect him, and he has been my mentor. Still, I have been planning for an alternative life for quite some time now.

It would have been unfair to leave in the middle of a crisis, but now I feel we can start a new life,' explained Vikram.

'What about Top Hat then?' enquired Ranbir

'Well, we can't catch them all. Besides, as Sanyukta once told me, there will always be terrorists and spies in this world. I don't think Top Hat is our problem anymore.'

The Pakistani media had kept Mamnoon's story alive and had been asking questions about the case and allegations against him. But after receiving the bribe and Mamnoon's word, the ISI had to control the matter, and to kill the story, Mamnoon was called for questioning to the ISI office in Multan every week. The idea was to slowly tell the public that the allegations were false and that no incriminating evidence had been found. Mamnoon's visits to the ISI were just for show.

One day, after one such visit, the sky became cloudy and it seemed like it was going to rain soon. As Mamnoon's car passed the shrine of Bahauddin Zakariya, he noticed the same corn seller selling corn on the cob.

Mamnoon instructed his chauffeur to stop next to the corn cart. The corn seller quickly prepared a corn cob as per Mamnoon's instructions and handed the savoury to the defeated and disgruntled man. Mamnoon took a bite, nodded approvingly, paid the vendor five hundred rupees and then grunted at his driver to leave.

For the vendor, this would be the last corn cob that he ever sold in Multan. Not because he had earned enough, but because it was time for the efficient R&AW field agent to return home, to India. He had executed his last mission perfectly by lacing the corn cob with thallium, a compound that is odourless, colourless and tasteless but is an effective poison.

The following day, the news of Mamnoon's death was widely circulated by both the Pakistani as well as international media.

Despite the poison having been detected, it was concluded that it was a case of suicide rather than murder. Most people felt that Mamnoon had taken such a step out of guilt. The ISI and the Pakistani prime minister too believed that the loss of reputation and power had proved too much for Mamnoon to handle and he had thus decided to end his life.

While the world was busy with Mamnoon's death, Naina was sitting in a café in Imphal, Manipur. For the past few weeks, Naina and her team had been tailing Sejun Pokharel, the young NID officer who had betrayed her in Nepal. Imay Lama, the other officer who had accompanied her to Jumla, had tracked Sejun to Indonesia. But after Sejun's money started running out, he had entered Manipur and had been working at a local café for the past few weeks. The café where Naina was sitting was across the road from the one where Sejun was working. Sejun did not recognize anyone from Naina's team.

The R&AW agents knew that Sejun was running out of money and he would soon contact Top Hat.

Mamnoon's death had jolted Sejun. He knew that Top Hat had been in cahoots with the dubious finance minister.

Sejun had remained in touch with Top Hat. So, when his frustration over his circumstances peaked, he called him and said, 'You had promised me money and a job but every time I call, you delay our meeting and payment on the pretext of letting things cool down. Well, I'm tired of your excuses and am coming to meet you. If you refuse, I will go to the police and reveal your identity.'

'There is no need to get angry. I got you a job in the NID and at the café in Imphal. I still have a job for you and am not going back on my word to pay you. Why don't you come down to Coorg?' stated the turncoat calmly.

The following evening, Sejun embarked by bus on the long journey to Karnataka. It took him about a week to reach Coorg. Naina and her team were close behind.

Naina followed Sejun to Old Kent Estate and Spa. There she noticed Sejun surreptitiously approaching the secluded writer's bungalow. He did not go to the reception, rather was being guided by Top Hat who was on the phone with him. After walking for about fifteen minutes, Sejun reached the bungalow.

Naina waited with bated breath to see who would open the door of the bungalow. She couldn't believe that she would soon discover the identity of the turncoat.

A few minutes later, much to Naina's surprise, Defence Secretary Shekhar Banerjee stepped out and said, 'Hello Sejun. Welcome. How was your journey?'

'Let's cut the pleasantries and get straight to business. Where is my money? What do I do now?'

'I have your money, and I have got you a job as a senior assistant at this property. You shall help the manager, Ayush, manage and maintain the estate.'

Sejun was visibly irritated. He had been seriously downgraded. The meagre amount of money that he had saved over five years of service at NID had mostly been spent while he had been hiding in Bali and on the run. However, he felt this was not the time to argue. Something was better than nothing.

Naina, who had been hiding in the bushes, moved to gain a better vantage point. Ignoring the rustling of the bushes, Shekhar beckoned Sejun to come inside. Once the duo had entered the bungalow, Naina and her team moved slowly and silently towards it. As they entered, they heard noises coming from upstairs. Just as Naina climbed the first few steps, she heard a loud bang.

A moment later, Shekhar Banerjee came running out with a gun in his hand, and looking at Naina and the agents he said, 'Oh, thank God you are here. A thief broke into my room, and he tried to kill me. I had to shoot him in self-defence.'

Forcing a laugh, Naina said, 'We know you are the turncoat. We know that you are Top Hat.'

In a flash, Shekhar became calm again, dropped the gun and with a smug look on his face, confidently said, 'It shall be your word against mine. What proof have you got against me?'

'Who said I was looking for proof,' said Naina, and pointing her gun at Shekhar, shot him twice in the stomach.

As Shekhar slumped down and lay dying, Naina said, 'The official narrative shall be that Sejun, who was your partner in crime, shot you when you refused him his payment. And we shot Sejun in self-defence. You see, Mr Shekhar, to kill a shadow, I had to become one myself. And just to let you know, Hamid Ansari was planted by the NIA director, Vishal Chauhan, to uproot Mamnoon Qureshi's plan. He was never a traitor. Although his patriotism may have taken him too far, Hamid never acted against the people of his country.'

Wincing in pain and spitting up blood, Shekhar asked, 'How did Vishal know about Mamnoon's plan?'

'A terror financier called Mirza Ghulam Khan told him, before the NIA team executed him.'

Laughing at the turn of events and at his fate, Shekhar said, 'I was the one who informed Vishal about Mirza Ghulam. He was the link between Mamnoon and me. He helped Mamnoon garner finances from various like-minded people. But just before the plan was to be executed, he declared that he wanted greater control and a bigger piece of the pie. He wanted Mamnoon to establish him as a minister in the newly formed government and grant him protection from international persecution. But he was too well known around the world for Mamnoon to publicly embrace him. Mirza had outlived his utility, and so I had him executed by the NIA. It seems that the brute financier died before he could take my name, yet he did spoil our plot. Maybe if I hadn't...'

But before he could complete his sentence, the life ebbed out of him.

Naina silently wondered whether the greedy and shrewd man had wanted to apologize for his actions or if he just regretted the miscalculation in his nefarious plan. She would never know but would always wonder.

After executing Shekhar Banerjee, Naina left for Mangalore airport. She was going to report the developments to Secretary Wasim Khan.

While waiting for her flight, Naina decided to browse through a convenience store for some magazines and snacks. After picking up a chocolate and a can of cola, as she was walking towards the payment counter, she noticed a man wearing a loose white linen shirt and a pair of black jeans emerging from the adjacent aisle. Naina was taken aback as she recognized the man from multiple file photos. The man was Satya Kulkarni.

Extending her hand, Naina said, 'Mr Kulkarni, where have you been? We have been looking for you.'

Satya shook her hand lightly and said, 'Seeing the people around me drop dead scared me. Everyone involved with the development of Vita is dead. I did not know whom to trust.'

'Not everyone in the government is corrupt or a traitor,' replied Naina with a half-hearted smile.

'Yes, but one bad fish dirties the entire pond, and in this case made the game so dangerous that I had to flee.'

'Don't worry, we have our ways of sniffing out the traitors. We are tactful in our weeding process,' replied Naina with a sly smile. Her subtle hint was lost on Satya for she had neither confirmed nor denied the killing of the traitor, Shekhar Banerjee.

'Yes, but there are many more out there,' replied Satya, his face grim.

He then walked out of the store, his shadow becoming one with the many passengers hurrying to board their respective flights.

Acknowledgements

"Creativity is the greatest rebellion in existence." – Osho

In the journey of life, through all the ups and downs, many thoughts come and go. Some remain in the soul as inconsequential brainwaves. Weaving together such inspirations and ideas I created a story which I believe I would have loved to read. The idea was to take the reader on a fast-paced journey at the end of which they would have something to think and talk about. If reading the book generates even a casual conversation, I as an author shall feel that I have succeeded.

I shall forever be in gratitude of my Nani ma, Late Smt. Leela Devi Somani, who initially inspired me to write. I hope she is looking over me from the heavens above and is proud of my journey.

I am indebted to my parents, Anand and Sunanda Maheshwari, who have taught me everything I know and who have, through impeccable sacrifices, turned me into the person I am today. All my experiences in life and the practical

Acknowledgements

knowledge towards approaching an issue stem from their knowledge and hard experiences. I cannot thank my father enough for everything that he has done for me. A special shout out to my mother, whose eyes twinkled in excitement and who showed faith in me when I told her that I had started writing. Her critique and support made it possible for me to write the story. She acted like a sounding board while I discussed my raw plot line with her.

I thank my elder brother, Aditya Vikram Somani, who painstakingly went through the first draft and suggested the much required changes and formatting. He gave me insightful critique at every step and was a constant support throughout the journey.

I also wish to thank my dear friend, Abhijai Singh, who too gave me incisive critique and helped me shape the raw outline into a meaningful story.

I thank my wife, Sakshi, for her on point critical analysis of the story and for patiently bearing with me while I typed away in solitude on countless nights.

I thank my agent Suhail Mathur and his literary agency The Book Bakers for pitching the story to OM and for being a guiding light throughout the journey. He has been exceptionally patient with me.

I thank my friends for being an immense pillar of support at all times.

I thank OM Books International for giving me the opportunity to tell my story to the world and for patiently holding my hand and guiding me through this endeavour.

I thank all my readers. I sincerely hope you will enjoy the book.